Debra Webb, born in Alabama, wrote ~~~~~~~~~~~~~~~~~~
nine and her first romance at thirteen. It wasn't until she
spent three years working for the military behind the Iron
Curtain – and a five-year stint with NASA – that she realised
her true calling. A collision course between suspense and
romance was set. Since then she has penned nearly a hundred
novels. The *Faces of Evil* is her debut thriller series. Visit
Debra at www.debrawebb.com

Praise for Debra Webb:

'Webb keeps the suspense teasingly taut, dropping clues
and red herrings one after another on her way to a chilling
conclusion' *Publishers Weekly*

'Fast-paced, action-packed suspense, the way romantic
suspense is supposed to be. Webb crafts a tight plot, a kick-
butt heroine, a sexy hero with a past and a mystery as dark
as the black water at night' *Romantic Times*

'Compelling main characters and chilling villains elevate
Debra Webb's *Faces of Evil* series into the realm of high-
intensity thrillers that readers won't be able to resist' *New
York Times* bestselling author C. J. Lyons

'Bestselling author Debra Webb intrigues and tantalizes her
readers from the first word' www.singletitles.com

'Masterful edge-of-your-seat suspense'
www.aromancereview.com

By Debra Webb and available from Headline

Revenge

Debra Webb

headline

Published by Forever Yours in 2013, an imprint of Grand Central
Publishing, part of Hachette Book Group, Inc.

First published in Great Britain in 2013 by
HEADLINE PUBLISHING GROUP

1

Cataloguing in Publication Data is available from the British Library

ISBN 978 1 4722 0700 5

Typeset in Palatino by Avon DataSet Ltd, Bidford-on-Avon, Warwickshire

Printed and bound in Great Britain by Clays Ltd, St Ives plc

Headline's policy is to use papers that are natural, renewable and
recyclable products and made from wood grown in sustainable forests.
The logging and manufacturing processes are expected to conform to the
environmental regulations of the country of origin.

HEADLINE PUBLISHING GROUP
An Hachette UK Company
338 Euston Road
London NW1 3BH

www.headline.co.uk
www.hachette.co.uk

Revenge . . . its delight is murder, and its end is despair.

– Johann Christoph Friedrich von Schiller

To Fran, a true Southern Lady.

There was just no way around it. She'd have to go down to the garage and take care of the breaker herself. Resetting the damned thing wasn't a big deal. Not really. After getting Dan out the door last night, she'd hurried through a shower and switched on her hair dryer and *poof* the lights had gone out – just like tonight. Thankfully her landlord had still been puttering around in his kitchen then, so she'd knocked on his door.

He'd explained that her apartment and the garage were on a subpanel, which also clarified why there was no service disruption in the main house when her lights went out. Inside the garage last night, she'd carefully watched him reset the breaker and even remembered which one it was. Fourth from the top.

'Easy as pie.' Jess shoved her cell phone into the pocket of her worn-comfortable robe and strode to the door. She could do this without bothering her elderly landlord.

On the deck outside her door, she verified that Mr Louis's house was indeed dark before descending the stairs. She hoped the garage side door wasn't locked. That could be a problem. Dammit. She hadn't thought that far ahead. People generally locked all doors at night. Then she'd have no choice but to pester her landlord.

'Don't borrow trouble, Jess.'

At the side door, the knob turned without resistance and she was in. Thank the Lord. She roved the flashlight's beam over the cavernous space to get her bearings. Smelled like wood shavings and vaguely of oil. Last night she hadn't really noticed. She'd been too focused on how to get the power back on in her place. This go-round, her curiosity got the better of her.

There was just one vehicle in the garage, a classic black Cadillac Eldorado. That she had spotted last night. The car fit the man, she decided. The thought of Mr Louis and his horn-rimmed glasses behind the wheel of that big, formidable-looking automobile reminded her of a character straight out of *The Sopranos*. Like the moneyman or the bookie.

Along the back wall, a workbench and stack of wood in varying sizes awaited the next DIY project. Exposed stone walls were lined with shelves on the other two sides; all were neatly organized with cans of paint and tools. The brush lying across the top of a can of white paint had her remembering and wondering about her landlord's sudden decision to freshen the door to her apartment the other evening. She should ask him about that. Not that it really mattered at this point to the homicide case she had just closed, but he needed to understand that in her line of work sometimes trouble followed her home. And if some jerk decided to leave her a personal message, it was essential that she see it – all of it, no matter how unpleasant – before it was whitewashed.

4

The sooner she made that point clear to him the better. Maybe tomorrow when she spoke to him about the electrician.

Jess padded across the rough concrete floor and settled the light on the gray metal door of the breaker box. She opened it and sure enough breaker number four from the top had jumped into the *off* position. 'So you don't like my hair dryer. Is that it?' She reached up and snapped the breaker into the *on* position. She watched for a moment to ensure it wasn't going to repeat its unruly behavior. When the breaker remained in the proper position, she closed the door to the box and turned to go. She stubbed her toes and cringed.

'Damn, damn, damn!' She hopped on one foot while she stretched the injured toes. Aiming her flashlight at the offending object, she glared at the large wooden box. Looked like a homemade toolbox or storage container. Another of her landlord's little projects. The man appeared to be building, patching, or painting something every waking hour. If she was that bored when she got old, she hoped someone took pity and gave her cold case files to analyze – anything to keep her away from power tools and paintbrushes.

Something on the floor just to the left of the annoying box prompted a second look. The floor was uneven, not smooth at all. Looked as if it had been poured in sections in different decades. But the small round object that snagged her attention glittered in the light . . . *silver*. Jess leaned down and picked it up. A ring. Not just a ring . . . a *wedding band*.

She couldn't read the inscription since her glasses were upstairs. The ring made her think of the one she had stopped wearing recently, only this one was larger, a man's maybe, and hers had been gold—

The garage filled with flickering lights.

Her breath stalled somewhere in the vicinity of her throat and she squinted at the flood of harsh fluorescent glare.

'Is there a problem, Chief Harris?'

Mr Louis, her inordinately patient landlord, waited at the door she'd entered and left standing wide open maybe two minutes ago.

Uh-oh. Busted. So much for not troubling the man. It was a wonder he hadn't barged in toting a twenty-gauge. This was Alabama. Folks took three things very seriously: religion, football, and the right to bear arms. Not necessarily in that order.

Jess shoved her hand, along with the ring, into her robe pocket. 'Just that breaker again.' She smiled, knowing damned well she must look as guilty as sin. 'I should've known better than to use my hair dryer until I checked with you. I hope I didn't disturb you.' She gestured to the breaker box. 'I thought I'd try to take care of it myself this time. It's so late and all.' She clicked off the flashlight and waited for a reaction. He didn't exactly look angry. Maybe frustrated or unsettled.

'The electrician will be here in the morning.' His lips shifted into a smile, banishing the less pleasant expression he'd been wearing. 'I apologize for the inconvenience.'

'No trouble.' Truth was she felt like a nosy Nellie. This man had kindly offered his garage apartment when she had no other place to go – besides her sister's, and that was just not doable for a whole host of reasons – and here she was treating him as if he were a suspect. Dan's paranoia about her renting from a stranger was evidently rubbing off.

No, that wasn't fair. She couldn't really blame it on Dan. She'd always overanalyzed people and situations. She walked straight up to her landlord and held out the ring. 'I found this on the floor.'

He accepted the band, turned it over in the light. 'Why, thank you. I'd wondered where it had gotten off to.'

She wasn't about to ask the questions pinging at her. A certain level of nosiness came naturally after twenty years in the business of criminal investigation, but he might not understand or appreciate that undeniable and sometimes bothersome fact.

Before she could apologize again for the trouble, he said, 'You have company.'

At this hour? Surely Dan hadn't come back. He'd

taken her to dinner earlier this evening and they'd discussed the ongoing investigation into the bomb that had been planted in the BPD vehicle she'd used last week. They'd gone over the business about Captain Ted Allen. The head of BPD's gang task force had been missing for going on seventy-two hours now. The close timing of the vehicle tampering and a cop going missing had everyone on edge. Especially since the missing cop had been seen in the vicinity of the vehicle in question before going AWOL. She booted the idea that a fellow cop could have wanted to get even with her that badly. The fact that she'd had a rather tense conversation with Allen the last time she saw him was amping up her guilt factor. It shouldn't. Dammit! Barging into his investigation into the Lopez family drug business here in Birmingham had been the right thing to do.

Don't think about it, Jess.

'Company?' She started for the door where Louis waited. 'Must be police business.' It had better be. Knowing Dan, he'd returned with one more reason she should be wearing full body armor at all times or hiding behind him.

The man took overprotective to a whole new level, particularly with the bomb scare and Allen's abrupt disappearance.

He really had to get past this obsessive need to see after her every minute. Soon! If he was at her door again, she was going to give him what-for. For heaven's sake it was Monday and they were having enough difficulty already leaving their personal relationship with the weekend. That was the deal they made when she accepted this position. During the workweek, he was the chief of police and she was one of his deputies. No exceptions.

She'd been back a month and that rule had gotten broken with tonight's dinner and dessert that segued into getting naked afterward.

God, she had to get this mess that was her personal life in some sort of order.

Starting right now, she promised herself silently.

'Sorry again,' she said to Louis. 'I'm sure you weren't expecting all this middle-of-the-night activity when you offered to rent the apartment to me.'

'Your presence keeps life interesting, Chief Harris.' With that he stepped aside for her to exit the garage.

'You should call me Jess,' she suggested. It was silly for them to be so formal, considering she was living on his property.

He ducked his head in one of those shy nods she'd come to associate with the older gentleman. 'Of course, and you should call me George.'

'Well, George, thank you and good night.' Jess gave him a nod as she walked past him.

'Good night, Jess,' he called after her.

She almost paused and turned around at the way he said her name. Familiar almost, like they'd known each other for a long time. Instead she kept going, slowing only to check the driveway. He was right about her having company but thank God it wasn't Dan.

A white sedan she didn't recognize sat in the drive behind her Audi. The slightest inkling of trepidation trickled through her veins as she rounded the rear corner of the garage and peered up at the top of the stairs leading to her apartment. The light outside her door illuminated a woman who knocked firmly, most likely not for the first time. She wore khaki slacks and a matching blouse. Her gray hair was tucked into a neat bun. Her bearing looked vaguely familiar. As Jess watched, the woman reached up and knocked again.

'Hello,' Jess called as she started up the stairs.

Her visitor turned toward the sound of Jess's voice and recognition jarred her.

'Ms Frances?' Of all the people . . . 'Is that really you?'

Frances Wallace had been Jess's ninth-grade English teacher. She was unquestionably the only reason Jess didn't quit school the day she turned sixteen. In truth the woman had been the closest thing to a mother in Jess's life since she was ten. What in the world was she doing here? Jess hadn't seen her in ages. She hated to admit it but she hadn't even been sure the woman was still alive.

Yet here she was.

'The one and only,' Frances confessed. 'I've been following the news about you since you returned to Birmingham,' she announced as Jess climbed the final step. 'You always did do things with panache, young lady.'

It had also been ages since anyone had called Jess a young lady. She liked the sound of it. 'I had an excellent teacher.'

Frances Wallace was a genuine character. No one got anything over on her and she did everything – including her teaching – exactly the way she wanted, the rules be damned.

For one long moment Jess got so caught up in the memories she lost all sense of decorum. 'Come in, Ms Frances. Please.'

She opened the door and ushered her former teacher inside. 'Have a seat.' She gestured to the new-old sofa she'd discovered at a thrift store on Saturday. 'Would you like coffee?' She should have had wine to offer but she and Dan had finished it off before getting naked. A flush of embarrassment went through her at the idea of even thinking about sex in front of Ms Frances.

Her former teacher took a moment to survey the apartment. Jess felt that same heat rise in her cheeks as her gaze lit on the tousled sheets of the bed.

'I'm still getting organized—'

Frances turned to Jess then, and the unabashed fear on her face stole the rest of what Jess was about to say.

Without a word of explanation, Frances drew her into a fierce hug. 'I need your help, Jess,' she whispered with the same ferocity as her embrace. 'I think I'm about to be charged with murder.'

Chapter Two

Despite the lack of lights and sirens, within half an hour of the police's arrival, the residents of Vestavia Village were gathering in the food court for complimentary coffee and the promise of a briefing. Excited chatter and curious stares accompanied their meandering path through the solarium that served as a lobby. Not a single member of the geriatric crowd paid the slightest bit of attention to Jess and her team. They were far too busy attempting to get a glimpse of the *body*.

Word had already spread that someone was dead.

Jess couldn't exactly fault their curiosity. These folks had lots of time on their hands, and the fact was no one was more curious about the dead than her. Maybe because her parents died when she was so young. Jess didn't really remember when her interest was stirred but that morbid curiosity made her very good at her job. She turned back to resume her survey of the crime scene. They'd cordoned off an area that extended along the corridor leading from the solarium to the offices of the administrator and his staff up to and including the main entrance of the facility. With two ways to reach the administrator's office – via the main entrance and the solarium lobby – it was necessary to protect both until any evidence was recovered.

The timing of the call from dispatch, not fifteen minutes after Frances whispered her stunning announcement in Jess's ear, would have been freaky bizarre except that impeccable timing had always been another of her favorite teacher's notable attributes. The man Frances suspected she would be accused of murdering was indeed dead. Which was no coincidence since Frances had found him that way before rushing across town to pay Jess an impromptu visit.

Further proof that Jess drew killers like bees to honey, except Frances Wallace was no killer. Her explanation of tonight's events was a little scattered and a lot thin but Jess had gotten the gist of things. Even at seventy-five, the woman wasn't going to be hoodwinked by some whippersnapper – said whippersnapper was, unfortunately, the murder victim.

Since her options were limited, Jess had brought

Frances to the crime scene with her. She was ensconced in the library in the company of one of Birmingham PD's finest. Not that she was going anywhere, but Jess had no intention of letting her talk to anyone else until she got to the bottom of exactly what had transpired.

The janitors who found the victim and called 911 were sequestered to a staff lounge on the east end of the building where Detective Lori Wells was taking statements. The crime scene unit techs had arrived and were documenting and gathering evidence in and around the primary scene. Lieutenant Valerie Prescott was monitoring that activity while Officer Chad Cook wandered amid the residents in the dining hall. His job was to take note of anyone who appeared nervous or visibly out of sorts. BPD uniforms were searching the grounds. The deputy administrator of the senior living facility had arrived and was waiting to give his statement as well. Jess had given him a few minutes to get the residents settled.

Someone from the coroner's office was en route. Wouldn't bother Jess one bit if Sylvia Baron got the case. The snarky doctor was spot on in her assessments, and . . . Jess was curious about her – or more precisely her sister, a former Mrs Daniel Burnett. And, if she were completely honest with herself, Jess kind of liked Sylvia. They were friends . . . sort of.

'Chief,' Sergeant Chet Harper said, drawing her

attention back to the reason she was here. 'According to his personal secretary, the victim, Scott Baker, remained in his office last night after she and the rest of the staff left for the evening. No meetings were scheduled and, to her knowledge, he wasn't expecting any visitors. She says it's not unusual for him to work late.'

'So,' Jess said, following Harper along the corridor that led back to the administrator's office, 'between half past five and quarter to eleven, Baker was here alone except for a visit from the Grim Reaper. The janitors came in to clean the office and found his body. Called nine-one-one. And here we are. Anything on the surveillance cameras?'

The question she kept to herself was: *Is a little gray-haired lady showcased in any of the footage?*

Harper shook his head. 'The surveillance system is digital and motion activated. It generally runs twenty-four-seven, which would've shown anyone entering or exiting the facility. But the system was turned off just before six last night. Pete Clemmons, the deputy administrator, insists that only Baker could have done that. Not even Clemmons has the code. And no one outside the security company has the ability to delete stored data in the system.'

Jess crossed the threshold into the administrator's office for the second time since her arrival. The forensic folks wouldn't start in here until after she'd had her look and the coroner's office had done their thing.

The body lay on the floor in front of the broad mahogany desk. That he was in front of the desk rather than behind it suggested to Jess that he'd been engaged in intimate conversation with his visitor. Scott Baker's suit jacket hung on a bronze coat rack in the corner near the door. The white shirt and navy trousers showed a day's wear. A small pattern of blood splatter soiled the left shoulder of his shirt. His striped tie and the first two buttons of his shirt were loosened as if he'd had reason to be exasperated or maybe he'd had a long day. Possibly his visitor may have pumped up his frustration level.

Baker's dark hair was matted on the left side of his head where it appeared two violent blows to the temple area had taken him down. Probable fractures and certainly internal hemorrhaging had ensured he didn't get back up.

The scenario that he had tripped and fallen went out the window pretty quickly as far as Jess was concerned. The desk – and the table, flanked by two chairs – was clean of blood and tissue that would surely have been left behind had he hit his head there. Nope, Scott Baker had not accidentally gotten that lethal injury. His most likely right-handed visitor had given him a hell of a wallop upside the head, then another for good measure, before walking away.

The victim had been dead a few hours. Rigor had a good start. Jess eased into a crouch to get a better look at the damage to his temple area. 'Did you find anything that might have been the murder weapon, Sergeant?'

'If it's still in this room,' Harper offered, 'it's been wiped.'

Jess pushed to her feet and mentally inventoried the potential weapons. A crystal paperweight was too roundish to have caused the gouges in the scalp. The stacks of manila folders may have given the man a headache but they hadn't killed him. Framed photos of a young wife and son weren't heavy enough. Besides, a blow like that would have broken the glass. With gloved hands, she lifted and gauged the weight of an Administrator of the Year Award.

'This feels solid enough.' Jess studied the marble base. Like Harper said, no sign of blood or tissue but the sharp corners would have done the trick. She squatted next to the victim again and had another look at his wounds. 'The corner of this base could be it.' *If* the killer hadn't taken the murder weapon with him.

'I'll have one of the techs bag it as soon as the ME has a look,' Harper agreed.

Jess settled the trophy on the desk and dusted her gloved hands together as if that aspect of her work was done. Notification of next of kin was still a no-go. According to the deputy administrator, Baker's wife and son were down in Mobile for a final getaway before school started. That would need to be confirmed to clear the spouse.

Jess moved around behind the desk and opened drawer after drawer. More files. Sharpened pencils and a stash of peppermints. Her attention returned to the framed photos. Young, beautiful family. She'd checked his wallet and driver's license. The man lived in one of Birmingham's wealthiest neighborhoods. The car keys in his pocket belonged to a Jaguar that was parked in his slot out front. The school uniform the young son wore in one of the photos told Jess he attended Birmingham's most prestigious academy.

However good life was for Scott Baker and his family, someone had wanted him dead and that someone had managed to get the job done. In light of the after-hours timing and the shutting down of the surveillance part of the security system, Baker had not only known his final visitor quite well, but he'd also been anticipating the visit. Could be a village resident? Frances Wallace's image taunted her. She couldn't have done this. Sure would have made Jess's job a lot easier if that video surveillance had been left on.

'Why in the world did you turn off the video surveillance, Mr Baker?'

'If he answers you,' an irreverent female voice announced, 'I've wasted my time coming here.'

Jess turned to greet the medical examiner. 'Looks like we'll be working together again this week, Dr Baron.'

'I've survived worse.' Dressed in a color-blocked sheath of dove gray and burgundy with open-toed stilettos in a deeper shade of gray, Sylvia rounded the desk and crouched next to the victim.

Maybe the idea that they were sort of friends was a bit premature. Before Jess could levy a witty comeback, Sylvia asked, 'You get settled in your temporary apartment?'

'I did. Thank you for asking.' The belted ivory dress, her favorite, Jess had opted to wear for this middle-of-the-night outing suddenly felt like a flour sack compared to the sleek-fitting one Sylvia wore. Then again, it might not be the dress. The woman was gorgeous, tall and stat-uesque. Things Jess would never be.

'Carrie Bradley mentioned she saw you and Dan out shopping on Saturday.'

'Carrie Bradley?' Jess didn't know the name. On Saturday, Dan, Chief of Police Burnett – her boss, she amended – had taken her to a few local thrift stores in search of stuff for her apartment. She'd found a surprisingly nice sofa and chair, along with a coffee table, a chest of drawers, and a bedside table. For now, she was set.

'Carrie's redecorating her master bedroom,' Sylvia

explained. 'She donated everything in the room to the Second Life thrift store. She saw you there.'

'Oh.' Great. There was nothing like having Burnett's uppity friends know that she shopped at the same place they donated. 'That's nice,' Jess said with about as much enthusiasm as the guy on the floor had for his current predicament. 'I'll have to remember that next time I redecorate.' She could redonate the stuff. Ha-ha.

Sylvia made a noncommittal sound. 'I guess you found everything you needed.'

'For now, yes.' No point going overboard with the decorating since she didn't know how long she'd be living in the garage apartment. Not that she was in any hurry to start house hunting. Her house in Virginia was still on the market and she needed the cash from that sale before going more deeply in debt. Besides, the elderly man who was currently her benevolent benefactor seemed nice enough. Good, trustworthy landlords were hard to find. This one went to church every Sunday. Her sister told her so.

That reminded Jess, she should check in with Lily to see how she was feeling. Waiting on the results of all those tests to determine what was going on with the crazy symptoms plaguing her was driving them both crazy. Not to mention Jess was also supposed to drop by their estranged aunt's house to pick up that medical history she'd compiled. The weekend had slipped by and

Jess had completely forgotten.

Or maybe she'd forgotten on purpose. Seeing her aunt again ranked about as high on her looking-forward-to list as getting a mammogram. Why she even referred to the woman as her aunt was a mystery. Lily was the only family Jess had. End of story.

'I was the new kid on the block at the coroner's office when his sister died,' Sylvia said, her attention on the victim as she measured the body's core temperature.

Another of those deep frowns puckered Jess's forehead as she elbowed aside the distracting thoughts of her sister and Dan's snobby friends. She rubbed at the creases with the back of her hand. 'Whose sister?'

'Your new landlord's. He took care of his sister until she died. She was a total invalid. MS, if I recall correctly.'

Burnett had told Jess that Louis hadn't been married. Lily had gotten the part about him being a widower wrong. Based on what Sylvia had just told her, Lily probably thought the sister had been his wife. Not that it mattered to Jess but Burnett had insisted on doing a background check. He didn't like the idea of Jess living over a stranger's garage. Which was ridiculous. Most any landlord in the city would be a stranger to her.

Wait a minute. The frown was back. If Mr Louis had never been married, who owned the ring she'd found in his garage? Had his sister been married? Probably. Maybe he even had nieces and nephews. He hadn't entertained any visitors this last week as far as Jess knew. Then again he might not have any relatives in Birmingham. Not that it was any of her business.

'You know him?' Jess asked. Sylvia hadn't mentioned knowing him when she'd dropped by with a house-warming gift the other night. 'Course, they'd had other worries at the time.

'Not really,' Sylvia said, her attention still on the victim. 'I pronounced the sister. Louis and I met. That's basically it.'

Jess had to admit she was a little curious about the man. Okay, maybe she was a lot curious. Mostly she was immensely thankful for a place of her own, even if it was basically just one big room. Of course, if she'd known Lori was going to move in with Harper so soon, she could have sublet her place. Probably not a good idea. Having a tenant in her place would only ensure Lori stayed in the relationship with Harper even if she started to have second thoughts.

Good grief, there she went assuming the worst of the couple's latest step. Just because Jess hadn't been able to sustain a decent romantic relationship for any length of time didn't mean Lori and Harper wouldn't be able to.

The fact was Jess's issue with relationships went way beyond the romance kind. She'd never really had a lot of friends. She was always too busy. After she'd put

Birmingham in her rearview mirror twenty some years ago and joined the Bureau at Quantico, she'd hardly come back for a visit. Lily reminded her often how much she'd missed.

Something else Jess had to fix.

'I'd estimate time of death at between eight and ten last night,' Sylvia announced, dragging Jess back to the here and now. 'Judging by the location of the visible injuries, I'd wager cause of death is middle meningeal arterial hemorrhaging from the trauma to the temple area. Depending on the damage to the artery, death may have been very swift. Possibly only minutes.'

'How long before we have a preliminary report?'

Baron stood and peeled off her gloves. 'The mayor is going to inform the victim's parents so they can get word to the wife. She's out of town. He called me en route to Scott Baker's parents' home and asked that we make this case a priority.'

'This victim's related to the mayor?' Jess didn't know why she was surprised. Birmingham's upper crust liked to stay within their class. They all seemed related somehow. In the South, old money had a habit of circling the same pocketbooks.

'No.' Sylvia turned to Jess. 'Your victim's great-great-grandfather was one of the railroad barons who helped build Birmingham. Old money and lots of it. The Pratt family fortune has roots in that same history.' She shifted her attention back to the victim. 'Dan didn't tell you about Baker?'

'He called but I haven't had time to call him back.' If Burnett had any ideas of giving this case to the Crimes Against Persons Division, he could forget it. This was her case. Jess had ignored his calls for that very reason. Seemed every time some who's-who from the lifestyle pages got murdered, her colleague Deputy Chief Harold Black cherry-picked the case.

Not this time.

'I'll have something later today, early tomorrow at the latest,' Sylvia told her. 'Can't keep the mayor or his friends waiting.'

Jess tugged off her gloves. She had folks to interview. 'I guess that's something that won't ever change about Birmingham. Even when you're dead it's all about who you know.'

The doctor's eyebrows arched. 'Or who you blow.' She bent down and retrieved her medical bag. 'I'll let you know as soon as I have a preliminary assessment.'

Jess wondered if Sylvia and her younger sister were anything alike. Her cell clanged that old-fashioned-phone ringtone, prodding her beyond the distraction. Jess dug for it as she called a thanks to Sylvia. The woman waltzed out of the office more like a runway model than a medical examiner. Jess shook her head. Why was looking that good so easy for some women?

Lori Wells's name and image flashed on the screen of Jess's phone. Was she finished taking statements already? 'Harris.'

'Chief, you need to talk to Mr Foster *now*.'

'The janitor who made the nine-one-one call?' Terrence Foster was the lead janitor and he hadn't given the impression that he possessed useful information when Jess first arrived.

'He swears he knows who the killer is.'

Talk about an about-face. 'I'll be right there.'

Jess went in search of Harper. He was taking the deputy administrator's statement. Jess pointed in the direction of the east end of the building and headed that way.

At the staff lounge, she entered the room and both the janitor, Terrence Foster, and his assistant, Moe Brewer, started talking at once. Lori looked way out of patience.

Jess held up her hands and the two gentlemen shushed. 'One at a time, please. But first' – she turned to Lori – 'Detective Wells, why don't you take Mr Brewer—'

'Foster's right,' Brewer interrupted, determined to get his two cents in. 'I hadn't thought about it until he said it.'

Before Jess could respond, the obviously agitated man said to his coworker, 'Tell her, man.'

'Mr Baker's been fighting with the widows for months,' Foster explained, picking the story up from there.

'Widows?' Jess looked from one to the other. Oh hell. She had a very bad feeling where this was going.

Foster nodded, his eyes wide with equal measures certainty and worry. 'The widows are big-time upset about the new building that's going up. During the last meeting, one of the women threatened Mr Baker.'

'You heard this yourself?' Jess countered. She needed clarification. If he was repeating hearsay, that was something else altogether.

Brewer shook his head before Foster could answer. 'We didn't exactly hear it. Claire Warren heard it. She runs the dining hall. The meeting was in there and she was still closing up after serving dinner.'

'We'll need to take her statement,' Jess said to Lori. 'Mr Brewer' – Jess looked from him to the other man – 'Mr Foster, who are these widows?'

'Residents,' Foster explained. 'They've had the others staging sit-ins. Once they even formed a picket line out front. They keep everybody here upset about one thing or another. It's always something.'

'The widows are residents,' Jess reiterated just to be sure she'd heard correctly, really hoping she hadn't, 'of this facility?'

Both men nodded adamantly.

They were talking about *old* people, like Frances. Whoever killed Baker had to have been strong enough to wield a heavy object. Jess wasn't so sure an elderly female

– she wouldn't name names – would be able to manage such a feat. 'Exactly how old are these widows?'

'The youngest is seventy-five,' Brewer said with a nod to Foster for confirmation. 'She's the ringleader.'

'She sure is,' Foster agreed. 'That woman is a mess.'

'Who's the ringleader?' Again Jess looked from Brewer to Foster, bracing for the name she did not want to hear.

'She's been riling up those other old ladies since day one,' Foster said, his tone firm.

With a big emphatic nod, Brewer added, 'She's the one threatened to kill Mr Baker – there's witnesses to that.'

'I need a name, gentlemen,' Jess nudged. She appreciated their thoughts on the woman but a name would come in far handier.

'Frances Wallace,' the men said in unison.

And there it was. Frances had admitted to motive. Certainly she'd had opportunity. Now, for all the world to see, there were witnesses to the public declaration of her motive.

Oh God. This was going to get complicated…

The medical examiner had just estimated time of death between 8.00 and 10.00 P.M. Frances had showed up at Jess's door around eleven or shortly after with her shocking announcement.

Dread settled on her shoulders. Jess had spent a lifetime looking up to Frances Wallace. Making sure this case was investigated properly and the real murderer found would be a piece of cake.

Protecting her friend's reputation was going to be the fly in the frosting.

Chapter Three

3.40 A.M.

Jess entered the Vestavia Village library and suggested the officer watching over Frances Wallace take a short break. When he'd closed the door behind him, Jess turned to the woman who'd curled up like a cat and fallen asleep in one of the large, comfortable chairs scattered around the book- and magazine-filled room.

Whatever other mischief Frances had gotten herself into during the past twenty-four hours, murder was not among her activities. Jess would lay odds on that. There was, however, no way to prevent viewing her as a person of interest and pursuing the necessary accounting of her movements during the past six or so hours that would clear her. Even Frances would understand that reality. In any event, she had a hell of a lot of explaining to do.

Preferably before Burnett and the mayor got involved

in the investigation any more deeply than they already were. That kind of interference always complicated an investigation. Made Jess want to tear out her hair.

She set her bag down and dragged over another chair. As she settled in, Frances opened her eyes and straightened. 'Had myself a little nap.' She fanned away the loose strands of hair that had slipped free of her trademark bun and adjusted her blouse. 'Did I miss anything?'

With monumental effort, Jess resisted the urge to roll her eyes. 'You mean, other than the body down the hall?' Jess shook her head. 'You didn't miss a thing.'

'Well.' Frances cleared her throat and folded her hands in her lap. 'I warned you that was coming.'

Somehow, while listening to her sketchy story on the way here, Jess had hoped to discover the victim's death had been an accident. Maybe he'd tripped and hit his head. It happened. Hundreds of Americans died every year just getting out of bed.

'Yes, ma'am, you sure did.' Jess retrieved her notepad and pencil. 'Why don't you tell me what you were doing before you decided to pay a visit to our murder victim?'

The older woman's head reared back just a little. 'So it was murder?'

'The official ruling will come after the autopsy but the ME has indicated we have a homicide on our hands.'

'Good heavens.' Frances put a hand to her chest. 'Am I going to jail? My daughter will never forgive me. It's a good thing Orson is dead already or this would kill him.'

'Whether you're going to jail,' Jess assured her, 'is entirely dependent upon whether you *only* threatened to kill Scott Baker in front of about a dozen witnesses.' Frustration puckered Jess's face, which only irritated her all the more. 'For Pete's sake, you couldn't have told the man in private that you were going to kill him?'

Fingers twiddling with the collar of her blouse and the antique brooch fastened there, Frances let a hint of trepidation show. 'Well, gracious no, Jess. The whole impact would have been lost had there not been any witnesses. I was making a point,' she insisted, as if Jess should understand perfectly what she'd intended.

God, she needed coffee. But going to the dining hall would be like jumping from the frying pan into the fire with all the village residents camped out there. 'Why don't you start at the beginning and bring me all the way up to now,' Jess suggested, 'and tell me what the point was. While you're at it, explain this *Widows* club thing you've got going.'

Frances grunted. 'We're going to need to send that nice young man who's been keeping me company for tea. This might take a while.'

Jess sent Officer Gillam for tea and coffee before settling her full attention on Frances once more.

'Nine years ago, Orson and I bought into this retirement facility. We paid big money for condos in the building that overlooked the lake. As did a number of our friends, at our urging, I might add.' She visibly struggled to contain the hurt that still lingered with the loss of her life mate. 'Many invested their whole life savings. Then two years ago there was a change of command. Out with the old and in with the new. Suddenly we had Scott Baker and a new corporation, Your Life, who cared only for making more money on this investment.'

Anger lit in Jess's belly. That was something she despised more than most anything else. Those who bullied or took advantage of children and the elderly.

'What steps have they taken to that end?' Jess jotted the names Frances had mentioned.

'They're constructing a new building between ours and the lake. Stealing our bought-and-paid-for view of nature and giving us a massive brick wall in its place.' Her lips tightened in fury. 'Perhaps some would consider that a nonissue but we have the right to the quality of living we were promised. I've been spearheading the group of widows fighting the project. That's all I'm guilty of, Jessie Lee. Beyond a few not-so-pleasant thoughts about Baker and his cronies.'

'Which brings me back to the question,' Jess countered, refusing to allow her adoration for the lady to throw her off her game. 'Why were you in his office tonight?'

'I'd just come in from dinner at my daughter's home.

She and I had discussed how Baker was ignoring all our efforts and I was a little worked up.' Frances lifted her chin and said the rest. 'I saw his car was still here and I decided to demand some answers. But he was dead.'

Well, there was a truckload of motive. Jesus. 'Did you see any other vehicles in the parking lot?' Jess went on, hoping for additional answers that would clear the lady, not make her look guiltier. 'Any other persons, even from a distance? Think hard, Frances. Was there anyone else in the parking lot or lobby area? Did you meet another vehicle as you were driving up to the facility?'

Frances opened her mouth and then snapped it shut. She furrowed her brow in thought, then said, 'You know, I did meet another car after turning into the entrance.'

Anticipation pumped through Jess. Now they were getting somewhere. 'Can you describe the car?'

Her shoulders slumped. 'No. Their headlights were on bright. I cursed them all the way to my parking spot.' She shook her head. 'I wouldn't even have recalled that nuisance if you hadn't asked.'

Jess's disappointment at not getting a description must have been visible since Frances tacked on, 'Get ready for it, Jessie Lee. That's how it is when you get old. Can't see, can't hear. Forget every damned thing. The children you gave everything to are just glad you're some place like this instead of in their way more than one evening a week.'

Jess's heart broke just a little. 'It's the same whether a witness is eighteen or eighty, Frances. There's a lot they forget to mention unless asked specific questions. Why don't you just relax a few minutes and I'll be back in a bit.'

4.49 A.M.

As hard as she tried to keep her emotions in check, Jess dabbed at her eyes as she left Frances cuddled up in that same chair with a cup of hot tea. Jess left her cup on the table. The dining hall had run out of regular coffee. The only thing worse than no coffee at all was decaf. She closed the door behind her and gave the waiting officer strict orders not to allow anyone in or out of the library.

Burnett was here and he had sent Jess a text demanding to see her pronto. He couched the string of words with *please* but that was just code for *Don't make me send someone to get you.*

She took a breath and reached for the door that stood between her and the man who'd made love to her only a few hours ago. He was going to let her have it for ignoring his calls all morning.

Wouldn't be the first time or the last, she suspected.

He was on his cell when she stepped into the room. Whoever was on the other end, he wasn't making Burnett happy, or maybe it was the other way around. Oblivious to her arrival, Burnett gestured in frustration with his free hand – or more specifically the hand holding a cup of Starbucks coffee. Jess licked her lips in anticipation. Another cup sat on a nearby table. Was that one for her? If it was, that would be an answered prayer. Considering how long she'd kept Burnett waiting, the coffee was no doubt cold but she didn't care. She seriously needed caffeine.

He snapped a cutting remark at his caller. Something about keeping the investigation low-key for now. Usually unable to control her curiosity, she would try figuring out who was on the other end of that conversation. Not this morning. She had bigger issues with this case. But neither the case nor the promise of Starbucks could prevent the way she studied his every move. He had his back to her and there was absolutely nothing wrong with that side of him. Broad shoulders, narrow waist, and, well, things just got better from there. The elegantly tailored suit accentuated his every asset. Most of them, anyway. There were some that were best admired without any sort of embellishments.

A smile tugged at her lips when she thought of the way his skin smelled. Clean and masculine. He'd always been subtle with his aftershave or cologne. They shared that habit. Give Jess a softly scented lotion any day over perfume.

He ended the call and turned as if he'd suddenly sensed her presence. Her breath hitched. Looking at him head-on had always managed that feat. How could he be more handsome now than he had been as an ambitious senior in high school? His dark hair scarcely showed even a hint of gray. Jess had to get her roots touched up most every month. It was the bane of her existence.

Not fair.

And how the hell could so much time have passed? They'd known each other since they were kids. God she felt old. Forty-two really sucked so far.

Those blue eyes of his zeroed in on hers. 'I called.'

She nodded. 'Four times.'

He dropped his cell into his jacket pocket, then bracketed his coffee-free hand at his waist in an author-itative maneuver. All the move did for Jess was point out that, like Sylvia Baron, Burnett always looked expertly put together. Crisp, creamy white shirt and tan trousers topped off with a navy jacket and tie. When he wore that color, those blue eyes of his appeared even more vivid.

'You enjoy ignoring me like that?'

Jess sighed. She could lie but he would know. 'Immensely.'

Burnett frowned but he moved on. 'Sylvia says this appears to be a homicide.'

'I never had a doubt.' Vaguely she wondered if he'd

been speaking so sharply to Sylvia. But mostly she was amazed at how the sound of his voice disrupted her heart's natural rhythm even now when the topic of conversation was murder. That was something she probably should never say out loud. And just went to show how very much sleep deprivation affected one's ability to reason and stay on track.

Get to the point, Jess. 'Is SPU keeping this case?'

The hesitation before he answered had her heart thumping for a completely different reason. Her Special Problems Unit often had to go to war with Crimes Against Persons for cases like this. Jess had her own motives for needing to see this one through, but she didn't want to bring up Frances Wallace just yet. Knowing Burnett, he would insist a conflict of interest existed and the case would go to Deputy Chief Harold Black.

'Harold has his hands full with the Ted Allen situation.'

When a cop went missing, the first assumption was always foul play. Between that and the bomb planted in the department vehicle she had been driving last week, there were lots of questions and endless speculation going around. *For example, had her interference in the Lopez case gotten Allen killed?* That was one place she had no desire to go at the moment. She had done her job. Still, she hadn't missed the suspicious glances being cast her way around the department. The clashes between her and Allen were well and widely known.

Yes, he didn't like her. Yes, she felt no love loss toward him. But making him disappear was not her way of handling departmental rivalry. Otherwise there were a number of others who would go missing as well.

Not funny, Jess.

Whatever happened, she held no power over Leonardo Lopez and the actions he chose to take.

'It's certainly nice to be needed,' she said, hopefully diverting the course of the conversation away from another reminder of how she took too many risks. 'Why is it that every single time my team is assigned a case of this caliber it's because Black is busy?'

Burnett gave her that look – the one that warned she was being petty. She was. She waved him off. 'Forget I said anything.' She'd gotten in the dig. He'd remember her smart-ass remark next time that same old tug-of-war surfaced. And he would think twice about letting Black have first dibs just to prove her wrong. She knew him like a book. Dan Burnett was all about fair. Fairness and justice. He didn't like breaking the rules – that wasn't to say he wouldn't, but he didn't like it.

'I *need* you to tread carefully on this one, Jess,' Burnett continued, ignoring her question entirely but, thankfully, skipping the I'm-worried-about-you spiel. 'The victim's family roots go all the way back to the founding of Birmingham. Try not to offend anyone – especially if his or her name is Baker. He has an older brother who's a lobbyist in Montgomery and I'd like to keep him on good terms with the department. His support is invaluable.'

If her eyes had rolled any farther back in her head, she would have seen her roots going gray even as she stood there enduring this needless lecture. 'I wouldn't dream of stepping on any toes, especially any important ones.' One month in the department and she had a reputation that ensured her boss felt compelled to give her a talking-to before each case. 'Anything else you want to correct about my work before I get back to it?'

His gaze narrowed. 'No one who matters can fault your performance on the job, Jess. For your information, Mayor Pratt suggested you were the one he wanted on this case.'

Jess snorted. She cleared her throat and resisted the urge to ask if Pratt had somehow acquired amnesia. Like so many of her colleagues, as well as the brass around here, Pratt didn't like Jess's style or her methods. He spent more time complaining about her tactics than the city's anti-establishment reporters.

'Pratt asked for me?' There had to be a motive she wasn't going to like.

'I think you've shown him what you're made of,' Burnett said. 'He knows no one else will do the job better.'

Okay, this was too over the top to handle with no caffeine. She desperately needed a second wind about now. 'Is that Starbucks for me?'

He picked up the cup and passed it to her. 'It would still be warm if you hadn't ignored me when I first arrived thirty-five minutes ago.'

It was warm enough. The strong, rich taste had her stifling a moan. 'Thanks.'

He gave her a moment to relish her coffee before starting his interrogations. 'What's the deal with this group of widows Baker was having trouble with?'

He'd been briefed on the statements they'd collected so far. Good. Kept her from having to repeat the whole sordid story. 'There's a group of seven elderly residents who, along with their husbands, who've since passed on, bought into the village nine years ago when it was in the development phase.'

Burnett took her by the elbow and guided her toward the chairs. 'Let's sit.'

Did she look that exhausted or was he just being a gentleman? Some of both, she imagined. Actually she was exhausted, so she sat. Waited until he did the same and resumed her story. 'The building these ladies signed on for included spacious condos with balconies overlooking the seven-acre lake designed for the property. They've all lived happily ever after in their nice condos with their lovely views until the takeover by some money-hungry corporation. Now a new building that will draw in more elderly investors is going up.'

He nodded. 'The new building will block that *lovely* view.'

'Completely. The condos where the widows live is going from prime real estate to nowhere near prime. They've demanded construction be stopped or that a generous portion of their initial investments plus interest and so on be refunded.'

'Ouch.' Burnett crossed his legs at the ankles and tried to get more comfortable in the hard plastic chair.

'Since the new building is already sold out, stopping construction would be a financial catastrophe for the corp's investors.' Didn't take an accountant or a crystal ball to see that one.

Burnett slowly turned his cup between his fingers. 'One of these women publicly threatened Baker. What's your take on that?'

Jess hoped he didn't remember the name from when they were kids. 'Frances Wallace. Her husband was a distant relative of *the* George Wallace. Frances comes from old money, just like Baker, so this ongoing war over the new building wasn't about money. She could have bought a condo in the new building without blinking. She's fighting for the rights of the other six who used their life savings to buy into the village. They're being taken advantage of and no one on the board seems to care. It's a classic scam.'

Not to mention just another example of how bullies were tolerated far too often in today's society. Kids weren't the only targets. The elderly were often manipulated, deceived, and pushed around.

'You've interviewed her already?'

This was where things got sticky. 'I have. I don't believe she possesses the physical strength to do what the killer did to Baker.'

'What about the others?'

'We'll get to each one before the day is over, but' – Jess looked him square in the eye – 'I'm telling you now that none of these ladies are physically capable of murder in this manner simply by virtue of their advanced ages.' For God's sake, Frances was the youngest of the seven.

'Could they have pooled their resources and hired someone to do the job?' Burnett shrugged. 'Maybe they felt Baker was ultimately responsible for their problem and decided to get him out of the way.'

Jess couldn't rule out that scenario just yet but Frances would not have been party to that kind of scheme. No way. 'I will investigate that possibility. What we should keep in mind are two important facts that are irrefutable. Scott Baker was expecting company. His guest was someone he knew well enough to shut off the surveillance system in anticipation of their arrival, which seems to indicate he didn't want their meeting documented. Maybe Baker was caving to the widows, and someone with much to gain with the construction of this new building wasn't happy.'

'His final actions open up a variety of questions and motives,' Burnett suggested.

'He may have been meeting with a lover,' Jess offered. 'His own or his wife's. There may have been trouble with one or more of the board members involved with the corporation. Maybe with the contractor or a media source who'd gotten wind of the trouble with the widows. There are a lot of avenues to explore. I'm starting with the most well known – the ongoing battle with the widows.'

'Keep me in the loop. I don't want any surprises showing up in the news. There's already a mob on the street at the property's boundary.'

Not surprising. Getting the inside story on a murder kept ratings up. Jess stood. She had to get back to work. 'Yes, sir.'

Burnett pushed to his feet, his eyes searching hers again. 'Do we need to have *that* talk again?'

'We do not. I'm keeping an eye out for trouble. I'm definitely not taking any risks.' None worth mentioning anyway.

'Until we learn how that bomb got in the car you were using and what the hell happened to Allen, I won't feel comfortable about your safety or that of any other cop in the department.'

Except he wasn't hovering over any other cop. Jess had spent the last twenty-four hours chewing on this. She might as well say it. 'There is a chance that Allen wanted to get rid of me that badly, isn't there? He was in the motor pool the day you ordered the Taurus for me.' It was true. Dammit, she hated to think badly of a man who was most likely a victim, probably dead. But it was true. He'd made no bones about his less-than-friendly feelings toward Jess. Would he try to kill her, though? 'Maybe he knows he's caught and he disappeared to avoid the investigation.' Not to mention prison.

'I don't want to believe one of my own people would go there, but I can't deny it's possible,' Burnett admitted.

Jess had been ignoring one theory about why and how Allen had vanished. Birmingham's former drug and gang kingpins, the Lopez family, had warned that someone inside the department had it in for her. It made sense that Allen, being head of the gang task force and well known to the Lopez family, was the someone they meant. Particularly since he and Jess had butted heads so often. Now that the patriarch of the Lopez family had left Birmingham, had he neutralized the threat to which he'd alluded? Jess had gotten word that she shouldn't worry about that particular problem anymore. She had an *angel de la guarda*. A guardian angel, according to Lopez's messenger.

That was the part that worried her the most. The bomb, Allen's disappearance, the Lopez business could all be related. But why would Lopez go that far for Jess? Why would he play her guardian angel?

'Maybe Lopez wanted revenge for Allen's part in the downfall of his family,' she offered. 'For whatever reason, he may have decided I should get a reprieve.' Except there had been a bomb in the car she was supposed to use . . .

'Be smart, Jess.' Those blue eyes that had the power to draw her into his arms with a single inviting look showed her the fear and the worry he felt. 'Revenge is an ugly business, as you well know. If someone had it in for Allen for his perceived part in tearing apart the Lopez family, they may still have you on that same list. We can't rule out anything at this point. Lopez could have someone watching you right now.'

'That's me,' Jess said with a laugh she hoped passed for the real thing, 'Miss Popular.'

She doubted she would be so popular after she informed the widows that they were all persons of interest in a murder case.

With no other leads at this time, Jess's first order of business was to find a way to confirm Frances Wallace and the rest couldn't possibly have murdered Baker.

That would be a whole lot easier as soon as she found someone with a better motive for wanting the guy dead.

Chapter Four

Birmingham Police Department, 10.20 A.M.

'Captain Ted Allen has been officially missing more than seventy-two hours.' Jess paused for a beat before continuing. Guilt tried to intrude but she sent the pointless emotion packing. She wasn't responsible for the head of BPD's gang task force going missing. At least she hoped she wasn't. She exiled theories about guardian angels. 'I've just spent the past half hour in a closed-door session with Chief of Police Burnett, the mayor, and the other chiefs for a quick update.'

She'd barely gotten back to the office and started her case board on the Baker homicide when she'd gotten the call to report to the conference room. The press was about to be informed about Allen, and Burnett wanted everyone on the same sheet of music.

Jess surveyed her team, that infernal anxiety gnawing at her again. 'Our team was not assigned the case but we should press any unique sources we have for information. Check in with your informants. The investigation has zero leads right now. We need something. Every law enforcement agency in the state has been alerted to the situation. We recognize there is a strong likelihood that if Captain Allen did not leave of his own volition, he's already dead. There has been no demand or contact of any sort related to his disappearance. Be that as it may, until we have a body, this case will be pursued as if he is alive and in imminent danger.'

She braced for the barrage of questions the four members of her team would no doubt raise. She'd heard the watercooler talk. Most everyone thought Allen's disappearance had something to do with her face-to-face meeting with Leonardo Lopez, the so-called messiah of the MS-13 in LA and the father of the son and daughter who had effectively destroyed each other here in Birmingham mere days ago.

But Jess hadn't set up that meeting. She had been as surprised as anyone when Lopez sought her out last week as a means to convey his message to the powers that be in the city. He hadn't sent her that message about having a guardian angel until much later. She kicked the idea out of her head again. There was just no evidence at this time to make that connection.

Still, she recognized how it looked, and human nature had taken its course.

Chad Cook, the lowest-ranking and youngest member of the Special Problems Unit, spoke first. 'I guess Black getting the case was a good thing since that leaves us free to focus on the Baker homicide.'

'Deputy Chief Black and Crimes Against Persons will be primary on the Allen case, yes,' Jess confirmed, 'but make no mistake, the entire department will be involved in finding one of our own. This is not a competition. Keep that in mind, please.' Jess hoped no one in the room noted her lack of conviction in that last statement. Finding the bad guys was always a competition, starting with who got the case.

'Are *you* a suspect in the captain's disappearance, Chief Harris?'

Jess expected no less from Lieutenant Valerie Prescott. She might not overcome her frustration of being passed over for SPU's deputy chief in this lifetime, which inevitably meant that she would remain a thorn in Jess's side. Which was also another reason Jess didn't trust the woman one little bit. Two years older than Jess, Prescott was every bit as ambitious as her. She disliked her new boss and had no problem telling the world.

During the silence that followed the blunt question, the other members of SPU, Sergeant Chet Harper, Detective Lori Wells, and Officer Chad Cook, gave

Prescott the evil eye. At least the majority of Jess's small but skilled team respected and liked her. Unfortunately that reality didn't make the lieutenant's question any less relevant.

'I would be surprised if I wasn't considered a person of interest,' Jess admitted. 'But it won't be because Captain Allen had issues with the way I handled my end of the Lopez case or that he made those issues abundantly clear. Our close involvement in the Lopez case will be thoroughly investigated, as will that of numerous other detectives and federal agents. That's investigation one-oh-one, Lieutenant.'

'I haven't heard any rumors of trouble in his personal life,' Harper commented, redirecting the conversation. 'No marital or financial problems.'

'His record at BPD has been exceptional,' Jess added, thankful to be moving in the proper direction. Captain Allen's visit to the motor pool, just before Jess picked up the explosive Taurus, was known only by the few, like Chief Black, involved directly with the investigation into his disappearance. Until there was solid evidence Allen had crossed the line, that was the way it would stay.

Detective Lori Wells twisted in her chair. 'What about you, Valerie?' she said to Prescott, who was her superior in rank, but the younger woman didn't seem to care. Lori and Jess had bonded too deeply not to call each other good friends, off and on the job. 'Are you a person of interest, considering you were Allen's link to the scuttle-butt regarding Chief Harris? The way I hear it, you kept him informed of the chief's every move where Lopez was concerned.'

Though she appreciated Lori's support, this wasn't the time. Jess held up a hand before Prescott could utter what would no doubt be a frosty comeback if the icy glare pointed at Lori was any indication. 'Let's get back to the case board and what we have so far on Scott Baker. I just wanted y'all to know what's going on. And now' – she squared her shoulders – 'you know. So, let's move on.'

'Baker was only twenty-seven when he was selected to be administrator of Vestavia Village,' Harper said. 'That's a little young, so I did some asking around and it seems he has a friend of the family, a retired army general, on the board who ensured he was chosen for the position before the sellout to Your Life.'

'The Baker family,' Lori Wells picked up where Harper left off, 'required the victim and all three of his brothers to obtain an MBA and then to work in the private sector for at least three years and to reach the age of thirty before receiving their trust funds. Scott was set to receive his in less than one week.'

'I guess Daddy wanted to make sure his sons knew how to work for a living.' Seemed to Jess that more parents should do the same before turning over their money to their offspring.

'Makes you wonder how badly his wife wanted full access to that trust fund,' Prescott suggested.

'Good point,' Jess acknowledged. She wanted Prescott to be a part of this team. Mostly she wanted the woman to get over the fact that she didn't get the job and that Jess was her boss, for better or worse. 'How much is this trust fund? And does the wife get it or does it go back into trust for their son?'

'Ten million,' Lori said. 'I'll have to find out where it goes now.' She made a note in her phone.

'Ten million is a lot of motive,' Chad Cook said.

'By anyone's standards,' Jess agreed. 'Where are we on the statements from the other six widows and Claire Warren?'

'Cook and I have two more scheduled this afternoon,' Prescott said. 'Those two were out of town for a long weekend.'

'We asked what questions we could by phone,' Cook added. 'The important stuff, you know. Just to be sure they didn't go changing their stories after talking to anyone else.'

'Excellent strategy. I'm certain the first thing both did as soon as you spoke with them was to call their fellow widows.'

'I interviewed Ms Warren when she arrived at the Village this morning,' Prescott noted. 'She's been the dining room director since the Village opened. Her statement is a carbon copy of Foster's and Brewer's. She heard Frances Wallace say something to the effect that she would see Baker dead before she would allow him to get away with the new construction.'

'I can't see those ladies taking Baker down that way,' Harper countered. 'He was a young guy in good physical condition. His secretary said he played racquetball twice a week and ran three or four miles every day. He was strong. It took a hell of a blow to take him off his feet and keep him down.'

'And a sudden, lightning-fast move,' Lori tossed out. 'Baker had no defensive wounds. He didn't try and deflect the blow. He obviously wasn't expecting it.'

'It may have taken two blows to put him down for good,' Jess noted, remembering the way the gash in his temple looked. 'The first one may have rattled him enough that he didn't have time to react before the second blow landed.'

'Doesn't sound like one of the widows,' Harper reiterated. 'These ladies are seventy-five and beyond.'

Jess studied the images Lori had printed from the ladies' Facebook pages. According to Lori, everyone had a Facebook page these days. Jess didn't mention that she didn't have one. She was way behind on social media. Who had time? Her attention settled lastly on the photo of the face she knew so well. Frances Wallace. She'd asked Jess if she needed a lawyer. The only answer she could give was yes. Though Jess was convinced of her innocence, this situation could get complicated fast.

'They all have alibis.' Lori cleared her throat. 'Except Ms Wallace.'

'Ms Wallace has an alibi up until nine-fifteen,' Jess countered. 'Between nine-fifteen and ten o'clock, she arrived on the property where she met another vehicle departing. She couldn't hazard a guess at the kind of vehicle since the headlights blinded her.'

The silence that lingered signaled that everyone present understood Frances Wallace was a sensitive spot for Jess.

'Despite the concept,' Jess said, getting past the awkward moment, 'that these elderly women likely don't possess the physical prowess to have killed Baker, as Sergeant Harper pointed out, we can't overlook the possibility that they banded together and hired someone to do the job for them.'

'I can explore that avenue,' Prescott piped up. 'I worked a case last year where a wife hired a professional to have her husband murdered. I did a good bit of research that could come in handy.'

Jess was impressed with Prescott's sudden team spirit, if not convinced of her allegiance. 'Since you and Officer Cook are interviewing the widows, I'll leave the follow-up on that scenario to the two of you as well.'

Prescott looked pleased with herself.

As much as she would like to assume this was a fresh start for her and Prescott, Jess still had reservations. 'Sergeant Harper, dissect Baker's personal life. Find me a motive for murder. Someone out there wanted Scott Baker dead. We need to know who had a compelling enough reason to make it happen when the opportunity presented itself. We can assume since the murder weapon was most likely the Administrator of the Year trophy that the killer didn't come to Baker's office planning to kill him.'

'Unless,' Prescott argued, 'the killer had been there before and knew the trophy would do the trick.'

'Valid point.' Jess couldn't dismiss her reasoning. The woman was on the ball this morning. 'We do know the killer was in all likelihood right-handed. I'm hoping the feedback we get from the coroner's office can tell us if the killer was shorter or taller than the victim. If we're really lucky, trace evidence from a handshake or embrace will be found and can provide something more to go on.'

'I can follow up with the lab,' Lori offered. 'See if I can prod some faster results.'

Jess flashed her a smile. 'All right, then. Officer Cook, you'll continue to assist the lieutenant. I'll go back to Vestavia Village and poke around.'

When everyone else had gone, Lori asked, 'You reinterviewing some of the residents?'

Jess shook her head. 'Nope. You and I are going to see the body and talk to Dr Baron.'

Lori dug her keys from her purse. 'You worried Prescott's still keeping tabs on you for some reason?'

'Without a doubt.' Jess reached for her bag. 'We both know that's how Captain Allen knew my every move during the Lopez case.' That bad feeling she got every time she thought of the man scrambled up her spine. 'And look what happened to him.'

'You better watch out,' Lori teased. 'That could be construed as a confession.'

Jess decided to get the real confession part over with. 'If I went with my gut instinct, I'd have to say that whatever happened to him just might be related to me or something I did. I don't know what it is or how it connects to anything. But that guardian angel message from Lopez keeps nagging at me.' Another knot tied deep in her belly. 'I don't like that feeling one little bit.'

Jefferson County Coroner's Office, 11.39 A.M.

An autopsy, even a partial one, was an excellent tool for an investigator. Oftentimes it was the results of the tests conducted by medical examiners that turned around a case going nowhere or, worse, in the wrong direction. Jess was banking on the story Scott Baker's body could tell to help clear Frances and point them in the direction of the real killer.

Baker lay on the cold steel table, his arms at his sides, his naked body a somber gray. Before this day was over, every inch of him would be tested in one way or another. The tiniest speck of trace evidence could make the difference in finding the identity of his murderer.

'The CT scan revealed depressed fractures right here.' Sylvia Baron indicated his left temple where the visible gashes were located. 'His attacker hit just the right spot and he hit it hard. Two distinct blows. The first may have knocked the victim off his feet, but it was the second one that got the artery and caused a massive bleed. The worst I've seen that didn't involve a vehicle or a bullet.'

Judging by the visible tissue injury, Jess would have thought he'd have had a concussion, a bad headache and little more. Unfortunately, Mr Baker hadn't been so lucky. But Sylvia's conclusions confirmed the theory that Frances Wallace couldn't have been the one wielding the murder weapon.

'It's rare,' Sylvia continued, 'but I'd say he was dead in under five minutes. The good news is he may have died happy.' Her lips quirked. 'There were significant traces of semen and vaginal fluid in his boxers.'

So Frances Wallace wasn't the only female visitor to show up at Scott Baker's office on the night of his murder. 'No wonder he turned his surveillance system off.'

'When the cat's away the rat will play,' Sylvia said with a sour glance at the victim.

Couldn't exactly blame her. She'd lost her husband of ten years to another woman.

'Too early for any toxicology?' Jess knew better than to ask but she couldn't help herself and it felt like a good way to move on from Baker's indiscretions.

'Just the BAT,' Sylvia offered. 'Point-oh-five. Under the legal limit of intoxication for operating a vehicle but the man definitely had a drink before that wallop to the side of his head. Which didn't help his survival odds. Apparently it didn't help his morals either.'

'There was no alcohol in the office or in his car.' Jess resisted the urge to frown and add to the wrinkle population already residing on her face. 'I guess the killer opted not to leave that behind.'

'He did, however' – Sylvia indicated the gash in Baker's temple again – 'leave you the murder weapon.'

'The trophy?' Jess had thought as much.

Sylvia nodded. 'I spoke with the detective overseeing the analysis at the lab. Whoever cleaned the trophy last used a wood polish on or near the base. It sat on the desk – maybe the polish came from the desk.' She smiled. 'There's just no way to think of every little possibility when you're trying to commit the perfect murder, especially if one's thought processes are still hazy after orgasm. At any rate, the desk was cleaned recently and furniture polish was used liberally. Maybe the killer missed one of his or *her* prints as well in the wipe-down. The lab's still working on that aspect.'

'There's always one more thing the killer should have thought of,' Jess agreed.

'I don't want to get your hopes up,' Sylvia went on, 'but a trace of the victim's blood was discovered between the marble base of the trophy and the miniature brass statue of a businessman. So the wipe-down wasn't as thorough as the killer likely intended.'

'Sounds less and less like a professional job.' In Jess's opinion, the killer didn't have murder on his – or her – mind when he walked into Baker's office. Just another reason to rule out the widows' involvement in any capacity.

The key to this case was finding out who had reason to want or need Baker out of the way. Every act of violence was prompted by motive. Motives were rooted in emotion. Emotions ensured mistakes. It was a no-win situation for the killer.

All Jess had to do was find the motive and the mistakes. It looked as if she had a new avenue. *Infidelity*.

'And more like Baker pissed off the wrong person,' Sylvia agreed. 'A person shorter than him, by the way. The angle of the blow appears to have come from an upward slant.'

That might not be as significant as she'd hoped since

the victim was over six feet. Lots of folks, female and male, would be shorter than him. 'All I need now is a usable print or DNA sample and I can set out just like the prince in Cinderella to find who it belongs to,' Jess said, only half kidding. That was the thing about DNA evidence and even prints – there had to be something to compare that kind of evidence to. If there wasn't a match in one of the many criminal databases, then she had to pound the pavement and find it.

'There's something else.'

Jess's instincts perked up.

Sylvia drew back the sheet and tapped Baker's right hip. 'I have no idea what it means. Some fraternities have symbols but this isn't one I've seen before.'

The tattoo was a set of five small circles intertwined with a number five in the center. The ink was black, faded a little as if he'd had it for a while. 'Looks like a brand.' Jess met the doctor's gaze. 'The way ranchers mark their livestock. Maybe it's a family thing.' But Baker had only three siblings, not four. Jess studied the tattoo a moment longer. 'No gang or business affiliation I recognize.' She fished for her cell and snapped a picture.

'I looked it up,' Sylvia told her. 'It's a Celtic five knot. Represents earth, wind, fire, water, unity.' She surveyed the victim. 'For now that's all I can give you.'

'I appreciate it.' Jess readied to head out. 'How's Leslie working out?' Leslie Chambers was the teenage sister of the key witness in the homicide case Jess had worked last week. Sylvia had pretty much taken the two kids under her wing. She was funding Leslie's college and the younger brother's attendance at a private school for autistic children. Sylvia had also gotten the girl an internship here at the coroner's office. The lady had truly gone above and beyond.

'She's a fast learner and a hard worker.' Sylvia tidied the sheet on the victim. 'She's a terrific kid.'

'She's lucky to have made such a good friend.' Jess didn't expect the other woman to acknowledge the compliment. For a woman who seemed so arrogant and full of herself, Sylvia Baron didn't take real compliments well.

Before Jess was out the door, the ME called after her, 'My family has their annual Labor Day barbeque coming up. Check your schedule – if you don't have plans already, you should come. Bring Dan along.'

Jess hoped her surprise wasn't showing. 'I'll let you know.'

So maybe they were friends, or at the very least on the road to becoming friends. The jury was still out.

Jess caught up with Lori in the long corridor outside the autopsy room, and the detective tucked her phone into the pocket of her trousers and gave Jess a look that warned she wasn't going to like the news.

Before Jess got any more bad news – she'd had more

than her share last week – she needed to pass along a revelation of her own. 'Let Harper know that Baker was definitely having an affair.' Harper was digging around in the victim's personal life. This news would give him a direction. 'And our perp is in all probability shorter than the victim.'

'Okay.' Lori sent the text, then settled her attention back on Jess. 'That was the chief.'

Jess expected as much. She didn't have to check her phone to know he'd called her as well. She'd seen the missed call when she snapped the picture of Baker's tattoo. 'Do I want to know?'

'He needs you in his office. Now.'

Which meant one of two things: either the mayor wanted her reassurance that she would have the Baker case solved ASAP or they had found Captain Allen's body buried in her backyard.

Since she hadn't harmed a hair on the man's head much less planted him anywhere, it had to be about the Baker case.

She hoped.

Chapter Five

The Grille, Five Points, Noon

'I can't believe he's dead.' Juliette Coleman felt sick to her stomach. She pushed away the menu. This was her favorite lunch spot but there was no way she could eat and have this discussion. It hurt too much.

This wasn't supposed to happen. Agony flooded her being. What did she do now? How did she move past this? Stop the images from flashing over and over in her head?

She shut down that line of thinking. She couldn't go there. Not right now.

'This can't be.' Elliott Carson turned his hands up and surveyed the rest of the group seated around the table. 'No way. What about his wife and kid? Jesus Christ.' He hung his head, obviously stunned and horrified by the news.

63

He was the one she would have expected to be torn up about this. Elliott had always been the most kind-hearted of all the guys. Yet he was the one who had the most reason not to be. With his former celebrity status as a Major League Baseball player for the Pittsburgh Pirates, everyone had expected him to turn into a self-centered ass, but he never had. Instead, after several amazing seasons and a shoulder injury that forced his retirement at the height of his game, he came right back here to Birmingham and started a training camp for young athletes. He spent a lot of time giving back to the community.

Somehow over the years she'd forgotten what a good guy Elliott was . . . How had they come to this?

Don't go there, Juliette.

'What the hell happened?' Aaron Taylor demanded. He had no patience for beating around the bush; he never had.

'You're kidding, right?' Kevin O'Reilly, the son of Birmingham's media mogul Clinton O'Reilly, directed this at Aaron and then spent a long, dramatic moment in silence, staring across the table from one to the other.

Even if they weren't discussing the death of a lifelong friend, Kevin would pull out his whole trunk of theatrics. He'd been a drama queen back in high school and he was still one today. Part of him was probably glad Scott was dead. One less person for Kevin to be jealous of. Juliette banished the ugly thoughts. This was not the time.

God, what was she going to do? Agony welled inside her all over again.

'I warned you this would happen if Todd Penney ever came back,' Kevin said knowingly. 'Scott should have listened to me. All of you better start paying attention.'

'Oh my God.' Juliette couldn't believe he'd just said that. Anger overrode the pain and regret. Kevin thought he was the only one who could solve a fucking problem. Worse, he was making this about him! He made her sick.

As if he'd read her mind, he glared at her in warning.

She glowered right back, hoping he saw just how much she hated his guts right now.

'You can't really believe *he* would do this?' Aaron challenged. 'What could he possibly hope to gain?'

Answer that one, you sawed off little bastard, Juliette wanted to scream at him.

Unlike Kevin or Elliott, Aaron was the logical one. It was the attorney in him. Like his father and his grandfather, he had been born to analyze and to challenge. But a courtroom was the only place where he pulled out those sizeable balls of his these days. The cocky football star from high school was as queer as a three-dollar bill but he didn't have the nerve to come out of the closet. Instead he'd taken a fake wife and pretended they were

65

waiting until their careers were established to have children.

Juliette resisted the urge to shake her head. And the gang thought she was the only one who lived a lie. This little family was in for a major wake-up call. As much as she had loved all these guys at one time . . . there was something rotting away between them. She could hardly bear to sit at this table . . . but she had to. They'd made a promise. She, for one, intended to see that they all held up their ends of that bargain. She was not going to prison for anyone or anything.

Not even for Scott . . .

Beneath all the bravado and self-centeredness, they all had one nasty little secret in common – they were cowards. Even Aaron's innate reasoning skill hadn't helped them that night twelve years ago.

A new kind of fear welled so quickly inside Juliette she could hardly breathe. If anyone ever found out . . . What was she thinking? *He* knew. And if Kevin was right, Todd Penney was back and wanted revenge for the death of his best friend.

After all these years.

This couldn't be happening. Not on top of everything else . . .

But it had happened. Her stomach twisted with agony . . . Scott was dead.

Anger warred with the other emotions whirling

inside her. Scott had been a coward too. A coward and a liar.

She bit her lips to hold back an anguished cry. *He's dead.* Scott was dead. She couldn't believe he was gone.

Kevin shook his head at them as if they were all pathetic. 'You just don't get it, do you?' He stared directly at Aaron as he spoke. 'He's back and Scott's dead. You can pretend it's a coincidence and that what I'm saying to you is ludicrous all you want, but when another of us dies, you'll see.'

'Okay.' Elliott glanced around the private banquet room they'd paid the waitress a huge tip to get. 'When did Penney return to Birmingham?'

'We don't know for certain but within the last week,' Kevin said in that I-have-all-the-answers way of his. 'He's staying with his mother because he's still a loser just like he was back then.'

'So,' Aaron said, 'you think this big mama's boy loser killed Scott? Listen to yourself, Kev. It doesn't make sense. More likely Scott messed with the wrong guy's wife.'

'How can you say that?' Juliette growled like a mother lion. 'He was our friend.' She knew for a fact that the only wife he wanted was his own. The pain twisting inside her sliced like barbed wire. *He's dead. He's dead. Scott's dead.*

Aaron turned to her, no sign of sympathy on his face. 'He *was* our friend, Jules. You need to get over the idea that you two were high school sweethearts. He dumped you for the minister's daughter, remember? Scott could be an asshole just like the rest of us when necessary. Not everyone can be perfect like you. And none of us have been friends like that in a very long time.'

Juliette stood. She'd had enough. This hostile survival-of-the-fittest mentality was the reason this group had fallen apart. 'I will not sit here and listen to this bullshit.'

Kevin grabbed her hand. 'Please, Jules.' His plea almost sounded sincere. What an actor he was. An Academy Award-winning performance. 'I'll admit right now that I'm terrified. We have to do something about this. We can't just pretend it never happened.'

Incredibly, even Aaron didn't have a smart-ass come-back for that assessment. It was almost worth listening to this crap just to see him squirm.

Juliette dropped back into her chair. 'Fine, but no more unnecessary remarks.' She looked straight at Aaron as she said this.

He held up his hands in mock surrender. 'All right, all right. I'm chill.'

Juliette suddenly wished it was Aaron who was lying in the morgue instead of Scott. Her chest squeezed. She should feel guilty about that thought but she didn't. After they were done here, she needed to go directly to confession. She'd already been once today.

That was what she'd done that night . . . a dozen years ago.

The night the five of them committed murder.

Chapter Six

'That's the part that has crawled way up under my skin,' Deputy Chief Harold Black insisted when Dan was past ready to let the subject go for now. 'Ted has fifteen years with the department. *Fifteen years*. Why go off the deep end now? You're the chief of police, Dan. You've known Ted his entire career – *your* entire career. Doesn't that theory feel wrong to you? Even with this new and seemingly damning development.'

Harold was right on all counts. But the facts, as they knew them at this time, spoke for themselves. If there had been any question that something was amiss with Allen's behavior, the records from his cell phone greatly diminished that doubt.

'Nothing would give me more pleasure,' Dan began, hoping to convey just how deeply this tragedy affected

70

him as well, 'than to have your division somehow prove that Allen was set up. That dead or alive, he is an innocent victim.'

'The truth is, Dan,' Harold reminded him, 'we can't prove what Allen did or did not do when he entered the department's motor pool that day just before Chief Harris picked up the Taurus.'

'I suppose,' Dan countered, 'that we also can't hazard a guess as to why he may have taken additional steps toward that same end just days later. Any way you look at this, he was up to something that involved Jess.'

There was a whole hell of a lot they didn't know but some parts were damned obvious.

'One could say this latest development might indicate Chief Harris knows more than she's saying.'

Outrage lit deep in his gut but Dan tamped it back. 'Do not take this investigation in that direction, Harold,' he cautioned. 'If you do, you will not like my response. Is that understood?'

'I'm a little concerned,' the determined man persisted, 'that perhaps you are right now reacting on emotion rather than logic. Using your position to protect Chief Harris in this matter won't go unnoticed, Dan. It—'

Dan halted him with a deadly look. 'We will not go there. Are we clear?'

Harold relented with a somber nod. 'Quite clear.' He gathered his notes. 'You know I'll do my best to solve this puzzle, but I'll be honest with you right now. After talking to Ted's wife, I just don't believe he took off and left his whole life behind. He's got two kids, Dan. This' – he threw up his hands – 'circumstantial evidence aside, there is absolutely nothing in his background to suggest a character flaw that deep.'

'Stranger things have happened.' Dan worked at cooling off. Harold had struck a nerve and seemed to want to just keep tap dancing there. 'I do agree this behavior is out of character. That said, until we find him or someone or something that can provide the answers we need, we have no choice but to consider that Allen may have crossed the line.'

Jess would be the first to point out that everyone, man or woman, possessed the potential for evil. It was not crossing that thin, often hard-to-see line that made the difference. They could speculate every day, including Sunday, and never know what led to the chain of events that played out those last few days before Allen disappeared. Another of Jess's favorite sayings whispered through his mind. *Find the motive, find the answer*.

'I would be remiss in my duties if I failed to do exactly that,' Harold admitted.

In his capacity as division chief of Crimes Against Persons, the task before Harold was a heavy one. Allen was one of their own. A cop Dan had known, as Harold pointed out, for many years. That was the part that made this whole mess so unpalatable. To that end, just as Dan would not permit this investigation to drag Jess more deeply into the muck than speculation had already managed to do, he didn't want questions about Allen's loyalty to the department to play out in the media.

'For now, as far as the world knows, Captain Ted Allen is a victim of unknown circumstances,' Dan clarified. 'We need the community's eyes and ears on this one without unnecessary scrutiny.'

'Someone somewhere saw or heard something,' Harold agreed. 'All we need is to have that someone come forward.'

Unfortunately that didn't always happen. 'Put a little more pressure on his closest buddies. One of them may know or suspect something they don't feel comfortable coming forward with just yet.' The code among law enforcement officers was strong, as it should be. No one wanted to be the reason another cop's reputation was sullied.

'I'll pursue that avenue personally.' Harold stood. 'You'll pass this news along to Chief Harris? Or, if you prefer, I can speak with her.'

Dan wished there was a way around giving Jess this news. For her own safety, she needed to be kept abreast of where the investigation was on Allen. 'She's waiting in my office now.' At least he hoped she was. He'd sent word to her via Detective Wells since she opted not to answer his calls more often than not lately.

'I won't keep you, then.'

'For the time being,' Dan said in closing, 'I have no choice but to consider potential interim commanders for the gang task force.'

'Schafer's a good man,' Black mentioned. 'He's worked closely with Allen for more than a year.'

'I'll keep him in mind.'

Dan followed Harold from the main conference room more frustrated than when he'd arrived half an hour ago, and he would have wagered that was not possible. Allen's vanishing act was troubling on several levels.

The truly unsettling part was the idea that they had just begun this investigation. A very good possibility existed that things would only get worse from here.

His secretary held up a fistful of messages as he passed her desk, but he waved her off. Those would just have to wait.

'Chief Harris is waiting for you,' she called to him as he reached his office door.

Dan hesitated and turned back to his secretary. 'Thank you, Sheila. I'll take care of those messages later this afternoon.'

She smiled. 'I'll hold your calls.'

Dan returned the smile. He gave himself a mental boot in the ass for failing to show his appreciation of his

support staff often enough. Sheila and Tara, his recep-
tionist, kept his office running smoothly. He'd be lost
without them. At times like this they only got noticed
when they did something wrong and *that* was wrong.

Jess was waiting. He took a breath and reached for the
door once more. Her showing up on time was rare. That
was the first good news he'd heard all day.

'I guess turnabout is fair play,' Jess announced as soon
as he'd cleared the doorway.

She stood in front of his desk, bag draped on her
shoulder as if she had been contemplating leaving. She'd
had a hell of a long night and day. She had to be exhausted.
Just a few hours before she'd gotten called out to a
possible homicide they had broken their number one
rule, not once but twice. On her bed . . . on the kitchen
counter . . .

Get your head in the right place, Burnett. 'I apologize for
making you wait.' He rounded his desk and took a
moment to decide the proper approach for giving her
this sensitive news.

As if he'd telegraphed the thought, Jess's gaze
narrowed. 'What's going on? The only time you stay over
there' – she pointed to his position behind his desk –
'instead of sitting over here with me' – she hitched her
thumb to one of the two chairs stationed in front of his
desk – 'is when there's trouble.'

He'd have to remember that next time. Though

generally whatever he'd hoped to recall went out the window when they were alone together without his desk between them. Today, however, it was important that he keep his head on straight. 'Let's have a seat and catch up on what we have so far.'

She stood there, arms crossed over her chest, for several frustrating ticks of the mega-tense muscle in his cheek. He resisted the urge to work his jaw or reach up and rub at the damned twitch. As if she understood exactly how long she could hold out before he exploded, she finally sat, crossed those long, toned legs, and stared at him expectantly.

For the first time in nearly two hours, he let his guard down and said aloud the words that had turned to stone in his gut. 'We found Captain Allen's SUV. It was parked at the Amtrak station over on Morris.'

She tried to hide her initial reaction but he saw the pain and worry creep into her expression. 'Was *he* found?'

Dan shook his head. 'Just the vehicle.'

They had no body. No evidence that Allen had been harmed or kidnapped. He'd simply vanished. How the hell did a fifteen-year veteran of the force go AWOL? Leave his family in the lurch? Possibly try to kill a colleague? It didn't add up. Particularly since none of his credit cards had been used and the money he and his wife had in savings was still there – every dime of it.

'Then we don't know any more than we did,' Jess said,

sounding disappointed and frustrated. 'No way he just vanished into thin air.' She seemed to be talking more to herself than to him. 'It's a simple matter of physics, mass occupies space.'

He didn't miss the hint of hope she tried to cover with the frustration in her tone. Her feelings were understandable. It wasn't that she didn't want Allen's case solved, but until his body was found, there was at least reason to hope that maybe, possibly, he was alive. But in Dan's opinion, they were kidding themselves to hold on to any optimism.

Besides, if Allen was alive, unless he was a prisoner, he had changed sides and was now a criminal. Was that better or worse than the theory that he'd been murdered?

Dan heaved a sigh. He couldn't put this part off any longer. 'We also got his cell phone records.'

Denial instantly started to cloud her expression. She instinctively understood that this had something to do with her. 'Have any calls been made since he dropped off the map?'

'No.' Like Dan, she didn't want to deal with the monumental and dark possibilities this case opened up but sadly it was necessary.

The silence hung between them like a black cloud.

'The last time his cell reached out to a tower, it was near your place, Jess. Around four Friday morning.'

For another three beats she stared at him. He saw the

moment when full comprehension dawned on her. Her shoulders slumped and uncertainty replaced the denial in her expression.

'My Audi was tampered with sometime before I got up that morning . . . I had to call Lori for a ride and . . .' She blinked, disbelief widening her eyes. 'So he really is the one.'

'We can't prove he installed the explosive in the Taurus you were driving last week. He was in the motor pool the day I ordered the Taurus for you. The clerk admitted he'd gone outside for a smoke while Allen was there. As for your personal vehicle, we can only assume that given what happened with the Taurus, Allen intended to do the same with your Audi and was interrupted or ran out of time for some reason. Since we can't prove either one just yet, we're keeping that part out of the media. But we both know how this looks.'

'Why would he do that?' Jess shook her head. 'I've made a lot of serious enemies in the past.' She looked away. 'But they're usually the bad guys. Not other cops.'

'If Allen did this,' Dan said, 'he is a bad guy, Jess. Just because he carries a badge doesn't make him immune.' He wanted to round this damned desk and hold her. Damn propriety.

As if she feared he would do exactly that, she stood and squared her shoulders. 'Anything else?' She smoothed a hand over her skirt to avoid eye contact. 'I have a murder case to get back to.'

Apparently he had been wrong about which part of this briefing he dreaded the most. This next part had his gut clenching. Or, hell, maybe it was just saying it all out loud to her. 'We need to go over your Audi again, Jess. Check for prints and anything else he may have left behind. And your apartment.'

Rather than argue as he'd expected, she wiped her face clean of emotion and said, 'I'm a person of interest. I understand that. I'll talk to my landlord and set it up. Anything else?'

'You understand how important this is and that it's not about you having done anything wrong. No one's calling you a person of interest, Jess.' Not as long as he was chief of police. He searched her face, her eyes, needing to be absolutely certain she was okay with how this was going down. He hated like hell that any part of this made her feel guilty or threatened.

'Of course they are. We all know what constitutes a person of interest. I'm connected to this, Dan. Good or bad, I'm connected. And just because the guy didn't like me and may have tried to kill me and then disappeared doesn't mean I did anything wrong. I'm sure no one thinks that.' She laughed, the sound hardly amusing. 'My landlord barely knows me but he surely won't think I'm guilty of any wrongdoing. I'm certain he's just wishing he hadn't picked such a troublesome tenant.'

He couldn't take it any longer. Dan bolted around his desk. As if he'd intended to grab her and throw her over his desk for an encore of last night's out-of-control lovemaking, she backed up a step, bumped into the chair. Damn it. He stood there, helpless, wishing he could hold her for just a moment, but she didn't want that. She wanted to play by the rules.

Rules he knew better than to break – for all the good that knowledge had done him last night. *Or now.*

'You absolutely did not do anything wrong, Jess,' he said, going for soft but sounding rough. 'Your landlord will understand. I'll clear it with him if you'd like.' He wouldn't mind an opportunity to talk to the guy again. He still had reservations about that setup.

'Not necessary.' Jess dug in her bag for her pad and pencil. 'Give me a time frame so I can run it by Mr Louis.'

'The sooner the better.' Dan forced his body to relax. Harold was actually pushing for today to get into Jess's apartment, but Dan wasn't springing that on her. It was past one now. The man would just have to cool his heels until tomorrow.

Jess made herself a note, then jammed everything back where she'd gotten it inside that bottomless pit of a leather bag she hauled around. 'I'll take care of it. Anything else?'

She'd asked that three times already, angling for some

indication that the meeting was over so she could get back to work. She was the strongest woman he had ever known.

Despite just how shitty this day had been so far, he felt a smile coming on. She hadn't dried her hair after her shower. Back in college, she had always complained if he tried distracting her before her hair was dry after a shower. Just like back then, that mass of blond locks looked all wavy and sexy. She'd made a halfhearted effort at a ponytail but wisps had worked their way loose. And the glasses. She didn't wear them all the time, but when she did, he couldn't help thinking of that old classic eighties video 'Hot for Teacher.'

'This is exactly what got us into trouble last night,' she warned.

He snapped out of the lust coma and slid his hands into his pockets. 'You're right. We broke your number one rule.' No point pretending he didn't know what she meant. She was the only woman who had ever made him want to break the rules.

'*Our* rule, Burnett.' She cocked an eyebrow. 'We should show a bit more restraint next time, wouldn't you say?'

'We should.' He would try. He really would.

'How long will they need my car?'

It took a sec for him to shake off the I-want-you fog wrapped around his brain and to focus on the answer to her question. 'You'll have it back tomorrow. You can use one from the motor pool tonight.'

'I don't think so.' Her laugh was the real thing this time. 'I can catch a ride with one of my detectives, thank you very much.'

'You could catch a ride with me,' he proposed. *Smart, Burnett.* Spend time alone with her in her apartment again tonight. Way to go, idiot.

She smiled and he felt a little twinge deep in his chest. That smile and those lips had haunted him for two decades. God, he was glad she was back where she belonged. *Home.* Close to him even if not *with* him, officially.

'I should get back to work,' she said with a pointed look that told him she had a good idea what was on his mind.

Before he could formulate a response, she gave him her back. At forty-two he shouldn't still have those moments of uncertainty as to what to say or do next, but here he was watching her go with no idea how to proceed either way.

Jess paused at the door. 'By the way, we're invited to the Barons' Labor Day party. Mark your calendar, Burnett. I wouldn't miss it for the world.'

Leaving him dumbfounded by the announcement, she was gone before he could ask how the hell that invitation had come about.

He heaved a big breath that did absolutely nothing to relieve the frustration banding around his chest. On top of all the rest, apparently between now and Labor Day he would need to explain his past with the Baron family. The *whole* story.

Something else he wasn't looking forward to. He'd spent ten years trying to put that nightmare behind him.

Chapter Seven

Vestavia Village, 4.00 P.M.

Jess finished her tea and placed the glass on the elegant crystal tray waiting on the coffee table in the middle of Frances Wallace's unexpectedly opulent gathering room. Not a living room or great room or den, she had explained to Jess. The condos had gathering rooms with mini kitchens equipped for serving cold refreshments. No *cooking* kitchens or dining rooms. There was no need. The residents' meals were served in the facility's dining hall.

At least this way there was no worry about anyone accidentally burning the place down.

'This won't stop them,' Lucille argued. 'The construction will continue anyway. Our situation has not changed. *At all*. Why would we want to kill Scott much less bother doing so?' The last she delivered with a look that proclaimed the mere idea grated like broken glass against her delicate sensibilities.

Lucille Blevins was as blunt as Frances and about as delicate as the Glock Jess carried. She was the eldest of the group and made sure everyone understood that detail carried certain privileges.

And the two janitors had called Frances the ringleader. Ha!

Frances sighed loudly. 'Mercy alive, Lucille. No one's saying that.'

'You said it.' Polly Neal lifted her thin chin in consternation. 'Said you wanted him dead. I heard you. So did everyone else.'

Molly Jones, Polly's twin, nodded adamantly. 'I heard it too.' She turned to the others. 'We all heard it. Didn't we?'

The heads of the other three, Geraldine Lusk, Colleen Sharp, and Pansy Cornelius, moved up and down in frantic agreement. They stole a glance at Jess and stopped abruptly. Then another of those free-for-alls started with everyone assuring Jess that Frances would never hurt anyone. Absolutely not. Not even Scott Baker.

No wonder Frances felt compelled to rally around these ladies despite every last one of them being a tattletale. Well into their eighties, all lacked the actual know-how to dive into a war against the facility's board unless their strategy was to frustrate them to death. The sort of ladies who lived their whole lives with husbands taking care of everything. Nothing wrong with that for those who chose that lifestyle. Had Jess's mother lived, she would have been the same way. Lily's relationship with her husband wasn't that different even now.

Jess could not imagine leaving all that control up to the man in her life – when she had a man in her life.

She supposed Dan was kind of in her life. Sort of.

No one made Jess's decisions for her. The last time that happened, she'd spent from age ten to eighteen in a carousel of foster homes. The day she turned eighteen she made up her mind that would never happen again. Her livelihood and happiness would never depend on anyone else.

She hauled herself back to the present. Following up on the statements made by the widows was nothing more than a formality. Lori had taken each, one at a time, to Frances's balcony and gone over her statement while Jess attempted to explain how the investigation worked and the roles the ladies played in bringing to light the events of the past twenty-four hours. Prescott and Cook had already done the initial interviews but Jess needed to do this. Mostly to reassure herself that she wasn't missing anything.

That was working out just great so far. *Not*.

Bless their hearts. Jess reached for more patience and waited out this latest squabble. They were cute as buttons and for the most part sweet as could be. Except maybe for the twins. Those two were vicious little old ladies from what Jess had gathered so far. Looked as if they were ready to throw Frances under the bus and back up a couple of times.

During a moment of silence as they all caught their breaths and wet their whistles, Frances stared longingly at her tea as if she wished it were something far stronger. 'Ladies,' she said in a surprisingly calm voice, 'I said nothing about killing Scott Baker or wanting him dead. What I said was,' she stated firmly when mouths opened to protest, 'I hoped to live long enough to see him *eat those words and die*. I didn't mean I wanted him to literally die. I meant he should go to hell.'

'You could've just said that,' Lucille demanded. 'Maybe then we wouldn't be in this hellacious predicament.'

A collective round of gasps from the others punctuated the statements.

Frances looked heavenward. 'God, help me.'

Jess cleared her throat. 'Ladies.'

All eyes shifted to her. At least she had their attention again. The question was, how long could she keep it?

'None of you are suspects in this case. You are only persons of interest. But your statements are important to the investigation.' Jess kept her hands folded in her lap in hopes of presenting a calm, cool demeanor. She sure didn't need any of these ladies having a stroke or a heart attack. Try explaining a scene like that to the press. 'Anything you remember beyond what you've shared in your statement could be useful in finding the person who did this awful thing.'

Molly and Polly shared a look. 'You mean we're not in any sort of trouble?' the latter asked.

'No, ma'am,' Jess assured her. 'We only needed to go over your statements regarding where you were last night and to discuss whatever you might know about any enemies Mr Baker may have had.'

'You mean beyond every single soul he met?' Lucille challenged.

'Do you know of any specific person or persons with whom Mr Baker had trouble?' Jess tried again.

'Scott Baker was a very savvy businessman, Jess,' Frances said. 'He told me once that he'd never met any-one he couldn't charm when it came to negotiations.' She lifted her glass in a salute. 'Besides me, of course.'

'No one other than the seven of you were against this new construction?' Jess tried a different tactic.

Heads wagged. 'They're all too afraid to speak up,' Lucille explained.

'Why would anyone be afraid to speak up?' That was the first time she'd heard that one.

The widows clammed up as if she'd asked which one lost her virginity first.

'We pay well for this luxury,' Frances spoke up when

no one else would. 'But there are rules. Opening hours for the dining room and the little movie theater we all love so much. He made it a point to learn our habits, what we enjoyed, and then when we crossed him about this, he took the things we cared about away.'

'Give me an example,' Jess prompted, her dislike for the deceased mounting.

'I have dinner with my daughter's family on Monday nights. Afterward I come back here and enjoy a cup of tea in the dining room with my friends before retiring for the evening. He instructed Ms Warren to stop serving tea after eight.' She waved her arms to indicate her lovely home. 'We're not allowed to cook in our condos, not even with a microwave. We can't even have a coffeemaker or a teapot.'

'He fired my hairdresser,' Polly said. 'I won't let anyone else touch my hair.' She patted her curly gray locks. 'From the day the salon opened, Deidra was my stylist. He fired her. I can't make arrangements to go to the new shop in town where Deidra works since one of the occupancy rules require we use the on-site salon.'

'I'm addicted to hot fudge pie.' Lucille wrapped her arms around her waist as if the confession drew everyone's attention to her healthy middle. 'As soon as I signed that petition to stop construction, the dining room stopped serving my pie.'

Jess leaned forward, outrage kindling in her belly.

None of these instances were exactly torture tactics but the man was strong-arming these old women. No, he was bullying them. 'Have you contacted attorneys to have your contracts reviewed?' There had to be a law against this mistreatment.

'It's all in the fine print,' Frances announced, the weight of the battle she'd been waging showing on her face. 'Baker was a brilliant businessman. He may not have charmed me but he certainly outmaneuvered me.'

'No enemies to your knowledge, other than the residents such as yourselves who were unhappy with him?' Jess should get this interview back on track. 'No one in particular who came around that stirred your interest in what he might be up to?' This was as close as Jess would get to outright asking if the man was having an affair. She wanted these ladies to give her information, not the answers they thought she wanted to hear.

'No one I can recall,' Frances said first.

Lucille shook her head.

Jess tried a different tactic. 'No problems with his deputy administrator or his secretary?'

'They're having an affair,' Polly said in a stage whisper.

Now they were getting somewhere. 'Mr Baker and his secretary?' Jess asked.

'Oh no!' Molly laughed. 'Baker was too boring for that. Mr Clemmons and the secretary are having an affair.'

Everyone in the room started tossing out the latest gossip they'd heard. Jess held up her hands to quiet them. 'We need facts, ladies. Just the facts.' Whatever the deputy administrator was doing, Scott Baker had sex with someone before his murder.

'If Baker was having an affair,' Frances said as if she were the final authority in the matter, 'he was very discreet. I've never heard a rumor like that about him.'

Jess waited for her to go on. As did the others, fortunately.

'Scott loved his wife. He loved his son. He loved his life.' For a bit Frances looked as if she might weep. 'I despised his business tactics but' – she drew in a deep breath – 'he would never have hurt his wife or any other woman like that. He wasn't that kind of man. He worked. He went home to his family. That's it.'

'How can you be so certain?' Lucille demanded, her gaze narrow with suspicion.

'I hired a PI.' Frances gave a little half shrug. 'So sue me. I figured if I could find some dirt on him, we could be rid of him. Maybe if there was evidence he'd used his position in some inappropriate manner to manipulate the Your Life corporation coming in and taking over, then we could undo this mess. What I discovered was that he was a cutthroat businessman. He lied to us at every opportunity and, worse, he stole the peace we all deserved.'

'And paid for,' Polly added for good measure.

'A private investigator?' All the frustration and impatience Jess had been holding back whipped out of her on those three words. 'You have a background investigation and surveillance reports and you didn't think to mention that?'

Frances heaved another big sigh. 'I didn't want to look any guiltier than I already do. Hiring a PI is a little extreme. I recognize that now. But I was flustered and it seemed like a good idea at the time.'

'I'll need those reports immediately,' Jess warned. 'As in right this minute.'

'You can have them.' Frances got up from her camel-back sofa and walked over to a table near the door. 'But the reports are full of nothing.' She crossed back to Jess and handed her a pathetically thin manila folder.

Jess stood. 'Thank you, ladies.' She surveyed the group. 'I appreciate your cooperation.' She smiled and just for the devil of it said, 'Now don't y'all be leaving town until I give you the go-ahead.'

She strode toward the door with Frances hot on her heels and the other six whispering loud enough for folks in the next condo to hear.

'Jess, you know I didn't mean any harm keeping that from you. I forgot, that's all.'

She wanted to be upset with her favorite teacher but that just wasn't possible, so she whispered back, 'This better be the only thing you didn't tell me about.'

'I swear.' Frances held up the two fingers signifying Scout's honor.

Jess opened the door but decided to give Frances one last counsel. 'Keep your widows under control.' Then she was out of there.

This widows' club didn't know a thing that would help the Baker investigation. Jess was confident of that assessment. Still, as a cop, the truth was that the only thing preventing Frances Wallace from becoming a full-fledged suspect was Jess's certainty that the killer had been far stronger and faster than her.

Lori waited in the courtyard, her cell phone pressed to her ear. Judging by her exasperated hand gestures, she was not too happy with her caller. She and Chet Harper had just moved in together. Was there trouble in paradise already? Chet had a three-year-old son. Lori was worried about whether the child liked her or not. Maybe that was the real issue.

Jess wished she could make the younger woman understand that these things took time and patience. Something she'd never had enough of. That was why, at forty-two, she was alone unless you counted her off-the-record affair with her boss.

The man she was supposed to have married twenty years ago.

Another hard lesson learned about not relying on others or love or money.

Jess booted the past back to its place deep in the nether regions of her gray matter. She had a homicide to solve.

Lori looked up as Jess drew nearer. She quickly ended the call but there was no speedy way to banish the mixture of emotions from her face. She was worried and frustrated. Jess was confident her frustrations had nothing to do with the widows.

'That was Harper.'

'Everything all right?'

Lori joined her progression toward the parking area. Jess put her hand on her arm and stopped her for a moment. 'Just look at that view.' She admired the calm water of the lake. The birds dipping down for a drink with the breeze playing with the lovely ornamental grasses nestled around its rocky shore.

When the sun dropped amid the trees in the distance, it would be a breathtaking sight. No wonder the board was anxious to squeeze more out of this view. According to the plans she had seen in Baker's office, the new condo tower would be far taller and larger than the one Frances and her friends occupied. Leaving them absolutely no scenic view whatsoever.

Jess moved on. 'You were saying Harper called?'

'Mrs Baker is back home and she wants to speak to the person in charge of her husband's case.' Lori hit the clicker to unlock her Mustang. 'Like right now.'

That was generally Jess's line. Since the wife had been

out of town and the mayor had been keeping word of her return under wraps, Jess was glad someone wanted to help with this investigation rather than hinder it.

'Let's hope there's something she can add to the investigation.' Maybe Mrs Baker knew what her husband was up to when she wasn't home.

Jess fastened her seat belt and waited as Lori maneuvered off the property. If she chose not to talk about whatever was going on between her and Harper, Jess would understand. She hoped their relationship wouldn't damage the SPU team. She wanted both Lori and Harper working with her. Keeping their personal lives separate from the job wasn't going to be easy. Jess knew that firsthand.

She opened the manila folder Frances had given her to have a look at the PI's report.

'He doesn't want me in his father's house.'

The words burst out of Lori as if a dam had cracked. Jess turned to her. Her profile told the rest of the story. Lori Wells was on the verge of tears. That was way out of character for the tough-as-nails lady who had survived days on end as the hostage of a ruthless serial killer.

'Give it time. It's too soon to expect a child so young to accept you.' Jess wished she had advice more immediately comforting. At three, Chet's son was old enough to be fearful and standoffish with strangers. And yet too young to understand that his father had a new friend he wanted to keep around.

'I don't know.' Lori's lips trembled. 'He doesn't want to be in the room with me. He stays hidden behind his father and he doesn't want me close. At all. Maybe I shouldn't be there when he comes over. I could go to my place. Make things simpler.'

'No.'

Lori braked for an intersection. She turned to Jess with a question or hope amid the despair on her face.

'If you give him that,' Jess promised, 'you will never become a part of his new normal. You have to stay the course. Be strong and steady. Be there. Keep smiling and trying to interact. He'll come around in time.'

'From your mouth to God's ears.' She tightened her grip on the steering wheel and took a deep breath as if needing the cleansing effect. 'Your friend is a character.'

Jess smiled. As much as she wanted to shake Frances right now, she still adored her. 'Yeah. I know.' Speaking of Frances, Jess turned her attention back to the manila folder. She scanned the first report. 'Do you know a private investigator who calls himself or his business *Tracker*?'

'Tracker?' Lori glanced at her. 'Are you serious? I mean, *the* Tracker?'

Jess rifled through the four pages in the folder. 'That's the only name on the reports.'

Lori grinned. 'Tracker. I can't believe it. I think you're going to want to talk to him. Maybe even before we talk to Mrs Baker. What time is it?'

Jess checked her cell. 'Five-twenty.'

Lori got one of those aha looks. 'I know where to find him. He's like clockwork. Rumor is every day at five he lands on the same barstool with a beer in his hand.'

'Who the hell is this guy?' What in the world was Frances doing dealing with someone who spent that much time in bars? Frances Wallace epitomized etiquette and principles – most of the time anyway.

'Some cops would call him a lowlife scumbag if you could even get them to say his name out loud. But' – Lori paused, seeming to choose her next words carefully – 'others say he's a damned good investigator when he wants to be. I was curious. I read up on him. Until a few years ago, Buddy Corlew was a legend in the department.'

'Did you say Corlew?' No way. 'Forty-something?' Jess snapped her sagging jaw shut.

'That's him,' Lori confirmed. 'You know the guy?'

Jess leaned back in her seat, almost anticipating the opportunity that had fallen into her lap. 'Let's just say that I knew him once.'

The Garage, 10th Terrace South, 5.25 P.M.

Jess had to hand it to her old friend. If he was going to spend his evenings hanging out in a bar, this place definitely had some charm. From the rusty sign out front to the wisteria climbing over the iron gate and garden statues, a welcoming atmosphere just reached out and enveloped anyone who got close. Inside, there was more of the same. Lots of friendly conversations at the rustic bistro tables and along the bar, even for a Tuesday night.

One man sat alone at the far end of the bar, a vacant stool separating him from the rest of the patrons. Buddy Corlew was an island. The only thing here that could touch him was the lively music blasting from the speakers.

While Lori melted into the crowd, Jess made her way to that unoccupied stool. He didn't look up as she settled in next to him. Just as well. Gave her a moment to study his profile. Not much had changed. The threadbare jeans and T-shirt and cowboy boots had always been the mainstay of his wardrobe. He still sported that trademark ponytail. Only the slicked back hair was more salt than pepper now. Crow's-feet had made themselves at home. He'd filled out a little around the middle. Definitely no longer quarterback material but then she had no room to talk. It was hell getting older.

'If you're that interested,' Corlew suggested without turning his head to meet her steady gaze, 'I'm happy to buy you a beer and give you my number.'

'I got your number twenty-four years ago, Corlew,' she advised, 'the night you tried to talk me out of my panties.'

He turned to her, the lopsided grin that had broken many an innocent heart making an appearance. 'I don't expect I'd be any more successful now than I was then.'

Jess smiled. 'I don't expect you would.'

'I heard you were back in town.'

'I'm pretty hard to miss.' Considering she'd been all over the news, that was an understatement.

'You and Dan back together?'

'He's my boss,' Jess skirted the question.

Corlew grunted. Could mean anything or nothing at all.

'I hear you've got your own shop now,' she prodded, since he didn't seem inclined to launch into conversation.

Corlew had gone straight from high school to the Marines. It was either that or do jail time for busting too many heads. Back in the day, Buddy Corlew was the badass of Birmingham – a tough guy who rode a Harley and stole the prettiest girls from the rich boys in town.

But there had been one girl, hard as he tried, he hadn't been able to steal away from the rich boy she loved. Jess shook off the foolish thoughts. *God, that was a long time ago.*

'That's right.' Forearms braced on the counter, bottle

of beer in hand, he turned to Jess. 'After I lost yet another battle with Burnett four years ago, I decided I was better off working for me instead of the establishment.'

On the way here from Vestavia Village, Lori had explained how Buddy Corlew had achieved the status of veteran detective with nearly a dozen years under his belt at the Birmingham Police Department. As the story went, he'd had his own way of doing things and spent more time stepping on toes than following the rules. He'd butted heads with Burnett one time too many. When Burnett was appointed chief of police, Corlew was out of there.

There was more to the story, Jess suspected. Eventually she would get the rest from Burnett.

'Frances Wallace hired you to find the dirt on Scott Baker. According to the reports she showed me, you didn't have any luck.'

He bunched up one shoulder, then let it relax in an indifferent shrug. 'You can't find dirt that doesn't exist. Besides, you know I can't discuss a case with you.'

Jess reached into her bag for her badge, then placed it on the counter. 'In case you haven't heard, Scott Baker is dead. Murdered. It's my case. Frances gave me the file you provided. You have a question about that, you can call her. Otherwise, I have a few questions, Mr Corlew. You want to answer them here or you want to take a ride downtown?'

He downed the rest of the beer and pushed the empty longneck aside. 'Scott Baker was squeaky clean, *Chief Harris*. Not even a parking ticket. His wife too. Hell, I even checked out that swanky retirement facility he runs – ran. Nothing shady there either except a slick business-man determined to make his daddy proud.' The waiter grabbed the empty bottle and plunked down a replace-ment in a passing swoop.

Corlew gave the waiter a nod, then carried on with his story. 'They're building another swanky joint called Windswept Village down in Orange Beach. These guys aren't interested in murder. They're too busy making money off folks like Frances Wallace and her wealthy friends.'

Jess stowed her badge and fished out a business card. New ones that no longer listed her as a special agent for the FBI. She'd picked them up on her lunch break yesterday. 'If you suddenly remember something you believe relates to my case, I'd appreciate a phone call.'

He gave the card a thorough perusal as she slid off the stool. 'If I don't remember anything relevant,' he asked, 'can I call you anyway?'

Jess suppressed a laugh. Same old Corlew. 'You can try.'

Just like twenty-four years ago, she walked away without looking back.

Chapter Eight

As Lori slowed for the turn into the Baker driveway, the barrage of reporters camped at the street shouted questions at Jess. The onslaught lasted until the security gate opened and they rolled through, leaving the more unpleasant noise of a higher social status behind. Already Cook had notified Jess that she'd made not only the midday news but the five o'clock as well.

Apparently the most popular trend in the local media was whether Birmingham's elite could handle Jess Harris's brand of police work.

Funny, when she'd hit the road after high school graduation, the city's elite, beyond the Burnetts, hadn't a clue who Jess Harris was. Now she was a regular household name.

Whoop-de-doo.

The home Scott Baker, or his daddy, had bought for his family was a multimillion-dollar masterpiece of European design. The place was ten thousand square feet in size if it was two. What in the world did a couple with only one child need with a house this size?

His wife, Trisha, dressed modestly. Her slacks and blouse were your everyday generic garments found at any department store. The contrast between her wardrobe and the decadent silk brocade sofa where she chose to sit was almost distracting. The lady flaunted no French manicure. Very little makeup. Chances were she would have cried that off by now anyway. A trusty box of tissues sat next to her on the fancy sofa. The woman wasn't at all what Jess had expected. Totally unpretentious.

The in-laws, on the other hand, were exactly what Jess had anticipated. Scott's father had threatened to call the mayor if Jess excluded him from her interview with his son's wife. His own wife had taken their six-year-old grandson into the kitchen to make cookies. When Jess refused to be bullied by the overbearing man, he finally agreed to leave the room. Lori was taking his statement. That appeared to appease him. Jess reminded herself that the elder Mr Baker had lost his son. Maybe under different circumstances he would have been more cooperative.

'I apologize for my father-in-law's temper,' Trisha said as Jess settled in the chair across from her. 'We're all just devastated and not at all at our best. Scott's brothers haven't gotten into town yet. I'm hoping they can help *him* . . . with this. Scott's mother can't do anything with him. She and I are . . . in shock and just trying to muddle through.'

'That's completely understandable,' Jess assured her. Trisha was likely still in the denial phase. Her husband's death didn't feel real yet. This was a good time to interview her – before the inevitable emotional crash and burn. 'Mrs Baker, I don't want to keep you from your family, so I'll get right to my questions if that's all right.'

She nodded and Jess readied her pencil. 'Do you know of anyone at all, a friend or relative or a colleague, who might have felt ill will toward your husband?'

Trisha glanced at the closed doors.

'No one in your family,' Jess offered, hoping to set her at ease, 'will have access to your statement.'

Trisha's fingers knitted together in her lap. 'My husband spent a lot of time at work. He didn't really have a life.' She smiled a little but her lips trembled with the effort. 'My father-in-law's demands on his sons are so harsh and unforgiving that failure is just not acceptable. It's all about who can achieve the biggest deal. Scott was about to get his trust fund. Finally. Then his life would have been more his own.' Her shoulders rose and fell with the agony she clearly felt. 'I don't want my father-in-law to do that to my son. Scotty would never be able to tolerate that kind of treatment.'

'Do you feel this competition between Scott and his brothers may be related to his murder?'

Trisha shook her head, then glanced at the door once more. 'Before Scott reached thirty, there was only one way his trust fund would transfer to me and our son with no strings attached to his father. And that was if he died. He worried a lot about that.'

A new layer of tension started to work its way through Jess's muscles. 'There's less than a week to go before his thirtieth birthday. Why would that be a problem now?'

'I'm not certain.' Trisha swiped at her eyes, struggling valiantly not to break down. 'Lately Scott has been saying that even after he got his trust fund his father would never let him go. He worried that our son was doomed to the same fate. He asked me to take our Scotty out of town.' She moistened her lips. 'That was last Friday. He said I should go and stay put until one of two things happened: I heard from him or ... it was over.' Her eyelids fluttered wildly to hold back the tears. 'I tried to get him to tell me what was going on and he wouldn't say.' She dragged in a big shaky breath. 'He just kept telling me our son's troubles had shown him how wrong he'd been and now he might have to pay the price.'

'And you have no idea what he meant?' Jess wasn't getting the point here. 'Is your son ill?'

Her head moved side to side and tears spilled down her cheeks. 'Scotty's in first grade. He's small for his age

105

and painfully shy. Some of the boys make fun of him. He comes home from school crying almost every day. My husband couldn't bear it. I think that's why he began staying at work later and later. He said this was his penance.'

'Was your husband bullied or a bully himself growing up?'

'That's what's so crazy about this.' She cleared her throat, tried to dry her eyes with a wad of tissues from the box she now clutched like a trusted friend. 'Scott was one of the popular boys. Everyone loved him. He was a star lacrosse player. President of his senior class. He was a good guy. I never heard anything about him hurting anyone.'

'And you?' Maybe he was protecting her somehow. 'Did you have any issues in school? Or perhaps now?'

'I was a wallflower in school. I went to a private Christian school and he went to Brighton Academy. We rarely crossed paths. Once in a while at sporting events when our schools competed. He was the only boy who ever really noticed me.' She attempted a smile but her lips didn't want to cooperate. 'Not much has changed there.'

'Let me be completely honest with you, Mrs Baker,' Jess said. 'I can find your husband's killer a lot faster if I know about any problems you were having. Marital or otherwise.' Scott had sex with someone just prior to his death. And that someone was not his wife, since she had been out of town. If there were problems in the relationship, Jess could damn sure use a firsthand account.

'We didn't have any.' The new widow lowered her head for a moment before meeting Jess's gaze once more. 'Other than the worry he had about something he thought he did wrong in the past and it somehow impacting our son, our lives were as close to perfect as anyone could hope for.'

Jess absorbed the ramifications of what Trisha's statements implied. She would come back to that in a moment. 'Can you tell me the significance of your husband's tattoo? The number five?'

Trisha blinked as if she didn't understand the question; then she pressed her hand to her chest. 'The *Five*.' She laughed. The sound was painful to hear. 'When Scott was in high school, he and four of his friends formed a kind of secret club – the Five.' She made quotation marks in the air. 'They intended to rule the world. But he said they had to settle for Birmingham.' She stared at her hands where she ripped at the wad of tissues. 'Now it's too late for Scott.'

'I know this is very difficult, Mrs Baker, but could you give me the names of the other members of the Five?'

'Kevin O'Reilly and Juliette Coleman. Those were the two Scott talked about most. There's Elliott Carson and Aaron Taylor.'

Only one of the names was familiar to Jess. *Coleman*. She wondered if Juliette was related to Birmingham's beloved reporter Gina Coleman. 'These other members of the Five still live in Birmingham?'

'They all left for college with big dreams, except Scott and Kevin,' she said sadly. 'Their lives were plotted out for them right here so they all came back eventually.'

That story sounded way too familiar to Jess. Had she been back home more than a month now? Didn't seem possible. She'd left for college with those big dreams too.

'Do you think any of those friends would have some idea why Scott was so worried about whatever it was he felt he'd done wrong in the past?' There were a lot of things that could explain Scott Baker's guilt. An affair? Maybe he had another child somewhere that he had ignored.

'I suppose it's possible,' she confessed. 'I'd never heard him talk like that until Scotty's problems at school started.'

Jess glanced at her notes. 'You said that he asked you to take Scotty to Mobile and for you to stay until you heard from him or it was over. Do you believe he had a meeting planned with someone?' Scott Baker had met with someone – his killer. And whoever killed him had known him. Maybe even intimately.

'I wish I knew. While Scotty and I were in Mobile, my phone conversations with Scott were normal, as if nothing was wrong. If I asked him if everything was okay, he would suddenly need to go.'

'Did he give you the impression that you and your son were in danger?'

'No. He . . .' She looked away again, her hands wringing together as if the words were far too unbearable to say aloud.

'Mrs Baker, we need your help on this,' Jess urged. 'Whatever you know or think you know may make all the difference.'

The grieving woman drew in a shuddering breath and met Jess's gaze. 'I think something very bad was about to come out – something he felt was connected to him or his family somehow. So he did what he had to do to protect our son's future.'

The grim certainty in the woman's eyes had Jess's instincts screaming. 'What is it you think he had to do?'

'The only way to protect our son's financial future was for him to die.'

'But your husband would have gained control of his trust in a few days. Wouldn't that have achieved the same result?'

'I just don't know. But with him dead, the trust fund goes to Scotty with me in control.' Her lips flattened into a thin line of fury. 'And then I'm taking my son and I'm going as far from here as I can go. I'm never coming back.'

No wonder she hadn't wanted to talk in front of her father-in-law. 'But your husband was murdered. How does that play into what you're telling me?'

'Scott's family is Catholic. Suicide is unforgivable.'

What the hell kind of family were the Bakers? More important, was she saying what Jess thought she was saying? Holding her breath, Jess waited for Trisha to say the words. She could not put them in her mouth.

'I think he hired someone to kill him,' Trisha said. 'He sacrificed himself to save our son.'

With that stunning statement ringing in her ears, Jess thanked Mrs Baker and did the best she could to smooth over things with the father-in-law. He wasn't happy that some lesser cop had interviewed him while his unimportant daughter-in-law had gotten the deputy chief. He'd promised to inform the mayor of her treatment.

Oh well. Mayor Pratt was the one who'd suggested her for this case. She suspected he was not going to want to hear this scenario. As off the wall as it sounded, Jess had no choice but to give the wife's suggestion of suicide by murder a proper look.

Outside the palatial home, Lori fired up her Mustang and sent Jess a look. 'I hope you got more than I did.'

'I certainly got one hell of a theory to chew on.' She gave Lori the condensed version.

'It's not totally impossible,' Lori offered with a look that said *Yeah right*.

'Scott Baker was in to something,' Jess agreed. 'Something he wanted to hide from his family and that ultimately cost him his life. An affair? An illegal business scheme?'

Who knew? Jess ignored the reporters as they exited the property. Luckily none bothered to follow. They were far more interested in what the Bakers would do next than what the police would do.

Lori laughed, the sound a little strained. 'You're not going to believe this but I think we have a tail.'

Jess resisted the urge to turn around and stare out the back window. 'Anyone we know?' If Dan had her under surveillance again, she was going to . . . thank him and let it go. That war was getting old. Lopez's messenger had assured her she had nothing to worry about from that former empire, but taking the word of a gang lord as gospel wasn't exactly her style.

Uncertainty stirred when she considered another possibility. Nah. Eric Spears, the serial killer who had turned her life upside down and who had gotten away, was far too brilliant to make a move using such a pedestrian tactic.

'Navy or black four-door sedan,' Lori said. 'It's old. Maybe a Corolla.'

'Unless he makes an aggressive maneuver, just let him follow us.'

'You don't think it's any of Lopez's former allies?'

She pulled down her sun visor and had a look at the car via the mirror there. 'I don't think even the low man on the Lopez totem pole would be caught dead in a ride like that.' The last time she'd gotten a visit from Leonardo Lopez and his clique, they'd been driving high-end SUVs.

'The economy's bad all over,' Lori reminded her.

'That's why my house is still languishing on the market,' Jess grumbled. As long as the house in Virginia didn't sell, she couldn't look for permanent housing here. Cutting her Realtor some slack, it had been only a month. Maybe the place would find a new family soon. Someone who would actually be home occasionally. Unlike her. When she'd worked at Quantico, she'd spent most of her time at the office or on the road.

Lori took a right. A block later she made a left. 'He doesn't seem to mind that we've obviously spotted him.'

They could continue playing this boring game or, 'Let's find out what he wants,' Jess announced.

Lori shot her a look. 'You want me to stop.'

'I do.' Jess braced for her move. 'Maybe we can get his license plate number when he goes around.'

Lori let off the accelerator and then eased down on the brakes. Tires squealed in protest but the Mustang came to a smooth stop in the middle of the road.

The dark sedan careened to a stop far enough behind them that making out the driver's face was impossible. Jess turned all the way around in her seat to stare at him.

She wanted him to know he was caught.

He did nothing. Just sat there. A horn blew as a minivan drove around.

'Well, aren't you just full of yourself,' Jess muttered. 'What now?'

'Start backing up. He won't have any choice then.'

The instant the Mustang was in reverse and the backup lights flashed a warning, the driver of the other car backed up, then spun around and raced off in the direction they'd come.

Jess committed the first three numbers of his California license plate to memory but that's all she got. 'What're you doing so far from home, Mr Corolla?' She turned and settled back into her seat.

'You want me to follow him?'

'That won't be necessary. If he has something to say, he'll find us again.'

'Home or the office?'

Her Audi was at the lab. 'Do you mind dropping me at my place?'

'No problem. So what's the deal with Corlew?' She glanced at Jess. 'You two looked pretty tight in there.'

Jess had wondered when Lori would get around to that question. 'We went to high school together.'

'Was he pre-Burnett?'

'I knew Corlew first, if that's what you mean. He and Burnett were mortal enemies. Their football rivalry was legendary. Burnett was the rich kid from the right side of the tracks and Corlew was his opposite in every way.' Except that they were both devastatingly handsome and too sexy for any female's good. That part she would just keep to herself.

'You and Corlew had a thing?'

Jess considered how to put the answer. 'We had a *moment*. That moment is dead and gone. I had known Corlew for years and I can't deny having fantasies about him. Any girl breathing at the time would have admitted the same. But he never paid any attention to me until Burnett and I became an item. Then he wanted to take what belonged to Burnett.' As young as she'd been, she hadn't been stupid. 'It wasn't really about me. It was the rivalry between those two.'

'But you had a moment,' Lori reminded her.

'The night before the homecoming game of our senior year, I was angry at Burnett for something. We were always fighting and then making up.'

'Does that ever stop?' Lori sent her a look. 'I mean, really, do you ever outgrow that need to best each other?'

Jess wasn't so sure she could give Lori an answer she wanted to hear. 'I don't know. I'm still waiting for that to happen.'

Lori groaned. 'So you were mad at Burnett,' she prompted.

'I guess word got around that we'd had an argument

and lo and behold, who shows up at my door on his big
sexy Harley?'

'He took you for a ride.'

'He did.' Jess would never forget that night. The wind
in her hair and the absolute terror as he raced down a
long dark stretch of highway. She'd held on to him for
dear life. At some point they'd ended up at one of his
hangouts and he'd tried every way in the world to seduce
her.

'Earth to Jess,' Lori teased.

'We kissed. That's it.'

'Does Burnett know about that night?'

'If he found out, he never mentioned it.'

'The chief might need to worry,' Lori noted. 'I saw the
way Corlew looked at you. That moment might still have
a little life left in it.'

'I don't think so.' Jess shook her head.

'So you and Burnett made up after that *moment*?'

'He climbed into my bedroom window sometime after
midnight. My foster mother was out of town. Gambling
in Mississippi with her old lady friends, if I recall
correctly.'

Lori laughed, a rich deep, guttural sound. 'I can't see
the chief climbing in through a bedroom window.'

'We were young and in love. The only thing that
mattered was the moment.'

They'd had other moments . . . like ten years ago

when Jess had come back to Birmingham for Christmas with her sister and her family. She and Burnett had run into each other at the Publix supermarket.

They hadn't seen each other in ten long years and somehow they'd ended up at his place . . . tearing each other's clothes off.

Jess didn't know whether to laugh or cry at the idea that Burnett had somehow managed to invade every decade of her adult life.

Maybe it was a sign.

Chapter Nine

9911 Conroy Road, 7.55 P.M.

Jess waved to Lori, then turned to face her garage apartment. She had to start remembering to leave a light on inside. Mr Louis had added a sensor to the outside light on her landing so that it came on at dark. Still, no matter how old she got, there was just something unnerving about going into a dark house.

This evening, though, she was too beat to work up any real misgivings. Wasn't that always what happened with the characters in horror flicks? They were either too tired or too distracted to pay attention.

'Just go up the stairs, Jess,' she grumbled to herself.

'You're home.'

Jess jumped, made one of those silly sounds those characters in the movies she'd just been thinking about make. Her landlord stood at the corner of the garage wiping his hands on a small cloth or hand towel.

'I didn't mean to startle you.' Louis gestured to the garage. 'I was just cleaning my paint brush. But I was hoping to catch you.'

'Well, you caught me,' Jess assured him. She put her hand to her chest and ordered her heart to take it easy. 'I was trying to convince myself to climb those stairs.' When a seventy-plus-year-old man could sneak up on her like that, it was time to polish up those old basic awareness skills.

'I painted your railing.' He gestured to the iron railing leading up the landing outside her apartment. 'It was looking a little weathered. We can't have rust setting in.'

The deep bronze color did look a little browner but it was difficult to tell with dusk setting in. She was glad she hadn't touched it.

'I was about to have dinner. Come along, you can join me. Give yourself a rest before you have to climb those stairs.'

Jess almost cringed. She had a long hot soak and a glass of wine on her mind. 'I couldn't impose.'

'It's no imposition. Dinner is done already.' He motioned for her to follow. 'I insist you join me.'

How did she say no? 'If you're sure.'

Besides, she really needed to have that talk with him about her door. Last week she'd come home late, like now, and found him slathering a fresh coat of paint on her door. It wasn't that she didn't appreciate a well-maintained home, but she suspected there was more to that decision than the sudden urge to spruce things up. After the message she'd been left in her apartment by an intruder before her locks were changed, she had a feeling that same intruder had left her an ugly message on her door.

Maybe Louis was OCD and couldn't bear to put things off. She'd need to make him understand that he couldn't go cleaning up what might be connected to one of her cases.

She had a feeling he was so going to wish he hadn't rented this place to her.

He opened the door and waited for her to go in first. She opened her mouth to thank him but the most amazing aroma short-circuited her ability to speak. The scent of cloves and paprika hung in the air.

She finally found her voice. 'That smells amazing.'

'Why, thank you.' He ushered her inside.

She really should feel guilty imposing like this but he looked so excited at the prospect of having her company, and her appetite was doing somersaults at those incredible scents. She did have questions for him. The least she could do was spend a little time with a lonely old man.

And taste whatever smelled so freaking heavenly.

This was her first time in her landlord's home. The craftsman architecture of the century-old house carried through to the interior. The living room was neat and sparsely furnished. The lack of efficient lighting left the room a little dark for Jess's taste. She hadn't once seen the heavy drapes open on any of the windows except the kitchen. Nothing wrong with preferring privacy.

'I hope you're not a vegetarian.' He motioned for her to follow him. 'The kitchen's this way.'

'No, sir,' Jess said in response to his comment as she trailed after him. 'No reason to ignore any food group, the way I see it.'

'The pork's been cooking all day.' He pulled out a chair for her at the oak table that stood in the middle of his kitchen. 'The sauce is a family recipe.'

Barbecue pork. Jess couldn't remember the last time she'd had a barbecue sandwich. Or attended a cookout. She needed a life. As soon as this case was solved, she would make a concerted effort. Starting with the Baron Labor Day cookout. That was as good a beginning as any.

With a twisted ulterior motive.

She needed therapy. Serious therapy. She wondered what a shrink would say about her fascination with Burnett's exes.

While Mr Louis readied their plates, Jess considered how to broach the subject of the paint job on her door without offending the elderly gentleman. She guessed he was about the same age as Frances. Jess didn't have a clue whether or not he had any family here in Birmingham.

As independent as she was, she understood how difficult it would be to reach his age and be alone. Proof positive that her brain was done for the day. She needed that glass of wine and long hot soak.

'I saw on the news that the administrator of that nursing home was found murdered.'

'Retirement home,' she corrected. Considering those feisty widows, the Vestavia Village was definitely not a nursing home. 'It's more like luxury condos for those who don't want to cook and clean for themselves.'

'I see.' He crossed to the table and set a plate before Jess. 'Water? Iced tea?'

Too bad beer hadn't been one of the offerings. She loved beer with barbecue. 'Water would be nice.'

He delivered a glass of tap water on ice and a linen napkin for Jess before preparing his own plate. Then he sat down across the table from her and waited expectantly.

So this was awkward. Jess propped a smile into place. 'Do you want to say grace?'

'You may, if you'd like.' He adjusted his eyeglasses.

She smiled. 'Why don't we just eat?'

'Yes.' He nodded. 'Let's eat.'

She picked up the sandwich with both hands and took a small bite. The flavors filled her senses and she moaned before she could stop herself. 'This is delicious,' she managed around the chewing. 'The pork is so tender.'

'Hours of basting.'

Louis went on and on about how he'd prepared the meat. Jess tried to listen. She really did but mostly she just ate. By the time she'd finished off the sandwich, she felt like the hog she'd eaten. 'I am absolutely certain I've never had barbecue that amazing.' She was also certain she'd never devoured anything in front of a man who watched her every move so intently unless they had either just been intimate or were about to be.

'I'm pleased you enjoyed it.' One of those rare smiles lit his face. 'There's plenty more.'

Jess held up both hands. 'No. No. I couldn't.'

Silence stretched a second or two too long. She couldn't keep putting off discussing the subject of her door . . . or of the search Burnett wanted forensics to do of his property.

'So you're investigating that murder?'

She nodded. 'Yes, I am.'

'I'm certain you'll get the bad guy.' He cleared his throat and looked around the room as if he wasn't sure what to say or do next.

Just ask him, Jess. 'The other evening when I came home, you were painting my door. Had someone written something ugly there? Maybe a message for me?'

He reached up and adjusted his glasses again. 'What sort of message do you mean?'

There it was. The averted eyes. The monotone. Guilt. 'I investigate some very bad crimes, Mr Louis. Sometimes the folks who commit those crimes or maybe just some who don't like me very much get a kick out of saying or doing things they think will scare me.'

He cleared his throat again and glanced at her. 'You mean like threatening that you're going to die or something like that?'

So it was that kind of message was it? Her heart felt heavy at the idea. 'Yes, that sort of message.'

Still not looking at her, he nodded. 'It was very ugly,' he said softly, his voice growing lower with each word. '*Kill the bitch.*'

A similar message had been left at the crime scene she'd worked last week. 'I apologize that you had to see that,' she offered. 'And I do appreciate your trying to protect me from the unpleasantness. But the message may have provided clues to the case I was working on. I need to see any and all messages that come to me by whatever means.'

He stared at the table for a moment. Jess felt like a total jerk for scolding him. She didn't like it at all. He'd offered her a place to live and she made him feel awkward in his own home.

'Mr Louis, I'm sorry. I feel terrible even having to bring this up.'

He lifted his gaze to hers. Whatever he felt he'd erased it from his face. 'Don't apologize. You're right. I should have asked you first. I wasn't thinking.' He swiped his palms across the crisp white tablecloth as if trying to smooth invisible wrinkles. 'I was taught to respect and protect women. It's difficult for me to see such things. But I do understand.'

Relief flooded her tense muscles but she still had one more favor to ask of him. 'You remember on Friday my car had to be towed because someone tried breaking into it?'

He nodded but he didn't look at her. 'That's very unusual. We don't generally have break-ins in this neighborhood.'

There it was. Further proof that she'd brought nothing but trouble to his door. 'I'm certain you don't. We believe the person who did this was after me.' Jess moistened her lips. 'The forensics techs, the folks who gather evidence at crime scenes,' she explained, 'would really like to have a look around if that would be okay with you.'

He stared at the tabletop some more, smoothing another wrinkle only he could see. 'I suppose that would be all right.'

Jess wanted the floor to crack open so she could disappear. 'I appreciate your patience, Mr Louis. You've been so kind and I've been nothing but trouble.'

He stood abruptly. The table shook. 'Really. It's no trouble.'

Jess decided that was her cue to go. She gathered her bag and followed him to the front door.

'I'll have to return the favor sometime.' She gave him her brightest smile. 'I'm not nearly as good a cook as you but I am fabulous with takeout.'

He nodded. 'That would be very nice, but no Chinese. I don't eat Chinese.'

'All right, then.' More awkward seconds ticked off. 'Good night, Mr Louis.' She turned to walk out the door but his voice stopped her.

'George.' He cleared his throat. She had decided that was his nervous tic. 'You're to call me George.'

'George,' she repeated. 'Well, good night, George.'

'Good night, Jess.'

The night air wasn't much cooler than it had been before the sun went down. Sometime next month the heat would start to lose its ferocity. She couldn't wait.

Taking her time, she strolled across the yard toward her place. Mostly she worked at shaking off the creepy feeling she felt guilty about having. The man was just trying to be nice and she couldn't stop analyzing him and his nervous habits long enough to truly appreciate his generosity.

At least she didn't have to worry about dinner tonight.

Careful not to touch the railing, she climbed the steps to her door. As soon as she'd had that soak she'd promised herself, she intended to open a bottle of wine and relax in the glider that waited just outside her door. Another kind gift from her landlord. Lord, she felt like a total shit.

It was cool inside her place. She turned on the light, then, out of habit, locked the door and left her bag on the table. Grabbing her robe, she headed for the bathroom. If she had ever been this tired, she had no recall of the event. No sleep at all last night had taken its toll. Thank God Lori had done all the driving today. She opened the valves to fill the tub. Deep and extra hot was how she wanted it.

Jess thought of that dark Corolla that had followed her and Lori today. First thing in the morning she would put Chad Cook on trying to run down the possibilities with that partial plate number she'd gotten.

A rap on her door stalled her efforts at opening a bottle of white wine she wished was chilled but wasn't. She hoped Louis hadn't decided that he couldn't deal with all her issues and had come to give her notice of eviction. Or, worse, Harper was here with the report of another murder. Nah, he would just call.

That left only one possibility. She peeked at her visitor. *Dan*.

She opened the door and stared up at him. 'This is not a good time, Burnett. You're getting between me and my two best friends – wine and a long, hot bath.'

'I wanted to let you know that your Audi will be ready tomorrow around lunch.'

'You couldn't call?' There was more to it than that. 'Is there something new on Allen?' Surely not since noon today.

'Nothing new. Did you speak to Mr Louis about a search of his property?'

'Yes, I did. He agreed. You just need to set up a time.'

'Good.'

There was more. She waited. He stood there. This part always drove her nuts. 'You're here for what reason, then?' They were not having sex tonight. No way. No how. She refused to even be tempted, which required that she stay annoyed at him. They had bent that rule completely out of shape already this week. And she was exhausted. Totally, dog tired.

'Pratt called.'

Jess laughed. 'I should have known.' She turned around and headed back to that bottle of wine.

The door closed, locks engaged, and Burnett joined her. 'You need any help with that?'

'No, sir.' She twisted the corkscrew harder, taking her frustration out on it.

'Mr Baker complained about your tactics interviewing his daughter-in-law. He claims she was in no emotional condition to be interviewed.'

The cork came loose with a distinct *pop*. Jess didn't say a word until she had poured a hefty serving and downed a significant portion of it. 'She called and asked to speak to me as soon as possible. Ask Harper and Wells if you need verification. Besides, when exactly are family members of homicide victims in a suitable emotional condition for interviewing? Should we put the investigation on hold until whatever time that is?'

'I know.' Burnett's shoulders sagged. 'I don't need verification, Jess. I'm just here to let you know that feathers are ruffled. I smoothed things over but you'll need to proceed with caution. We talked about this.'

'That's *your* job.' She snagged the other stemmed glass she owned and passed it to him. 'You're the chief of police. You keep things smoothed over. I' – she waved her glass – 'on the other hand, ruffle things, including feathers.'

Burnett splashed some wine into his glass and sipped it.

She poured herself another serving. 'That's what you do for all your chiefs, right?'

He nodded. 'That's what I do for all of them, yes.' This time he downed the meager serving he'd allowed himself.

'You show up at Black's or Hogan's door like this when they step on toes?' She stared straight at him and waited for an answer.

'You know the answer to that.'

'That's what I thought.' Another gulp of wine for fortification. 'It's been almost a month, Burnett. At some point you have to stop treating me differently than you treat the others.'

He stared at his glass as if he wished he dared drink more and then drive home. *Because he was going home.*

There would be no sleepovers during the workweek.

'That might not be possible.'

At least he wasn't still denying that he was treating her differently. 'We'll have to work on that,' she suggested. 'If it makes you happy, I will try not to tick off any more of Pratt's uppity friends.'

'Have you heard from Duvall since he returned to LA?'

Now there was a question out of left field. 'He called to say he'd arrived safely.' She shrugged. Wasn't about to discuss the rest of what her ex-husband had said. 'I haven't heard from him since. Probably won't unless he learns something from Lopez that we need to know about Captain Allen's disappearance.'

'He wants you back.' Burnett placed his glass on the table and shoved his hands into his trouser pockets. 'You still sure that's not what you want?'

Where the hell had that come from? 'We talked about this already. I'm happy here and now. I'm not looking to go backward.'

He fixed that blue gaze of his on hers and grinned. 'See. That's how I feel every time something else about one of my exes comes up. Like this Baron cookout. You only want to go because you're curious about Nina.'

Well he had her there.

'I have to turn off the water in the tub.' She hurried to the bathroom before he could say more. The steam rising from the water as she shut off the valves had her considering just forgetting about Burnett and climbing in. But she couldn't do that.

Resigned to hearing him out, she padded back to where he waited. 'You could save us both a lot of trouble and just tell me the deal on Nina. Is she anything like her sister?' Jess liked Sylvia. She was brash and a total smart-ass, but she was tough and determined and far more fragile inside than she was outside.

'Good night, Jess.' He headed for the door.

That he refused to come clean with her about this Nina woman bugged the heck out of her. 'I saw Corlew today.'

Daniel Burnett stopped dead in his tracks. He turned back to her. 'How?'

'He's a PI now.'

'I know what he is,' he said with a sharpness she seldom heard in his tone.

Well, well. The two hated each other just as much now as they had back in high school it seemed. Why was it men didn't see how petty and immature that was? Women didn't walk about with chips on their shoulders like that. They found a way to get even.

'He did a background search and some surveillance on my vic.' She shrugged. 'I needed to follow up with him.'

Burnett held up both hands. 'Don't tell me, you found him in a bar.'

'How'd you guess?' Jess refused to rise to the bait. 'We had a nice little reunion. According to my sources, his services are highly sought after these days.'

'Watch him, Jess,' Burnett warned, anger simmering in those baby blues. 'He's not the same man he used to be. He's cold and calculating and he'll do anything to win.'

Jess frowned. 'That's funny. He sounds exactly the same.' Those parts of his personality she remembered vividly.

Clearly exasperated, Burnett changed the subject. 'You need a ride to the office in the morning?'

'Lori's picking me up.'

Apparently satisfied, he reached out and squeezed her arm. 'See you tomorrow.'

She cautioned him not to touch the railing and then she watched him go before locking up. At least the wine had her feeling a little more relaxed, despite his annoying warnings. Tread carefully with the mayor's friends. Don't trust Corlew. If she were totally honest with herself, she would have to admit that he used passing along the mayor's comments as an excuse to stop by when he could have simply called. He was still worried about her safety. Maybe she should be a little more worried herself. But she had to find a way to make him see that he could not continue to single her out from all his other deputy chiefs. Doing so made her look incapable and cast a bad light on him. How long would it take the others to notice Burnett was playing favorites to some degree?

The absolute last thing Jess wanted was for her return to Birmingham to damage his career. She had to make him see what others undoubtedly already had. He was hovering like a helicopter mom.

'I can take care of myself,' she muttered as she snagged her Glock and headed for that nice, long soak. She placed the handgun on the little table that sat next to her tub. Thirty seconds later her clothes were on the floor and she was neck-deep in nice, warm water. A little draining and then a lot of adding heated things back up, had the steam rising again.

She closed her eyes and allowed the images and voices of the day to filter slowly through her head. Scott Baker's wife was convinced that her husband had wanted to be murdered. The concept was a little too far-fetched in Jess's opinion. More likely Trisha Baker was in deep denial and talking crazy. Jess would need a lot more than her emotional plea to put much stock in that scenario.

The poor woman needed some rationale that her husband was dead and this made him a hero. He was protecting their son. Delusional or not, there could be some truth in the part about Scott Baker sending his wife and son out of town. Since Baker likely knew and anticipated his killer's visit, perhaps he felt that he and his family were threatened by this person and he wanted to ensure his family was safe.

Maybe the other woman had pulled a *Fatal Attraction*. If that were the case, why go through with the meeting without arming himself or having some manner of backup? Why not call the police? And why the hell did he turn off the security system?

The only logical reason for his decisions was that he had something to hide.

Jess groaned as her tense muscles started to melt.

If Baker had a secret, why didn't Corlew find anything? Even the best-kept secrets were never really safe. There was always someone somewhere who knew something.

Maybe Corlew had been paid to find nothing. By Scott perhaps. The Baker family was rich and powerful. If the son had troubles, they could certainly have made them go away without him ending up dead.

That was the part that didn't make sense.

The grind of metal on metal forced her eyes open. Jess held her breath and listened. Was someone at her door? The sound came again. She was out of the water and wrapping a towel around her body before the air released from her lungs. She claimed her Glock and eased to the bathroom door. She'd left it open a crack so seeing into the rest of her apartment was easy.

She slipped out of the bathroom and checked the door. Locked. One by one she checked the view out the windows. No vehicle in the driveway. No fleeing would-be intruder.

Just to be sure, she checked the lock on the door again. That grinding noise had sounded like the workings of a lock rubbing against each other.

Had to be Mr Louis doing something downstairs in the garage.

Satisfied that there was no one about, she cleaned up the mess she'd made. She'd tracked water everywhere. Then she finished her bath and climbed into bed. To hell with drying her hair. She'd forgotten to ask if the electrical problem had been resolved.

Just now she was too tired to care.

Her eyes drifted closed and her cell made that irritating sound that told her she had a text message.

Probably Burnett saying good night.

She reached for her phone.

Not Burnett.

Tormenter.

Eric Spears. The serial killer who'd gotten away. The one who'd tortured and murdered dozens of women. The one who'd gotten close enough to destroy her career at the Bureau and then followed her to her hometown. The sick son of a bitch who had killed a federal agent right here in Birmingham and almost killed Lori and Dan.

She'd gotten a smart-ass remark from him on Saturday.

Something about Burnett having won this round. He'd taunted her about her ex showing up. She'd ignored him. Maybe not a smart move. But his game was getting old.

Just something else for her to feel guilty about. Originally her plan had been to try and lure him into reacting so she could get another shot at taking him out. That had likely been foolhardy or just doomed from the start. Whatever the case, she was just too tired to play tonight.

But then if she didn't . . . what would his next move be? To start a new game with someone else? An innocent victim her actions might have saved?

'Just do it,' she muttered. She swiped the screen, opening the text from him. Her lips tightened as she read his message. Just one word. *Cheers*.

Her attention settled on the empty wine bottle and glasses on her kitchen table. He couldn't be here . . . watching her.

Impossible.

Her feet hit the floor, Glock in her hand. Again, she went from window to window and checked the perimeter for as far as she could see in the moonlight.

Nothing.

She ordered her heart to slow. The undeniable fear he had prompted dissolved and outrage roared in its place. 'Show your face, Spears.' Her fingers tightened on her weapon.

Let him come.

The next time he showed up in her life, she planned on being the last thing he ever saw.

Chapter Ten

Laurel Drive, Hoover, 9.20 P.M.

Elliott Carson studied the newspapers he had saved for more than a decade. His gut had turned inside out and then twisted into knots.

BIRMINGHAM HIGH SCHOOL SENIOR FOUND DEAD

Images from that night flashed like lightning through his mind. The seven of them seated in a circle on the roof with only the moon and a single candle for light. They had been drinking . . . a lot. Elliott and Juliette had smoked weed but the others had snorted coke. It was the first time any of them, to his knowledge, ever did drugs. They'd bought a whole load of shit. They were going to par-tay.

Look what it had cost them . . .

What had they been thinking?

Elliott braced his head in his hands and read the

headline that had appeared in the *Birmingham News* a week later.

BIRMINGHAM TEEN'S DEATH RULED SUICIDE

He closed his eyes and prayed fervently, his lips moving frantically to keep up with the words pouring from his heart. How could they have done this awful thing? How could they just cover it up and pretend nothing had happened?

They had taken a life . . . the five of them. All this time they'd pretended. They had gone on with their lives as if *his* hadn't mattered. Every day of every one of those years had been another he had not been allowed to enjoy because they had robbed him of that future.

It was time they made this right. Scott shouldn't have had to die for them to see how wrong it was to continue this lie. If Elliott hadn't been such a coward, he would have done the right thing long ago.

He was a coward. He had a boy of his own now. Just like Scott did . . . *had*. How could he expect his child to make the right choices in life if he didn't? Sweet Jesus, when his wife and son found out . . . his whole family would be devastated.

Scott's family would be further devastated.

They would all be devastated. Elliott's jaw hardened. He had no sympathy for the others. But their families were a different story. Their one mistake was going to cost so many so very much.

Elliott picked up the pages. Handwritten pages torn from a diary or journal someone had left stuck in his door like a religious pamphlet. Thank God his wife hadn't been home to find this ugliness.

Kevin was right. *He* was here and he wanted them to know he hadn't forgotten what they had done . . .

March 15

It was always the same. We ran into them at the mall. Probably wasn't a coincidence. Love did things to a guy. Made him stupid.

The Five were in the food court showing off. Ha! They thought they were celebrities or something. Thought their shit didn't stink. Avoiding the phonies would have been the best thing to do. Not so lucky. He had to sit as close to them as possible.

No point trying to save him. He was a lost cause. But a friend didn't leave a friend no matter that he was being a dork at the moment.

Elliott scrubbed at his eyes, his heart pounding, but he couldn't stop reading.

Hot Scott, that's what all the girls called him, was the leader of the Five but it was that smart-ass Elliott Carson who took a turn today. That's what they did. They took turns making other people feel beneath them. Using those less fortunate for their entertainment. It made him so angry . . . and still he took it because his friend was a sucker in love.

It was the stupidest move. If those assholes were smart, they would at least come up with more original ways of making everyone else look like idiots. Elliott asked him to go grab him another Coke. He'd even buy a round for our table. I told him not to listen to just ignore them. But he didn't. Poor bastard took the money and rushed to fill the order.

When he reached the table with the tray of Cokes, Elliott tripped him. Made a hell of a mess but mostly it hurt. Everyone stared at him and laughed. Maybe one day they would both get used to the humiliation. Not!

Life just wasn't fair sometimes. But he figured the Five would get theirs one day.

Elliott crushed the pages in his hand and pushed out of the chair. He remembered that day as if it were yesterday. He'd just been fucking around. He hadn't meant any real harm.

Goddammit! He walked around his desk to pace the room. His room. The private office and getaway he'd needed after his career-shattering injury had brought him back to Birmingham a lesser man. His wife had overseen the building of this big-ass mansion and getting them settled while he'd brooded, feeling sorry for himself. Eventually he'd gotten over it and started his new life – the one that didn't include baseball.

At least he'd had a life . . . The man he'd helped murder hadn't gotten that. All he'd ever gotten was laughed at after being made the butt of a joke.

How many times had Elliott been the one to initiate that kind of pain?

God, he didn't want to think about it.

Tonight, Elliott had sent his wife and son to her mother's. He needed some time alone to figure this out. A decision should have been reached by now. There was no excuse for this waffling back and forth. He knew what he had to do. If he'd had any doubts, receiving the pages from this journal had reminded him. All he needed was one ally in this mess.

Juliette was the most likely one he could count on. Kevin and Aaron would never go along with the idea of coming clean about that night. Both were too fucking selfish.

What they'd done back in high school was wrong.

His blood ran suddenly and completely cold. Would they get the death penalty for what they had done?

The law might decide to make an example out of them. Bullying and shit like that was on the news all the time now. All those generation Xers and Yers who whined about it now were the world's worst at belittling and bullying when they were in high school. Just like him. What a crock.

Okay. He had to make this right. Do this the proper way. The PI he'd called hadn't called him back and Elliott couldn't take the waiting any longer. He had to act. He could call that lady cop who was investigating Scott's murder. All he'd have to do was call the nonemergency line and get a message to her. She'd call him back when she got the message.

Elliott exhaled a big breath, let the tension flow out of him. Making that decision was a tremendous relief. He wished he'd made it years ago instead of listening to the others.

He touched the screen of his cell and pulled up the keypad. He tapped the first few digits. Something in his peripheral vision captured his attention. He stared at the wall above the credenza for two, then three beats before the reality of what he was seeing fully registered. His lucky bat was missing. His wife kept his trophies in a case in the family room, but that bat was extra special to him. He kept it here, in his home office.

Where the hell—

'Batter up!'

Elliott pivoted to face the person who'd shouted those two words. The ski mask and gloves concealing the intruder's identity registered, telling him nothing but stealing valuable time.

The bat swung.

Elliott saw it coming . . . but it was too late for him to duck. He'd been too startled, too stunned, too busy trying to figure out why someone in a ski mask would steal his lucky bat while he was in the house.

The bat slammed into his skull.

As he dropped to his knees, his lucky bat connected with his head again and the lights went out.

Chapter Eleven

Parkridge Drive, Homewood, 10.00 P.M.

Lori stayed in the bathroom as long as she could without risking Chet figuring out what she was doing.

She and Chet Harper had been living together less than a week and already they'd had their first major fight. He was angry because she pretended to have something else to do this weekend, which prevented her from going to the zoo with him and Chester. He couldn't say for sure she wasn't telling the truth. He *suspected* she wasn't because she had been up front with him regarding her reservations about his three-year-old son.

Little Chester hated her. End of story. He couldn't stand to be close to her. He clung to Chet whenever she was around. Nothing she said or did made any difference. The kid simply did not like her. Why would she make herself and the kid and Chet miserable by going to the zoo with them on Saturday afternoon?

Let the two of them enjoy the day and they could be miserable with her that evening. Because until the kid went to sleep that night, he would be miserable with her there. His father would be miserable because little Chester was miserable and Lori would be miserable at the whole idea.

She'd get her sister Terri to cover for her with some excuse of plans the two of them had with their mother. It shouldn't be a big deal. Except it was. Chet saw right through her.

He knew what she was up to.

She couldn't exactly hide in here all night.

Lori draped her towel over the side of the tub and secured the sash of her robe. Before making her exit, she ran her fingers through her hair once more, checked her teeth. She walked to the door that separated her from the confrontation waiting in her otherwise perfect relationship with a totally awesome guy.

The sound of the door latch echoed like a shotgun blast through the silent room. He'd already gone to bed. He was definitely upset with her if he didn't want to say good night.

The lights were out except for the one in the hall. She tiptoed to the bed. When the lump in there didn't move or say anything, she understood that he was through arguing for the night.

She would have liked to clear the air but Chet would prefer to avoid the problem. That concept made her angry all over again. Why the hell couldn't he understand her position? He was a father. He'd gone through the pregnancy with his wife and spent three years playing the part of daddy. She hadn't done any of that stuff. Yes, Chester was a precious little boy but he wasn't *her* little boy. She hoped one day they could be comfortable around each other but there was no way to rush the bonding.

Not for the child and not for her.

She yanked off her robe and tossed it aside before crawling beneath the sheet. This was exactly what she had feared. Before they had moved in together, the concept of becoming a pseudomother was just that – a concept.

Maybe she wasn't mother material.

Chet had no right rushing her into that step.

Something she obviously should have discussed in more detail with him before she'd moved into his home. The one that had a bedroom for his son – a point she had made when they had been contemplating the idea of moving in together.

What an idiot she had been! A child wasn't a piece of property. She should have given more weight to the reality that when she got the man, she got the kid. She couldn't love Chet without learning to love Chester.

She wanted to! She really did. But she needed time.

'I was wrong.'

His deep voice flowed through the darkness and skimmed her bare skin like warm silk. She couldn't hold back the shiver the sound prompted.

Lori rolled to her side. He did the same. It was too dark to see his face or eyes, but she already knew both by heart.

'I want to do this right, Chet.' She hoped her voice conveyed just how deeply she meant those words. 'But you're pushing your son and me to form a bond when we both need time. I can't make him trust me much less love me.'

For a few moments they lay in the dark, the silence widening between them.

'I love you, Lori.'

She couldn't bear it. She reached out, traced the strong line of his jaw. The dampness there made her breath catch. 'I love you.' She hadn't meant to hurt him . . . she'd made the strongest man she knew *cry*. Her heart squeezed in agony.

'I love my son too,' he murmured. 'I want you to love him . . . I want him to love you.'

Her lips trembled into a smile. 'It takes time. I will love him a little more each day just like I do you. But it'll take longer for him to love me. He doesn't understand.'

'I know. I didn't mean to push too hard.'

She moved closer to him, pressed her lips to his damp jaw. 'I know. We're both finding our way.'

'Chester and I will go to the zoo on Saturday. You go relax with your mom and sister. We'll catch up at dinner.'

Lori made her decision then and there. 'No. I'm going with you and Chester.'

'I don't want you to do anything you're not ready to do,' Chet urged gently, but she could hear the hope in his voice.

'Chester needs consistency. If I'm with you sometimes but not other times, he might get confused. I was wrong to be such a coward.' That was the truth. Jess had advised her to be consistent. Lori was a grown woman. It was ridiculous for her to be afraid of a child. She and Chet were making a life together.

That life included his son.

'I need consistency too.'

Lori frowned but he couldn't see her in the dark. 'Is something else wrong?' How else had she screwed up? Oh, man. This was worse than she thought.

He rolled her onto her back and burrowed between her thighs. 'I want to make love to you every day for the rest of my life. Missing a day doesn't work for me.'

'Who said we were going to miss a day?' She couldn't think of anything she'd rather do than spend her life making love with this man.

He pushed into her. Her whole body tensed with anticipation.

'I want to kiss every part of you.' He started at her forehead and began a methodical path over her face . . . but it was his hips grinding into hers with each firm thrust that had her unable to catch her breath.

'Here,' he murmured as he nuzzled her ear.

Her leg muscles tightened as she lifted her hips to meet his.

His mouth covered her breast . . . her fingers tangled in his hair as the waves of orgasm began. He cupped her bottom, pulled her harder against him as his own urgency drove him steadily toward that pinnacle of sensations.

Afterward he held her tight until her heart stopped pounding.

As she drifted off to sleep, she wondered how she would ever survive if she lost this man.

She hadn't wanted a relationship like this . . . but she hadn't been able to stop herself from falling so deeply in love with him.

How had this happened so fast?

Chapter Twelve

Birmingham Police Department,
Wednesday, August 11, 8.05 A.M.

Jess had gotten to the office early. She and Lori had updated the case board with what they'd learned from Baker's wife. The possible scenarios, such as an angry business partner and an obsessed mistress, had been added to the board. Alibis for six of the widows had been confirmed. Frances, dear, sweet, Frances, was the lone unsubstantiated person of interest among the group.

Buddy Corlew, the Tracker, had been added as a person of interest.

At Jess's request, Harper and Cook had made a run to the department's forensics garage to pick up her Audi. To finish clearing the SPU office, she sent Prescott to do some follow-up interviews with the two janitors at

Vestavia Village who had discovered Baker's body. Lori was tracking down fresh coffee.

Jess had maybe ten minutes before any of her team returned. She waited with mounting impatience for the call to connect. She'd intended to have this conversation with Supervisory Special Agent Ralph Gant, her former boss at the Bureau, before she left for work. But Lori had shown up earlier than expected and since she had been Jess's ride to work, that was the end of that.

'Gant.'

Finally. 'Good morning,' Jess said with all the perkiness she could muster. 'How are things with you?'

'Has *he* contacted you?' Gant cut straight to the chase without even a hello. Tension thickened his voice.

Jess made a face. Couldn't the man ask how she was or at least answer her question? She was the one who needed answers. 'I'm calling to see if you have anything new on Spears?' She held her breath, hoped her little maneuver would work.

'We haven't picked anything up on him since he left the country. Wherever he is, the bastard's flying way under our radar. I don't know why I'm surprised – that's his MO. I just don't like it, that's all. He killed one of my best agents, not to mention one of Birmingham's. I want that bastard.'

Jess didn't like it either. She turned to stare out the window behind her desk. What if he was out there?

Watching her every move again? To say good night at a time she was most likely in bed was one thing. Even to know when her ex-husband showed up in Birmingham wasn't outside the realm of easily obtained knowledge. Reporters had been all over the place the night her motel room was vandalized. Wesley's face may have shown up in one of the shots. But last night's text was a horse of a different color. How had he known she was having wine?

She shook off the troubling thought and decided there was no way to ask this question that wouldn't rouse Gant's suspicions but she had to know. 'What are the chances that he has slipped back into the country without detection?' She braced for a deluge of questions, though her query was perfectly logical. Despite the very best efforts, people slipped through the tightest security measures every hour of every day.

'I knew it,' Gant fairly shouted. 'He has contacted you. How the hell am I supposed to conduct this investigation if you don't keep me up to speed?'

Get around that one, Jess. 'I received a text from him. That's it. Short and sweet. Last night before midnight.' That was about as vague as she could get without being obvious. If he found out about all the other text messages, he would come unhinged on her. Gant might not be her boss anymore but he was in charge of the Spears investigation. He could make her life miserable if he suspected she was in any way impeding that investigation.

'What did he say? Did he threaten you in some way? What?' Gant demanded, his frustration loud and clear.

She grimaced in advance. This was not going to bode well. 'Cheers.'

All ten seconds that elapsed before he spoke again throbbed in her brain.

'Does that mean something in particular to you, Harris?'

Harris, not Jess. The frustration had been kicked aside in favor of an attempt at intimidation. Had he forgotten already that those tactics just didn't work with her?

'It means nothing.' Her sister would tell her she was going to hell for lying but Jess was pretty sure that particular sin was way down on the list of her transgressions. A fact she had no plans to point out to her sister. 'I mean, I did have wine last night but there's no way Spears could have known that.'

Gant didn't bother pointing out that somehow Spears had obviously known she was having wine.

Oh God. She rubbed at her neck. Why did this have to be so complicated? If he was after her, why didn't he just bust through her door? One more shot at him was all she needed.

'I'll need access to your phone records.'

Gant didn't trust her to give him the whole story. And he was pissed. Well, hell, why had she even told him? 'No need to go through all that red tape. I can tell you the number he used – if it was even him and if he hasn't dumped the phone already. I doubt checking it out will be worth your trouble.'

The chances of tracking him on a throwaway cell were slim to none but she liked throwing that remote possibility in Spears's face every chance she got.

'Why don't you let me be the judge of whether it's worth the trouble?' Gant demanded.

'Fine,' she snapped. 'Feel free to access my cell phone records, Agent Gant.'

Grudges are not attractive accessories, Jess. Just because Gant hadn't backed her up when the shit hit the fan a couple of months ago and her Bureau career had been crumbling was no cause to be a bitch now.

'Text me the number too.' Gant heaved a put-upon sigh. 'He may have someone local watching you. You need to be careful, Jess. This guy has a dangerous fixation on you. You know how this could go the same as I do.'

'That's why I'm calling.' No one comprehended the situation she was in any better than she did. She had two options. Ignore Spears and keep her fingers crossed that he was too afraid of getting caught to return to this country or bait him in hopes of nailing him if he did come back. She'd chosen the latter. Problem was, she couldn't share that with Burnett or Gant because all they wanted to do was shove her into protective custody. 'He made contact. I'm notifying you.'

'I'll let you know the instant I have anything new,' Gant assured her.

'Thanks. I appreciate it.' Jess ended the call. She stared at the pedestrians on the sidewalks below rushing to get to their offices. Spears could be out there. Or one of his henchmen. He could have someone watching her. He liked playing games. They didn't call him the Player for nothing.

She had let her guard down to some degree. Whenever she had a case, she lost track of all else. Between work and finding a place to rent until her house in Virginia sold, she had been a little preoccupied. Maybe Burnett and Gant were right. She needed to be more careful. She'd made at least two too many enemies.

Eric Spears she understood. For months she had studied the Player. She had known what made him tick even before she learned his real name. She knew what he wanted. He wanted her. To play with for a while and then to torture and kill her. That was his MO. She felt some degree of confidence that the way to stop him was to lure him back into a game with her. An up-close-and-personal game.

She needed him close . . . close enough to kill.

Captain Ted Allen was an unknown factor. He was supposed to be one of the good guys but that was up in the air now. He wanted revenge against Jess for screwing up his big case. At least, she presumed that was what he wanted. Everything else was a variable. Where was he? Who knew? What was his actual intent? No clue.

One thing was certain: she had good reason to watch her back.

Jess banished the thought and forced herself to relax by admiring the picture Devon Chambers, the key witness in last week's investigation, had drawn for her. At only eight years old, Devon was quite the little artist. He'd captured Jess, along with her bag and badge, on a perfect sunny day beneath a blue sky. She only wished she was as slim as the golden haired stick figure he had drawn.

'It took me a minute,' Lori announced as she breezed into the large conference space the Special Problems Unit used as a communal office. 'I had to brew a fresh pot.'

The scent that floated from the cups she carried had Jess meeting her in the middle of the room. 'That smells great.' She accepted a cup and cradled it in both hands so its warmth would chase away the lingering chill brought on by thoughts of Spears and Allen.

'It's all in the wrist.' Lori made a scooping motion with her free hand. 'Some of these guys make it so weak you can see through it. I'm here to tell you that ain't coffee.'

Jess tested Lori's theory. The brew was every bit as delicious as the stuff the detective made at home. 'If you ever decide to give up police work,' she told her friend, 'you could teach Starbucks a few things.'

Lori smiled but it looked a little overdone. 'I might not be the motherly type but I can bring down the house with my coffee-making skills.'

Jess felt her eyebrows rear up in surprise. 'Still worried about Chester, huh?'

Lori shook her head. 'I understand I have to give him time, but this is tough.' She shrugged. 'I feel like my entire life is on hold because a person less than three feet tall doesn't like me. By Friday I'm dreading Sunday and no sooner than we take Chester home on Sunday I'm already worried about Wednesday.'

Before Jess could scrounge up a witty answer, her cell phone clanged that vintage sound she loved to hate. 'Hold that thought,' she told her friend; then she laughed. 'Or maybe let it go for now.'

'That would make being around me a lot easier,' Lori assured her.

Jess checked the screen, didn't recognize the number. 'Harris.'

'Well, good morning, sunshine.'

Buddy Corlew.

No matter that she didn't want to, she heard Burnett's voice in her head warning that Corlew might have his own revenge on his mind. The two had been rivals back in high school but she'd had no idea about the troubles since.

Jess elbowed Burnett's warning aside. 'What can I do

for you, Mr Corlew?' She said his name with a pointed look at Lori.

Lori smirked. She didn't have to say the words. Jess knew what she was thinking. *I told you so.*

'I watched the news about your vic, Baker, last night and I remembered something from my dirt search on the guy that might prove useful to your investigation.'

'Really? And what would that be?' Like he hadn't remembered this whatever it was when she spoke to him yesterday. Maybe Burnett was right. Maybe Corlew wanted to play games. Well, she didn't have time for games. Unless he had the name of someone who wanted Scott Baker out of the way or he knew who Scott was having sex with besides his wife, then Corlew was wasting Jess's time.

'Not over the phone. Meet me at Cedar Hill Cemetery in Bessemer. Say in a half hour? I'll give you the big break you need on this case.'

'Cedar Hill Cemetery?' The call ended before she could demand a better explanation. She stared at her phone and bit back a slew of curses.

'We taking a road trip?'

Jess savored a sip of her coffee before surrendering to the inevitable. 'Yes. We are. Corlew is going to hand us the big break we need to solve this case.'

Lori grabbed her cell and purse from her desk. 'I knew he had the hots for you.'

'We'll just see about that, Detective.'

Cedar Hill Cemetery, Bessemer, 9.01 A.M.

Lori turned into the cemetery, rolling past the gates. Thankfully there were no services or service preparations going on this morning.

'That's him.' Jess leaned forward and studied the man leaning against the black Dodge Charger. He'd pulled over to one side of the main thoroughfare that cut through the landscape of headstones. 'What're you up to, Corlew?'

Lori pulled over behind him and shut off her Mustang. 'I guess we're about to find out.'

Corlew pushed off the muscle car and strode toward them. 'Nice wheels,' he said to Lori.

She acknowledged his compliment with a nod. 'Thanks. Yours aren't so bad either.'

'Got the Hemi engine to back it up too.'

Jess resisted the urge to step aside and give them plenty of space for a pissing contest. 'You said you'd remembered something useful to my case.'

'Follow me.' He turned and swaggered into the cemetery proper.

Cedar Hill had been a part of Birmingham history for more than a century. The grave markers spread for acres and acres. The best she recalled someone famous was buried here. A baseball or football player.

They were deep in the cemetery when her patience ran out. 'Corlew, where the hell are we going?'

'Right here.' He stopped at a marker and gestured to the name engraved there. 'This is your lead.'

Lenny Porter. Died at eighteen, just twelve years ago.

'I don't really need another dead man, Corlew.' Jess propped her hands on her hips. 'I hope you didn't waste my time dragging me out here.'

'Twelve years ago, Porter was poised to graduate with honors. He was headed to MIT with a full scholarship. Instead, the night before graduation, he walked off the roof of the old *Birmingham News* building. His death was ruled a suicide but there were those of us who believed otherwise.'

'What does his death, suicide or homicide, have to do with Scott Baker?' *Other than the obvious*, Jess kept to herself. The year of his death was the year Baker graduated from high school. 'Were Porter and Baker classmates?'

Corlew shook his head. 'They were miles apart. Like a couple other guys I once knew. Baker was the rich, popular kid and Porter was the nerd who spent his high school years glued to the wall wishing he had a life.'

Jess motioned for him to go on.

'Porter takes a nosedive. No one really cares but the police have to investigate, it makes the news, then fades away. Except' – those gray eyes of his glittered with mischief – 'his burial expenses were paid for by a certain wealthy Birmingham family you might know . . . the Bakers.'

'That's not so unusual,' she argued. 'The family likely heard about the tragedy and wanted to help. Folks do that down here.'

'And Scott Baker himself brought flowers out here every year on the anniversary of Porter's death. Every year. This was a kid Baker had no reason to know. None. Nada. And yet, he did somehow.'

Jess turned her hands up. 'This is all very interesting but I don't see the big lead you promised.'

'Baker's old man, the Samuel Scott Baker, has written a check to Porter's mother for the sum of two thousand dollars every month since his death. Do the math – that's a sizeable chunk of change.'

Now he had her attention. 'Was there an affair between Samuel Baker and Mrs Porter?'

Corlew shook his head. 'No connection whatsoever until her son's death.'

'The mother's still alive?'

'And getting that check every month,' Corlew confirmed. 'Funny thing is, the day before your vic bit the dust, Mrs Porter boarded a ship in New Orleans for a seven-day cruise. The first one of her entire life. I did some checking around and seems Scott Baker sent her on this luxury vacation. Made the arrangements just a week ago.'

Baker sent his wife and son out of town as well as the Porter woman. Interesting. That deep hum that signaled she was onto something started to vibrate inside her. 'Where's Porter's father?' Whether this was a lead in her homicide case or not, she wasn't sure. But it was definitely an interesting twist she needed to investigate.

'Not listed on Porter's birth certificate. Never in the picture as far as I could determine.'

'Sounds like maybe Samuel Baker had himself an illegitimate son.' Seemed the most likely scenario. But why did the mother only demand help after his death? Had Porter confronted Scott? Maybe the money was to prevent a scandal. And why send her out of town now?

'I was still in the department when Porter took that dive. I didn't catch the case but I heard rumors.'

'What kind of rumors?' Now she saw where this was going. 'Who did catch the case?'

'Funny that you ask,' Corlew said, 'but I believe you should ask Burnett for specifics. I think it was his friend Harold Black's case.'

Jess didn't like the idea that Corlew's goal could be to make Burnett and the department look bad, but if anything he had to say led her to Baker's killer, she wanted to hear it.

'I will ask him,' she guaranteed the cocky guy. 'Meanwhile, don't yank my chain, Corlew. I have an investigation to conduct. What kind of rumors did you hear?'

'That a group of teenagers, all rich kids, were involved in Porter's death. A friend of his, a guy by the name of

Todd Penney, told the police he and Porter had been invited to a private party by Scott Baker and his friends. But Penney later recanted the statement.'

'Did Baker and his friends have an alibi?'

Corlew laughed. "Course. They had each other. The *Five* they called themselves. These were the richest, most popular kids in Birmingham. The Five. Untouchable. Going places.'

The tattoo and the number five. Well, well, it appeared there was more to this little group of high school friends than met the eye. That feeling – the one that started deep in the pit of her stomach and wouldn't let up until she saw something through – started to build.

'We'll pull the case file. Check it out.' That was all she intended to say on the subject. If getting even with Burnett was the agenda here, she was having no part of that.

Her gaze settled on the headstone that proclaimed this plot as being home to Lenny, no middle name listed, Porter. If there was any truth whatsoever to Corlew's conjecture, Lenny deserved her attention.

Her cell clanged with an incoming call. 'I appreciate the heads-up, Corlew. I'll let you know if I find anything.'

Jess turned and retraced the path they'd taken through the cemetery. She didn't look back to see if Corlew followed. He'd handed her more trouble. That was what he'd done. She'd already ticked off most of the department with her brash methods and her less-than-subtle way of doing business. Now she was going to go digging around in an old case and maybe have to suggest her biggest competition in the department, Deputy Chief Harold Black, needed to lick his calf over.

Oh yeah, this was going to go over like a lead balloon. She'd gotten a taste of the blowback when she cast the shadow of suspicion on a cop last week. But she had no choice but to see this lead through.

By the time she dug her phone from her bag, it had stopped ringing and Lori's had started. Jess's caller had been Harper, as she suspected Lori's would be.

Jess kept moving toward Lori's Mustang as she listened to the one-sided conversation.

'We'll be right there.' Lori ended the call and tucked her cell into the pocket of her slacks. 'That was Harper.'

'Has he found us a real lead?'

'I don't know about that but we have another body.'

'Another homicide?' Jess didn't mean to sound surprised, but after the trouble she'd had with Black over who got what case, to get two in a row so close together was totally shocking.

'You got it. Male, age thirty, same graduating class as Baker, same type of fatal head injury. *And*, another member of the Five. Elliott Carson.'

The information Corlew had just passed along suddenly jumped to the front of Jess's priority list.

'You ladies decide you needed to properly show your gratitude and maybe take me for coffee?' Corlew asked, catching up since Jess had stalled to consider this news.

'Sorry, Corlew, but we got a call. You remember anything else you think is relevant, you let me know.'

'Will do.' He tapped his temple. 'Mind's like a steel trap.'

The man was incorrigible. 'I guess all those years of fast women and cheap booze didn't do any damage after all.'

He ignored her jab. 'So you got another murder?'

He'd hear about it soon enough. She might as well get his reaction. 'Elliott Carson.'

'Damn.' Corlew looked away.

'Damn what?' Jess demanded. If there was more he wasn't sharing, he was not going to like her bad cop side.

'Carson called me last night. Left a voice mail saying we needed to talk. I called him back but I didn't get an answer.'

'I guess now we know why.'

Chapter Thirteen

Elliott Carson had apparently done well for himself despite the early demise of his Major League career.

'This is some place,' Lori noted as they parked amid the barrage of official vehicles already on the scene.

'I Googled him on the way here,' Jess said as she prepared to climb out of the vehicle. 'His work with underprivileged youth has garnered him several big-time sponsors. Doesn't hurt that his wife is the daughter of a Texas oil baron.'

'That would explain the massive house.' Lori shoved her door closed and met Jess at the hood of her Mustang. 'Texans take big to another level.'

'That's what I hear.' Jess surveyed the home of the latest victim. Funny thing was, why the hell didn't these rich guys hire bodyguards if they anticipated trouble coming? Where was their sense of self-preservation?

Probably the same place as yours when you play games with Spears and complain because Dan feels the need to protect you.

Point taken.

Now there was something new. She was carrying on a conversation with herself.

Not a good sign. Maybe the department shrink was right when she suggested Jess needed additional counseling.

'News hounds picked up the scent,' Lori noted.

Jess snapped to attention and glanced back at the street. Three reporters hustled from their vehicles.

'Let's get a move on,' Jess suggested, mostly to herself. She had nothing to give the hungry reporters just now.

A curving stone staircase led from the sidewalk up to the porch. By the time they reached the door, she was cursing the four-inch heels of her new shoes. She'd lost everything when her place was destroyed a week and a half ago. Even her shoes had been beyond salvaging, save one pair that didn't match her new spiffy suit. She'd just bought these lovely new heels that did. Trouble was they were far from broken in.

'Remind me never to buy a house on a hill,' Jess grumbled as they reached the porch. After donning gloves and shoe covers, she smoothed a hand over her taupe pencil skirt and checked that the matching waist jacket wasn't riding up. Those reporters would be getting video feed, if not comments, for late-breaking news. It was bad enough to have them dissecting her every investigative step. She had no desire to have her appearance ripped to shreds as well. 'Let's get this done.'

The towering double doors of the front entrance opened and Harper greeted them with, 'I put in a call to the coroner's office to let them know this case might be related to the Baker murder. Dr Baron is on her way.'

'Thank you, Sergeant.' Jess appreciated his quick thinking and the confidence to take the steps he deemed necessary.

'And your Audi is waiting in your reserved parking space downtown.'

'I have a reserved spot?'

'You do. Right next to Deputy Chief Black.'

'Nice.' Now she had no excuse for not saying good morning to him every single day. Until she started questioning one of his old cases and a new war started. *Great*.

The Carson home was as ostentatious inside as it was outside. From the marble entry hall floors to the soaring ceilings, the home spoke of style and wealth. Evidence techs moved in and out of rooms like bees searching for pollen.

'Who discovered the body?' Jess settled her attention on Harper.

'The wife. She and their son spent the night at her

mother's home last night. This morning she dropped the boy off at baseball camp and came home to find her husband dead in his study.'

'I thought her parents lived in Texas.' That was what she got for relying on Google.

'They do but the mother keeps a home here so she can spend more time with her only grandchild.'

'Did the wife say why she spent the night at her mother's last night?' Jess fished for her glasses and tucked them into place.

'She says her husband asked her to. Said it was important.'

'I think I've heard that story before.' Scott Baker's wife had stated that he'd asked her to take their child and go away for a few days. Could be a coincidence, but considering both victims were members of this *Five*, she was thinking maybe not.

'Prescott and Cook are interviewing the neighbors,' Harper went on. 'The wife is in the family room.'

'Detective Wells,' Jess said to Lori, 'interview the wife again. See what she knows, if anything, about the Five and any of her husband's friends. Does she have some idea why her husband wanted her away from home last night?'

Lori gave her a nod and looked to Harper. 'Straight ahead,' he explained. 'The family room is at the back of the house next to the kitchen.'

Harper led the way to the study. An evidence tech was videoing the room. He lowered his camera and nodded to Jess. 'I'm done in here, ma'am. I'll just get out of your way.'

Jess thanked him and waited until he'd left the room before asking her next question. 'No indication our perp was after anything? Money? Jewelry?'

Harper shook his head. 'I didn't find anything disturbed anywhere in the house. I asked the wife if there was a special place they kept valuables or a hidden safe. She showed me the safe in the master bedroom but nothing had been touched. Other than this room, the place is clean.'

'We can certainly rule out robbery.' From what Jess had seen so far, this place would be a burglar's lucky strike.

'Found these wadded up in his pocket.'

Harper passed her two evidence bags containing pages torn from a notepad not unlike the one Jess carried. The handwritten pages were dated March, twelve years ago. As she read the victim's name, her breath stalled.

'The author's reminding him of why he had to die.' That cop instinct had kicked in hard. Had they overlooked something like this yesterday? 'When we're done here, go back to the Baker scene. Check his home.' She passed the evidence to him. 'If these murders are connected, there may be more of these.'

Jess turned her attention back to this murder. She surveyed the elegant study. Richly paneled walls lined with bookcases along one side. Another wall was corner to corner windows that filled the room with bright morning sun. Heavy drapes of red velvet were gathered on each end of the ornate rod that extended the full width of the generous room. A third wall featured framed photos and certificates from the victim's sports career. An organized desk and credenza sat in front of that wall. Directly above the credenza was a mounted rack that sported the slogan *Lucky Wood* but whatever the rack had held was missing. She frowned, but Harper had said nothing was missing.

'The bat's on the floor next to the victim.' Harper gestured to where the victim waited for Jess's attention.

'No sign of a struggle,' she noted, mostly to herself. Carson lay on the floor next to the wall of windows. His lucky bat at his side. Blood had accumulated on the floor beneath his head. The blow or blows had left him with a considerable gash.

'Lividity indicates he's been lying in that position for several hours. He's in full-on rigor. Been dead for a while.'

Like Scott Baker, Elliott Carson had been tall and athletic. Seemed strange that someone had overtaken him with his own bat without him putting up a fight.

'No sign of forced entry at any of the exterior doors?' The house surely had several points of entry. She supposed one could have accidentally been left open.

'Every door in the house was locked,' Harper confirmed. 'The only one left unlocked when the first officers on the scene arrived was the one coming in from the garage but the wife had unlocked it when she arrived home.'

'Was the security system set?' No need to ask if they had one. They would have one.

'She said he usually sets the alarm before he goes to bed each night. That didn't happen last night.'

Jess tried to visualize how the attack took place. 'He either knew the perp or the perp was here waiting for him.' She turned all the way around, looking for a good hiding place.

'I guess he could have hidden under the desk,' Harper offered.

'Too difficult to get into position without the victim noticing.' Jess looked from the door to the desk. 'If the perp had attacked as Carson came into the room, he would have fallen here.' She indicated the floor near the door. 'We need to check for blood spatter there. Our killer may have tried to clean it up.'

'What about behind the drapes?' Harper asked as he walked to the window. He shifted the full reams of fabric and hid behind it.

The drapes fell to a generous puddle on the floor. Jess had never understood this particular decorating trend.

Just something else to move when you vacuumed. 'That could be our hiding place,' she agreed.

'I'll make sure the glass is checked for prints.'

Jess looked from the curtains to the victim. 'Still seems to me that if our guy stepped out from the curtains, bat in hand, that Carson would have turned to him in surprise. Wouldn't he have fallen more here than there?' She pointed to a spot perpendicular to where he currently lay on his back.

'You think the perp moved him. Positioned him for some reason.'

Jess looked back at the door and then to where the victim lay on the floor, feet aimed at the door. 'I think our perp didn't want it to look as if he'd come up from behind his target. He wanted us to believe he'd come through the door.'

'A coward attacks from behind,' Harper suggested.

Indeed. 'Let's see if we can find any evidence that confirms our theory.'

'You know that murder weapon is worth some bucks.'

The victim's apparently famous bat lay on the floor next to him, discarded as if it were worthless. 'Proves our point that this wasn't about money.'

'Please,' a female voice said from the door, 'everyone knows that ultimately everything is about money.'

Jess turned to the newest arrival. 'Good morning, Dr Baron.'

Sylvia breezed into the room, her form-flattering dress an understated tangerine color that complemented her tanned skin. Speaking of money, Jess would bet a million bucks that beneath those tacky shoe covers the doctor's toenails matched perfectly manicured fingernails that sported the same sassy color as her dress.

How could any woman who spent most of her time with the dead look so elegant and classy? Did she sit up nights with her own private salon and spa staff? Jess was lucky to get a bath and shave.

Sylvia paused next to Jess and surveyed the victim. 'Oh my. I'll have to tell Daddy to mark him off the guest list for the Labor Day barbecue.'

If Jess didn't know that Sylvia's brash brand of humor was more about concealing her own vulnerabilities than anything else, she would be offended for the unfortunate victim. Sylvia immediately set to the task of determining approximate time of death and making a preliminary call on manner of death, not that it wasn't glaringly obvious. Only this time the killer hadn't bothered to clean the murder weapon.

Had he gotten careless or changed his strategy?

'I'll give the lead tech our punch list,' Harper offered.

Jess pulled her attention back to the present. 'Thank you, Sergeant.' The sooner the techs could wrap up this scene, the sooner this family could try and resume some sort of normalcy in their lives. That wouldn't happen before late today. Jess preferred two rounds of evidence collection. Two rounds was SOP when it came to large scenes with multiple victims. For one as clean as this and with only one victim, some might say once was enough. Not in her opinion.

'You and Dan are coming, aren't you?' Sylvia asked while she made a small incision for inserting a thermometer into the victim's liver. 'To the barbecue?'

'We'll be there.' Burnett hadn't actually said yes but he hadn't said no either.

'Good. My father wants to meet you.' Sylvia sat back on her heels and studied the thermometer. 'Your vic died between eight and eleven last night. The manner was certainly homicide.'

Jess made a note of the time frame.

'You might want to brace yourself for trouble,' Sylvia said as she examined the damage to the left side of the victim's skull.

'Why is that?' Beyond the fact that both her victims were high-profile Birminghamians whose forefathers were the city's founding fathers, which meant the press was sure to pick the investigation to pieces in the news. What could be worse?

'When I came inside, there was a little storm brewing out there.' She jerked her head toward the wall of windows that looked over the grand driveway and stairs that fronted the home.

'I expected the media to show up in droves.' Jess would have preferred to be on her way before the flock got too thick. Dealing with the press when you had nothing to give them was like getting your picture taken for the DMV. It never turned out well.

Sylvia looked up at her then. 'It's worse than that,' she warned. 'Buddy Corlew's out there demanding to be allowed inside.'

What in the world . . . The last thing she needed was for him to go running off at the mouth to any reporters.

'Thanks for the warning, Dr Baron,' Jess said as she headed for the door. 'I'll catch up with you later.'

At the moment she had to put out a potential fire.

'That man is trouble,' Sylvia called after her.

He was trouble all right. But right now he was mostly a pain in the ass.

On the porch she ran into the man in question, escorted by one of the officers charged with guarding the perimeter. At the street, no less than a dozen vans and cars representing various local media outlets lined the perimeter. Powerful lenses swung toward her. Jess could feel them zeroing in.

'Chief, Mr Corlew says you sent for him.'

She glared at Corlew. And there went that mischievous twinkle in his eyes again. 'Thank you, Officer Ashby.' She gifted the young officer with a big smile, then turned to Corlew. The smile disappeared and she gave him what she hoped was a murderous glare. 'Follow me, *Mr Corlew*.'

Jess marched back inside. As soon as the door closed behind the man, she rounded on him. This was as close to the crime scene as he was getting. 'I know we were friends once,' she snapped, 'but this—today—is not about friendship. This is about murder. If you have some real input that can help with this investigation, I'm all ears. Otherwise, stay out of my way, Corlew.'

He stared at her for a moment before he spoke. 'You finished reaming me a new one?'

Jess was too furious to respond.

'The reason I rushed over here,' he said finally, 'is because I just learned a major newsflash I think you're going to want to be aware of.'

She regained enough of her composure to speak. 'This better be good.'

'Remember I told you the dead guy from twelve years ago, Lenny Porter, had a friend who swore Lenny was with the Five when he died? But no one believed him,' Corlew kept going, giving her nothing new, 'because he didn't come forward for nearly a week after his pal took a nosedive off the *News* building.'

Other than the timing, she'd heard all this. 'What took him so long?'

'He was in detox. Seemed he'd been on a trip. Didn't lend credibility to his story.'

'What makes this newsflash any more relevant than it was an hour or so ago?'

'That's the part you're going to want to hear. Todd Penney, the friend, rolled back into town a few days ago. Drives a 1999 dark blue Corolla.'

Now that was worth listening to.

She considered the description of the guy's car. The one that had followed Jess and Lori from the Baker residence last evening had been a dark blue Corolla. Apparently Mr Penney still had something to say. Jess glanced toward the room where Elliott Carson's body lay on the floor with his skull bashed in. Or maybe he'd already said plenty and no one had been paying attention. She wanted to talk to this Mr Penney and she needed a handwriting sample.

As if he'd read her mind, Harper appeared. The guy had uncanny timing.

'Sergeant, track down Todd Penney for me. Caucasian' – she looked to Corlew for confirmation, and he nodded – 'approximately thirty years of age and drives a 1999 Toyota Corolla.' She flipped through her notes and gave Harper the first three numbers she'd gotten from the license plate of the vehicle that followed them last night. She'd intended to have Officer Cook look up Corollas this morning but she'd gotten distracted. 'And, Sergeant, since Mr Corlew has offered his invaluable insights into the case, you can take his official statement.'

'Yes, ma'am,' Harper said with a smile of satisfaction. 'It would be my pleasure.'

Lori had said Corlew was a legend in the department. Problem was, it wasn't in a good way and apparently most of the cops who knew him disliked him.

When Corlew started to argue, Jess cut him off. 'If you'd rather wait and go downtown with me to give your statement, that works too.'

'That's the thanks I get for trying to help.' Corlew executed an about-face and headed for the door.

'Watch him,' Jess murmured to her detective.

Harper smiled. 'I'm going to enjoy this.'

Later, when she had the time, Jess needed the whole story on Corlew and his legendary status in the department.

Her cell clanged, pushing her curiosities about Corlew aside.

Gina Coleman calling.

'Great.' The woman didn't want to wait for a statement. Fact was, Jess still owed her a favor. She might as well make good on that. The sooner the better. 'Harris.'

'We need to talk. *Now.*'

'I don't have anything I can release just yet,' Jess told her flatly, 'but the moment I do, you'll get it first.' That seemed fair enough.

'I'm not calling for a sound byte,' Coleman said sharply. 'I'm calling about my sister. I need your help and you owe me, Harris.'

'Has something happened to your sister?' Jess wasn't even aware the woman had a sister.

'We can meet at your office in fifteen minutes.'

'Hold up, Coleman. I'm at a crime scene,' Jess informed her. 'I can't just leave.' Jesus Christ! Just because Birmingham's hotshot reporter had Burnett and the mayor at her beck and call didn't mean Jess was there, too, even if she did owe her one.

'My sister thinks she knows the killer,' Coleman said. 'She says he isn't finished yet.'

Hold on a minute. 'Is Juliette Coleman your sister?'

'She's one of the Five,' Coleman said. 'Juliette is terrified that this guy isn't going to stop until he gets them all.'

Just went to show that Birmingham wasn't so big after all. It would have been nice if Coleman had announced this part first. 'Keep an eye on your sister while I finish up here. Meet me at my office at one-thirty?'

'We'll be there.'

Jess ended the call and went in search of Lori. She found her in the kitchen. 'I have a meeting in the office at one-thirty. If we're not finished here, I'll need you to handle the rest without me.' The words were hardly out of her mouth when she remembered that she didn't have her car. Damn it!

Sylvia Baron's husky voice demanding that someone

should get out of her way echoed all the way to the kitchen.

Perfect timing. 'I can catch a ride with Dr Baron.'

'Works for me,' Lori said. 'Mrs Carson's mother is on the way. I'm having her come in through the alley.'

'Good idea. They'll be taking the body out the front any second.'

'When things are wrapped up here, I can try to round up the others for lunch. Give you some privacy at the office,' Lori offered.

'That would be very helpful.' At some point SPU was going to need different accommodations.

After meeting with Gina Coleman and her sister, Jess needed to visit all remaining members of the Five. If Penney was the killer and he was out for revenge, chances were Gina Coleman's sister might be right – he wouldn't stop until he was done.

Two down, three to go.

Chapter Fourteen

9911 Conroy Road, 12.15 P.M.

Dan knocked on Mr George Louis's door. Jess's landlord had been exceedingly cooperative considering the short notice Dan had given him. The man hadn't asked any questions. Instead, he'd acted almost giddy at the idea of having cops crawling all over his property.

Strange man.

In any event, the search was necessary. This was the last location at which they had been able to track Ted Allen. Anything he may have left behind could prove useful to the investigation into his disappearance.

The evidence techs were scheduled for half past noon, but Dan wanted to stop in for a brief visit first. His excuse was that his visit was the proper thing to do but actually he wanted an opportunity to get a better overall assessment of the guy.

The door opened and Louis stared at Dan through the thick lenses of his eyeglasses. 'Chief Burnett, come in.'

'I wanted to stop by and thank you again for your cooperation,' Dan said as he followed the man into his living room. 'This is a serious and somewhat sensitive situation.'

'Of course,' Louis said with a nod. 'I understand.'

His home was clean and well organized. The walls were bare of photos and decorative items. Like the man, his home felt quiet and sedate. Yet there was something about him that unsettled Dan. Maybe just his over-eagerness to protect Jess. That was what she would call it anyway.

'You're welcome to have a look around inside as well,' Louis offered.

Dan had only asked for a search of the grounds. Seemed logical that Allen hadn't come inside the home or the garage since Louis hadn't noticed anything out of place or any locks that had been tampered with.

'That's not necessary,' Dan said with reluctance. That was exactly what he wanted to do but that would be overstepping his bounds.

'I insist,' Louis urged. 'I'll feel much better if you're convinced that there is nothing untoward going on in my home.'

Obviously Dan was a lot more transparent than he'd realized. 'I would be happy to assess the security of your home if you'd like but otherwise there's no reason for me to look around inside.'

'I have dead bolts on all the doors,' Louis explained as he led the way into the kitchen. 'The windows have been painted shut for years. It would take quite an effort to open one of those.'

The old man regaled Dan with vivid tales about how different life was now than when he was Dan's age. Jess had said her landlord was like a hermit. Maybe he had an identical twin, 'cause there was nothing withdrawn or quiet about this guy.

'Would you like to see the basement?' Louis almost seemed excited at the idea of showing off his basement.

He'd seen everything else. What the hell? 'Might as well finish the tour.'

'They don't build houses like this anymore,' Louis said as he showed Dan to the basement staircase.

Like the rest of the house, the basement was neat, organized. Not a single thing to prod suspicion.

'Would you like some tea, Chief Burnett?' Louis asked when they arrived back in the kitchen.

'Thank you, Mr Louis, but I should get back to the office. You let me know if there are any issues with the crime scene unit. They shouldn't be here more than a couple of hours. Again, I appreciate your cooperation.'

He showed Dan to the front door. 'Don't worry about Jess,' he said. 'She's very safe here.'

Outside Dan had a word with the search commander before heading out. As he turned around, he noticed Mr Louis watching him from an upstairs window.

His assurance that Jess was safe here hadn't helped to alleviate Dan's concerns in the least. He'd already done some digging into the man's background. So far, Louis had come up clean.

Yet that nagging sensation deep in his gut just wouldn't let go.

There had to be something Dan was missing.

Birmingham Police Department

Dan rifled through the stack of messages his secretary had left on his desk. His fingers stilled on the one from Special Agent Wesley Duvall.

Call ASAP.

Jess's ex wouldn't have left a message if it weren't important. He enjoyed talking to Dan about as much as Dan enjoyed talking to him – not at all. But Duvall was investigating the Lopez case. If he had learned anything on Allen or Jess via that connection, Dan needed to be briefed. Things here were going nowhere. Allen had basically vanished.

Harold Black's suggestion of investigating Jess's activities around the time Allen was known to have been close to her apartment elbowed its way into Dan's thoughts. The outrage he'd felt when Harold put the scenario on the table reignited even now. He'd had enough of Jess's peers in the department picking at her methods and grumbling about her.

Maybe Jess was right and he was overreacting. But he had persuaded her to take this position and it was his responsibility to see that she was treated with the respect she deserved. He knew firsthand how hard she had worked to rise above the hard knocks of her childhood to become the woman she was today.

'What now?' he grumbled as he thumbed through his contact list. He tapped Duvall's name. He waited through three rings and had decided he was going to get the guy's voice mail when a breathless, 'Duvall,' echoed across the connection.

'This is Dan Burnett returning your call, Agent Duvall.'

'Thank you for getting back to me so quickly,' Duvall said. 'I had a lengthy discussion with Leonardo Lopez this morning. He claims his people had nothing to do with your captain's disappearance. He went so far as to put out feelers among his associates and no one seems to know what happened to him. Any new leads on your end?'

As much as Dan wanted to scoff at the word of a high-powered drug and gang lord like Lopez, he couldn't ignore the possibility the man might be on the up and up about this. There were no legal repercussions for him to fear. Lopez and the Bureau had a deal. He would keep them abreast of certain activities and his daughter would get house arrest instead of prison time. There was no reason for him to lie.

In Dan's opinion the man had better watch his back. His daughter was schizo.

'We're still chasing our tails,' Dan admitted. 'We got nothing.'

'I presume your investigation is more focused on finding a body at this point rather than a rogue cop.'

'Frankly we don't know what to expect.' No need to sugarcoat the facts.

'There is a tremendous amount of money to be made in the drug business, Burnett. Put your best cop on a case like the Lopez one and opportunities invariably present themselves. Greed can be a strong motivator.'

Dead air hung between them for a long moment. Dan knew what the other man wanted.

'How's Jess?'

And there it was. 'As hardheaded as ever.' Dan suspected Duvall wouldn't be surprised by that news. 'She refuses my efforts at protection.' For the life of him he had no idea why he was telling this man a damned thing about Jess and his frustrations with her. Evidently his desperation meter had maxed out.

Or maybe it was just because he and the other man

shared something neither one could ignore. Each wanted Jess. They'd both had their shots and blown it. At least Dan had walked away before the walk down the aisle. Not to mention he had youth as an excuse. He'd been twenty-two and stupid.

Duvall couldn't cite either of those excuses.

'She prefers to take care of herself,' Duvall noted. 'Jess is fiercely independent. I'm confident she sees your hovering as challenging that independence.'

Hovering? Jess had tossed that at him too. There was a lot Dan could say to that but he chose to keep the conversation civil. 'I prefer to consider it watching her back.'

'Unfortunately, you may be more right to take that strategy than you know.'

A new kind of tension tightened Dan's gut. 'You have additional information that involves Jess?'

'I received a call from Agent Gant just before lunch today.'

That tension that had gripped his gut was suddenly at Dan's throat. 'Something new on Spears?'

'Gant says there's no confirmation he's back in the country but Jess has been receiving text messages from him or from someone he has watching her.'

What the hell? She hadn't said a word to him about this. 'How long has this been going on?'

'Gant couldn't confirm the exact number of times

Spears has contacted her but he believes she's keeping the information close to the vest in hopes of luring Spears into some sort of trap. She wants to get that bastard, Burnett. More than either of us fully comprehends, I suspect. Until he is caught or eliminated, she won't rest. Likewise, she won't be safe.'

The idea that she would keep this from him had an emotional hurricane twisting inside Dan. Or maybe it was the glaring fact that Duvall knew and he didn't. Be that as it may, he appreciated getting the heads-up from whatever source necessary. 'If you learn anything else, I hope you'll keep me advised and I'll do the same.'

'I take it she hasn't shared this information with you either.'

'She has not.' That admission was like a sucker punch to the gut.

'Watch her, Burnett. She's way too smart and far too determined to let this thing with Spears go. I'll do what I can from here,' he vowed.

The call ended. Duvall was right. Jess had no intention of playing it straight with him or anyone else when it came to Spears. The bastard was the one black mark on her record. A killer who didn't deserve to live. And she wanted him. Wanted to get him badly enough to avoid telling Dan the truth.

To prevent him from getting in her way.

A knock on the door yanked him from his frustrating

thoughts. Lieutenant Valerie Prescott waited at his open door.

'Your secretary's away from her desk. May I have a moment of your time, Chief?'

'Sure.' Dan cleared his head and gestured to one of the chairs in front of his desk. 'Have a seat, Lieutenant.'

'I'd like to request a transfer, sir. I thought I could handle the situation but I can't.'

'I was hoping you would see your way clear on this.' Prescott was a good detective. But she couldn't compete with Jess. Few could.

'I've tried,' Prescott assured him. 'I really have. I realized when I was working with the gang task force on the Lopez case that my loyalty just wasn't with Chief Harris. I feel we'd both be better served if I transferred from SPU.'

This was a prime example of the sort of disrespect Dan would not tolerate.

'I appreciate your honesty, Lieutenant. Captain Allen's disappearance has left us with a hole in the department. I'd like you to consider moving permanently to the gang task force since you were happy there.'

'That would be my first choice in assignments, sir. I'm up for captain, you know.'

'Yes, you are, Lieutenant.' Dan gave her a moment to gloat before lowering the boom. 'But in light of recent events, I feel your teamwork skills are lacking. For now,

Lieutenant Schafer will serve as interim commander of GTF. You're to report to him ASAP.'

Prescott's jaw dropped.

'I'll see that the proper paperwork is rushed through.' Dan turned his attention back to the messages on his desk. 'That'll be all, Lieutenant.'

She'd made it all the way to the door without saying a word when she stalled and turned back to him. 'Maybe I shouldn't mention this, but I'd feel disloyal if I didn't.' Her voice was tight, her face flushed with anger. 'Just before I left the scene at the Carson home, Buddy Corlew showed up demanding to see Chief Harris.'

What the hell was that guy up to? Dan had no doubt as to the lieutenant's intent.

'Chief Harris looked none too happy but Corlew managed to get into the scene just the same. He's like that, you know. He keeps on until you let him have his way just to shut him up. I'm sure you of all people remember how he can be.'

With that parting remark, Prescott left. She would need a state-of-the-art GPS to find happy again.

'Join the club,' Dan muttered.

His cell vibrated and he suffered a twinge of guilt until he confirmed it wasn't Jess calling. She wouldn't be happy that he'd transferred Prescott out of SPU without discussing the move with her first.

Sylvia Baron's name flashed on his screen.

Dan exhaled a big breath that failed to help with the frustration he couldn't seem to ditch. 'Sylvia, what's up?'

'I don't know about you,' she jumped right in without as much as a hello, 'but I'm rather busy with all these dead bodies your newest deputy chief keeps piling up, so I'll get right to the point. I'd like you to visit Nina with me on Sunday morning.'

Caught off guard by her request, he hesitated. Images and voices whispered through his mind. The weapon in her hand . . . the screaming . . . the pounding of his heart.

When he failed to recover quickly enough, Sylvia went on. 'Before you come up with a more than worthy excuse to beg off, hear me out.'

He worked at keeping an open mind despite the tension coiling in his chest. 'I'm listening.'

'They can't do anything else for her here, Dan. Once she's settled in at the new clinic in New York, she may never be back to Birmingham. If there's any chance at all my sister's in there somewhere, I want her to know you're not holding what happened against her.'

'Christ, Sylvia, you know that's not the case.' He dragged a hand down his face. How could she think that?

'I know it,' she agreed, 'but the point is that she knows it. Please, Dan. It would mean a great deal to me.'

Nina had suffered too much already. He couldn't bear to be the reason she might suffer more emotional pain. A moment was required for him to find his voice but he was certain of what he had to do. 'What time?'

'Ten, if that works for you. I assume you're still a heathen like me and don't attend church services.'

'I'll be there.'

'It's the right thing to do, Dan.'

Those words reverberated inside him over and over for long minutes after the call ended.

Dan pushed out of his chair and stared out the window. He hadn't visited Nina in years. There hadn't seemed any point.

Truth was, it was easier for him to sleep at night if he could close his eyes without seeing her face.

With every fiber of his being, he was certain the Nina he had known was gone. If he had been wrong about that . . . God he couldn't even go there.

For years he had tortured himself about what he might have done differently. After all, he must have done something wrong or that day wouldn't have happened. How could this beautiful woman he had married turn into a raging force of anger and hatred in the space of a day without some sort of event that caused the change?

Schizophrenia.

Her family had explained that the illness had always been there. But sweet, beautiful Nina had somehow managed to triumph over those demons. She'd finished law school, had a thriving practice.

Then she'd met Dan. They'd been so happy at first.

He'd let her down. He'd spent too many hours at work. Had too many commitments that didn't include her.

He hadn't been there when she needed him most.

He'd let her down just like he did Jess after college.

Now all these years later he had a second chance with Jess. He wouldn't let her down again.

But he would never forgive himself for letting Nina down.

Chapter Fifteen

1.30 P.M.

Jess had the office to herself for the meeting with the Coleman sisters. As promised, Wells had coordinated lunch with Harper and Cook to discuss the similarities in the two murder cases and what they had on each so far. Hopefully Harper had something on Todd Penney's whereabouts as well as Scott Baker's personal life. Prescott had dropped back by the office long enough to prepare her report from this morning's canvassing of Elliott Carson's neighbors. Just when Jess was sure she would need to ask the detective to find someplace else to work for an hour or so, she had promptly informed Jess that she needed the rest of the afternoon off.

Now, if her luck would just hold out for the next hour, Burnett wouldn't show up demanding an update or answers as to why she had been cavorting with Corlew.

Lori had already warned her that pictures of her and Corlew in front of the Carson home had made the breaking news. Speculation as to his involvement in the investigation would soon be rampant and Burnett would not be happy. In light of his nasty break with the BPD, most likely no one in the department would be happy.

Gina and Juliette Coleman now sat in front of Jess's desk, one looking as terrified as the other appeared determined.

'We started hanging out as a group our freshman year,' Juliette explained. 'We'd known each other our whole lives and' – she shrugged – 'somehow we just ended up as close friends. We got the tattoos when we were seniors.'

'Was there ever any trouble between the five of you?' Jess asked. They were taking this from the beginning. She needed a good handle on the dynamics of the group.

Juliette shook her head. 'Not at all. We backed each other up. We kind of made a pact that we would always be there for each other. You know, take over the world.' She laughed, a sad, bittersweet sound. 'We still try to get together when we can but everyone's busy. When we do, we share photos of kids and partners. Brag about our accomplishments.'

'I'm aware of Elliott's and Scott's accomplishments. What about the others?' Juliette was a political analyst with the local CBS affiliate. Her family had major connections all the way to the White House. No wonder Burnett and Gina Coleman had clicked.

Stop, Jess. This meeting wasn't about Burnett's sexual conquests.

'O'Reilly Enterprises was started by Kevin's great-grandfather. The company owns several newspapers and magazines in the southeast, including the *Birmingham News*. Kevin is the CEO. Aaron's father is an Alabama Supreme Court justice, as was his grandfather. The hope is that Aaron, who is a very successful attorney, will follow in that same path.' Juliette looked to her sister. 'Did I miss anything?'

Gina shook her head. 'You covered it, sweetie.'

'Impressive.' The mayor and every other uppity-up would be breathing down Jess's neck on this one. On top of that, with Carson a national celebrity figure, the case would be followed by national news. Complicated things, but there was no help for that.

'You and your friends met for lunch yesterday, you said?' Jess confirmed, making a note on her pad.

Juliette averted her gaze, squirmed a bit in her seat the way folks who didn't want to answer questions always did. 'Yes. Kevin was worried that Scott's death was somehow related to Todd's return to Birmingham.'

Juliette Coleman was scared to death and still she was keeping some aspect of the reason to herself; otherwise she'd have no trouble with direct eye contact. The woman worked in the limelight; she wasn't shy.

'Why would Todd's return have anything to do with Scott or any of you? Was there some sort of trouble with him before he left town twelve years ago?'

Juliette picked at her cuticles to prevent making eye contact. Certainly that fresh French manicure she sported didn't require any further attention. Her older sister stared at her and still the awkward silence dragged on.

'Tell her, Juliette,' Gina pressed.

'We were there,' the younger woman said. 'That night when Lenny Porter jumped.'

'Why don't we start from the beginning? Again,' Jess said firmly. 'Only this time let's start with that May night twelve years ago. How did you and the other members of the Five end up on the *Birmingham News* roof?'

Juliette glanced at her sister.

'If there's anything you'd prefer not to say in front of your sister,' Jess suggested, 'I'm certain she would be happy to take a walk.'

Juliette cleared her throat, as if she needed to get past the emotion clogged there. 'No. It's fine. I told her the whole story when I heard about Elliott.'

'And how did you hear about Elliott?' Jess had still been at the scene when Gina Coleman called.

Seemed some of Juliette's sources had gotten the word to her even before an announcement had been made to the press. Either that or the woman had a friend in the department.

'Kevin told me. He received a call from one of the paper's investigative reporters who has a source in the department.'

How nice for Kevin. All cops hated leaks unless they were the ones doing the leaking. 'All right, then. Tell me about that night. It was the night before your high school graduation?'

She nodded. 'Seniors didn't have school the next day, so we decided to have a private celebration. Since our parents were watching us like hawks – you know, a lot of seniors end up never seeing graduation because of last-minute celebrations that get out of control.'

Jess understood what she meant. Far too many seniors ended up in the morgue the nights before and after graduation. 'So you took your party to a place they wouldn't think to look.' How clever.

'We got together up there sometimes.' She smiled, apparently recalling fond memories about those days. 'When we were up there, we felt like we were on top of the world. That anything could happen.'

Something else Jess knew a little something about. She and Dan had a place like that as teens. They went back to Sloss Furnaces just a couple weeks ago. Her stomach quivered at the memory. How had so much time flown by when they weren't looking?

'We had a few beers. Talked about our futures and just chilled out.'

Jess waited for her to continue. From the distant expression on her face, she wanted to linger among the memories of that night before going on.

'Lenny Porter showed up.' She looked away. 'Kevin was mad as hell. Apparently Aaron left the door open when he went down to the parking lot to get more beer. That's the only way Lenny could have gotten in.'

'The roof couldn't be accessed via some exterior means? A fire escape maybe?'

Juliette shook her head. 'You had to come through the building, take the elevator or the stairs to the top floor and then the maintenance access door to the roof.'

'Was there any way Porter could have known you were going there?'

Juliette stared at her hands again. 'He sort of had a thing for me. He followed me around. Left me notes. Sat in the street in front of my house. It was sweet but' – she shrugged – 'it got a little creepy the last couple of weeks of school.'

'Creepy how?'

'He started coming to my door at home. I tried to be nice but he just wouldn't leave me alone. So the guys gave him a talking-to.'

'Did this talking-to include a physical confrontation or public humiliation?'

'I don't think so. Scott was my boyfriend at the time and he wasn't like that. He wouldn't have hurt anyone.'

'That still doesn't answer my question about how Porter found out where you were that night,' Jess countered.

'Don't you think it's obvious that he followed her?' the elder sister demanded. 'I was already living in my own apartment, but Juliette mentioned that she had a stalker. She laughed it off. Thought he was harmless.'

Jess gave Gina Coleman a patient smile. 'Why don't we let Juliette answer the questions?'

Gina crossed her arms over her chest and glared at Jess.

'She's right. I believe he followed me there.'

'The five of you were just hanging out and he appeared?' How convenient. Jess wanted to reach across her desk and shake the woman. Maybe what she'd read in those journal pages was making her less objective. Either way she wasn't letting Juliette off the hook. Jess needed the truth before someone else ended up dead.

'We were sitting in a circle on a blanket, drinking beer and just talking. He showed up, looked at me for a moment while the guys were demanding to know what he thought he was doing. Then he walked over to the edge of the roof and jumped.'

'Did any of the guys make a move toward him or threaten him in any way?'

She shook her head adamantly. 'No one even got up. We were all kind of in shock.'

'Did he appear to have been drinking or using drugs? Was he high?'

'I don't know. The papers said he was on drugs. The rumor was he was dropping acid.'

'Was he a drug user, to your knowledge? You said he hung around you all the time.'

'Not that I know of. He was like a genius. He and his friend Todd Penney were the top nerds at Carver.'

'Where was his friend Todd that night?' Jess kept firing the questions at her. She wanted to see the woman's emotions – her true emotions. Two of her friends were dead for Christ's sake.

'He was in the car . . . I guess . . . waiting for him. He claimed to have tried to talk him out of coming but Lenny wouldn't listen.'

'So his friend had no idea Lenny had come to the roof to jump?'

She shook her head and shrugged. 'I don't know.'

'Did Todd Penney come to the rooftop?'

Juliette hesitated before answering. Her gaze flicked around the room, looking for some place to light. 'No. He didn't.'

More evasive answers. 'Despite having not witnessed

any actions made by you or your friends, he blamed you for what happened.'

Juliette nodded. 'But the police didn't believe him. They believed us.'

Of course they did. These were the offspring of Birmingham's movers and shakers. No one was going to call them liars without serious evidence. 'Scott must have felt guilty over the incident. His father paid for Lenny's burial and has paid his mother two thousand dollars every month for all these years. I find that curious.'

'Scott thought that maybe something he said to Lenny pushed him over the edge, so to speak. He felt guilty about that night until the day he died. I'm certain he thought that was the right thing to do. That's the kind of guy he was.'

'He never mentioned to you that he was worried about Penney's return? He gave you no impression that he believed Penney was a threat to you or anyone related to any of you?' Jess pushed.

Juliette shook her head. 'No.'

'Yet his wife stated that he urged her to take their son and leave town. That's why she wasn't home when he was murdered. He also paid for Lenny Porter's mother to go on a cruise so she would be out of town as well. Scott never mentioned he was worried about his family?'

'No.' Juliette looked puzzled. 'I'm not sure I believe he said any such thing to his wife.'

'You and his wife aren't friends?' Jess didn't give her time to get a deep breath.

Disdain flashed on Juliette's face before she could stop it. 'Not really.'

'In fact, you never married,' Jess mentioned. Scott had sex with someone who wasn't his wife just before he died. Corlew claimed he'd found no evidence the guy was cheating. Juliette could be the reason why. They were already friends. As long as they were discreet, who would know? 'Were you and Scott still involved?'

'That's out of line,' Gina Coleman snapped. 'Juliette is trying to help with your investigation and you ask a question like that. I don't like your tone and I damned sure don't like your innuendoes. Do you want her help or not? We can end this right now.'

'Yes,' Juliette announced, shutting down her sister's protests. 'We got together occasionally. But no one knew. Neither of us wanted anyone to be hurt. I was perfectly happy being the other woman that no one knew about.'

'Oh my God.' Gina wrapped an arm around her sister's shoulder and hugged her. 'Why didn't you tell me?'

Juliette stared at her hands some more. 'It was too painful to talk about.'

At least she was honest about her relationship with

Baker. 'Did you see Scott the night he was murdered?' Jess would just see how honest she intended to be.

Juliette squared her shoulders and looked Jess in the eye. 'Yes, I did. We usually got together at his office. He worked late almost every night so no one would be the wiser if we met there.'

'What time was this?' Jess made a few more notes on her pad.

'At seven. I brought wine and cheese. We shared the bottle and had sex. I left around eight-thirty and . . . that was the last time I saw him.' Her voice trembled on the last few words.

Gina Coleman was speechless. That had to be a first.

'Did Scott mention having any other appointments that night?'

Juliette shook her head. 'He had work to finish up and then he was going home.'

'I assume he always turned off the security system, specifically the surveillance system, whenever the two of you . . . had your private rendezvous?'

'Yes, I believe he did.'

Jess would need to come back to this. 'You stated that after Scott's murder, Kevin called a meeting of sorts to discuss the possibility that Todd Penney was back in Birmingham for revenge.'

'Yes. Kevin got really nervous when Scott told him Todd Penney was back in town. Kevin had been warning us that we should be careful but no one paid any attention. We were cleared of any wrongdoing twelve years ago.'

'Maybe so,' Gina spoke up, suddenly finding her voice, 'but I told you that neat little closures like that rarely happen when emotions are involved. If Todd Penney believes the five of you had something to do with his friend's death, he may only now have devised a plan to see that justice is served. Isn't that right, Chief?'

'That's a possibility, yes,' Jess agreed. 'But there are others. There may be additional motives at play. If someone else was somehow responsible for Lenny Porter's death, he or she may be attempting a frantic cover-up before Todd starts digging around or stirring up interest in the case.'

If Elliott Carson hadn't turned up dead this morning, Jess would most certainly have considered Baker's wife a suspect, considering what Juliette had just shared. She couldn't have done the job herself since she was out of town, but she could have hired someone. With Carson's murder, the entire focus of the case shifted from Scott's enemies to the enemies of the Five.

She'd have to let the widows know they were no longer persons of interest in this case. Frances would be relieved. Jess was relieved. That was the only good thing to come out of this mess.

'There couldn't be anyone else,' Juliette argued Jess's

reasoning. 'There was no one else there that night but the five of us.'

'You said yourself that Porter didn't say anything. He just showed up and jumped. Either he was making a point, to you most likely, or he was coerced somehow. Maybe by his friend Todd. Maybe by Scott or another of your friends. Until we know what really happened to Lenny Porter, we won't know what happened to Scott or Elliott. Understanding the killer's motive will lead us directly to him.' That was Jess's experience in the business of investigating homicides. This investigation was following that same pattern.

'She just told you that none of them said anything to Porter that night,' Gina argued, none too happy with Jess's slightly aggressive interrogation.

'How did Scott know Todd was back in town?' Jess asked Juliette, ignoring her sister's comment for the moment.

Juliette shrugged. 'I don't know. Kevin said he knew. You'd need to ask him.'

'Do you remember this incident?' Jess placed copies of the handwritten journal pages in front of Juliette. 'Whoever wrote this was talking about you. I'm thinking since you stated that Lenny Porter was infatuated with you that his friend Todd Penney is the author.'

She read the pages, her sister reading over her shoulder. This time when Juliette looked up, she met Jess's gaze. 'Yes. I remember.'

'Oh my God, Jules. How could you let them do this and say nothing?'

'I said things,' the younger woman argued. 'I told them to stop or I would leave.'

How noble. Jess wanted to throw up.

'This was two months before Lenny took that leap.' Anger unfurled inside Jess. She tapped the first of the two pages. 'How often were your friends torturing Lenny Porter like this?'

Juliette shook her head. 'It was a joke. Something everyone did to someone at one time or another.'

Jess's long simmering anger built to a boil. 'Maybe Lenny decided he'd had enough. Maybe you and your friends were too inebriated to remember what really happened on that roof.'

Juliette shook her head and held up both hands. 'No. No. I had a couple of beers. Nothing more. I know exactly what happened. I'll never forget it.'

'She came here to help,' Gina reminded Jess. 'If she was guilty of some wrongdoing, would she be here right now?'

Gina Coleman would be surprised how many murderers came forward to provide assistance to the police. It gave them a feeling of power. Maybe Juliette liked the power. Her friends obviously had enjoyed it.

'If you remember anything else, be sure to let me know.' Jess needed to interview the other two members of the group. The sooner the better. What she didn't want was Juliette sharing her version of that night's events with the others. Though she suspected that had happened a long time ago.

'Juliette will be staying with me until this is over,' Gina said. 'I don't want her alone.'

'I think that's wise,' Jess agreed. 'Two of your friends are dead, Juliette. Murdered. If the killer is someone from your past who's out for revenge, he may have gone over the edge. He's killed twice using the same MO. We have reason to believe he's not finished. Until we've stopped him, you and your friends are all targets.'

'What if you can't stop him?' Juliette looked from Jess to her sister. 'I swear I didn't do anything to hurt Lenny but Todd might come after me anyway. What am I going to do?' She burst into tears. The older Coleman sibling hugged her close.

Somehow Jess was having trouble mustering any sympathy for Juliette. But then, she was prejudiced when it came to snobby rich kids. She'd endured enough of their crap in high school herself.

'We will stop him, Juliette,' Jess promised, cutting her some slack. 'As long as we have your full cooperation and the cooperation of your friends, you can count on it.'

Juliette swiped at her eyes. 'Thank you. If there's anything else I can do, please let me know.'

Jess had just shown the sisters to the door when Lori, Harper, and Cook returned from lunch. She was itching to start fleshing out what they had on a case board. The sooner they got the details hammered out, the more quickly they could stop the killing.

Within half an hour they had the timeline established with photos printed from the victims' and persons of interest's DMV photos. Not the most flattering shots, but no one cared.

'I confirmed that Todd Penney is driving a 1999 Toyota Corolla with California plates,' Harper said, dragging Jess's attention back to the here and now. 'His mother, Ramona Penney, who lives in Homewood, says he's here but she hasn't seen him since Monday. We've issued an APB in hopes of locating him.'

'He's a big-shot game developer now,' Cook threw in. 'The man needs to upgrade his wheels.'

Harper sent the younger man a look that warned he wasn't finished.

Cook held up his hands. 'Sorry.'

'Former Lieutenant Corlew swears he knows nothing about Scott Baker except what's in the case file from twelve years ago. He stands by the reports he prepared for Frances Wallace and the information he passed along to you.' Harper added the picture of a vintage Corolla to the case board beneath Penney's photo.

Jess was pretty damned sure her old friend Corlew was lying through his teeth. One way or another, she intended to find out. She considered the photo of Baker's wife, Trisha. 'Detective Wells and I will follow up with Baker's wife. I want to rule out the possibility that she learned about his ongoing affair with Juliette and hired someone to murder him while the trust fund would still transfer to her son.'

'Doesn't Carson's murder rule out that possibility?' Lori asked.

'Perhaps,' Jess allowed. 'But the journal pages set the two murders apart in a significant way. My instincts are telling me they're connected but we don't want to overlook the other scenarios. The story is still a little too cloudy to call it one way or the other.'

'Mrs Baker agreed to a search of her home. If the journal or pages from the journal are in the home, we'll find them.' Harper added the necessary notes under Trisha Baker's photo.

'Sergeant, I'd like you and Officer Cook to track down O'Reilly and Taylor since we haven't been able to get either one on the phone. I'm confident someone in this illustrious group knows more than they're telling. We need their statements and need to ensure they understand the potential danger to them from Penney or whoever is killing off their friends.'

'Do I get to play bad cop?' Harper asked with a grin. 'I think I could get them to talk.'

'Works for me,' Cook said as he pushed back his chair. 'I prefer the good cop role.'

Jess wasn't about to mention it to the young man but he was far better suited for that role. He wasn't much taller than Jess and a little on the thin side. And with that all-American fresh face, she doubted anyone would ever see him as a bad guy. Harper, on the other hand, adapted to the role of bad cop extraordinarily well.

'Detective Wells and I will interview Mrs Penney. We need Todd's side of the story and since we can't locate him, we'll try to get it from the next best source. I think the variable Penney represents takes precedence over the affair and the possibility that Baker's wife had found out.'

There were always two sides to every story. This one would be no exception. In fact, Jess suspected she might come closer to getting the truth from Todd Penney than any one or all of the Five. That bunch had far too much to lose and that was never conducive to getting the truth.

When Harper and Cook were gone, Jess paused before following them out the door. 'Let's take my car. If Penney is watching for us, he'll remember your Mustang.'

'No doubt,' Lori agreed.

Opting for the stairs instead of the elevator, Jess was grateful to escape the building without running into Burnett. Her cell clanged and she checked the screen. Corlew. If he had new information, he would leave her a voice mail. Let him stew. She wanted him ready to talk by the time she hauled him into her office. Whatever game he was up to, she didn't have time to play. And he was playing a game. Doling out tidbits like he was taunting a hungry pup.

A shiver went through her at the thought of players and games. She already had one game too many in her life.

Even now, Spears could be back. Watching her.

Wasn't that what she wanted? Another chance to take him down for good?

Her cell called out to her again. If Corlew thought blowing up her phone would get him the attention he wanted, he was wrong. But it wasn't Corlew. She frowned and immediately scolded herself for doing so. *Sylvia Baron calling.*

'Harris.'

'I don't have anything for you on Carson yet,' Sylvia said, getting straight to the point. 'But I did notice something you may find interesting.'

'What's that?' Her curiosity was piqued.

'Mr Carson had the same tattoo as Baker, as you anticipated. Even had it in the same spot. But he'd had his altered in an attempt to cover it up. Looks like a baseball now but you can just see the numeral five and the lines of the other circles beneath the red, white, and blue ink used to fill it in.'

Had Elliott Carson felt guilty? Or maybe his motive for attempting to cover the mark was resentment since his big career had stalled and the other four of the five seemed to be continuing to climb. But why didn't he just have it removed? Juliette admitted to having the same tattoo. She also admitted to having an affair with Scott Baker, something Corlew had missed in his investigation.

Or had he simply opted not to mention it?

'There's one other thing. Seems a little odd but it might not mean anything,' Sylvia went on. 'My assistant discovered a folded piece of paper in one of Baker's socks. It may or may not be relevant to your investigation but it reads like a confession of sorts.'

'I'll be right there.'

Jefferson County Coroner's Office, 3.40 P.M.

It took some doing to figure out all the words since sweat had blurred a few here and there. But between Lori, Sylvia, and Jess, they finally put it all together.

April 1

He cried tonight. I'd never seen him do that. He received flowers and balloons at school. He was really excited when he saw the big heart-shaped balloon. The note was an invitation to a movie. She was supposed to be there. I told him not to go, but he was too excited to be reasonable.

He went to the theater, bought his ticket, and went to the seats where she was supposed to meet him. The back row, way in the corner. No one who came to watch the movie ever sat there. It was for making out and doing other shit you don't want anybody to see.

Finally he admitted defeat. She wasn't coming. When he started to get up to leave, he couldn't. That bastard Baker had spread tubes and tubes of Superglue on the chair. The legs of his jeans were stuck. He was stuck since cutting off his pants in a theater filled with people was out of the question. The fucked-up Five were just a few rows down. They started laughing and whipped out their cameras. People crowded around, pointing and laughing.

The pics were everywhere the next day.

I hate Scott Baker and his friends. I hope they die screaming.

'Apparently Baker and his pals had an ugly side,' Sylvia observed.

Jess tamped down the outrage. 'Looks that way to me.'

Lori had bagged the page. The handwriting was the same as the other.

'We'll get this dropped off at the lab.' Jess prepared to

go. What she wanted more than anything else right now was to find Todd Penney or at least a sample of his handwriting beyond his DMV signature.

'I'll let you know when I have more on Elliott Carson.'

Jess thanked her and headed for the door. 'Let Harper know we have the journal page,' she said to Lori. 'And let's see if my Audi will move like your Mustang.'

'Let me drive,' Lori offered, 'and we'll find out.'

Pansy Street, Homewood, 4.50 P.M.

Ramona Penney's home was modest but well kept. She had offered tea or soft drinks but both Jess and Lori had declined. According to her DMV records she was only forty-five which meant she'd basically been a kid when she had her son. Yet she looked far older than her years. She smoked two packs a day and according to the story she'd given so far, she had worked two and three jobs until just a few years ago in order to survive.

She claimed her son was only in town for a couple of weeks and that he was off visiting friends. Jess found that excuse for his absence quite odd since the file on him from twelve years ago indicated that Lenny Porter was his only friend.

Maybe he'd made new ones in his detox stint after Lenny's death. Seven days in the psych ward after a bad trip on acid. His first, he had sworn. Jess had no idea if that was the case or not but he certainly had no other police record, here or in California.

Todd was a nice-looking man. Dark hair, dark eyes, and a kind face. He didn't look like a killer but then again few did.

Evil was rarely the expected.

'Todd has really made me proud,' Ramona said with a broad smile. 'He left here after high school and drove all the way to California in that old Toyota of his. He knew what he wanted to do and he made it happen. Every dream he'd had as a kid is his now. He develops video games for Sony.' She blinked at the tears shining in her eyes.

'He sounds like an extraordinary young man.' Jess gave her an understanding smile. 'I know you're proud. I hope he's one of those smart people who kept a journal about his journey to the top. Look at Steve Jobs. Your son's story could end up being a movie.'

Suspicion darkened the woman's expression. 'I don't think he kept a journal or a diary.' She shook her head. 'No. I'm sure he didn't.'

So much for catching her off guard with that one. Might as well get to the point. 'Can you tell us about his relationship with Lenny Porter?'

Her face turned as pale as a ghost's. 'I'm sorry. I have a terrible headache.' She stood. 'Migraines, you know. I'll have to ask you to go now.' She moved to the door. 'Nice to have met you.'

Jess and Lori exchanged a look. If the woman refused to talk, there was little they could do. Taking their time, they joined her at the front door.

'Mrs Penney, I realize this is a sensitive subject, but we desperately need yours and Todd's help. Two people are dead. Murdered. We believe their murders have something to do with Lenny Porter's death.'

'I don't know anything about that and neither does my son.'

'But twelve years ago your son insisted that Lenny Porter was murdered. Two of the people he claimed murdered Lenny are dead just days after Todd returned to Birmingham. I'm worried about your son, Mrs Penney. This is a very bad situation. If he refuses to talk to us, that's only going to make him look guilty.'

'I have nothing else to say to you.'

Before she could close the door in their faces and despite knowing the answer before she brought up the subject, Jess went for broke anyway. 'A sample of Todd's handwriting for comparison could rule out his involvement.'

'Next time you want to talk to me or my son,' she warned, 'call our lawyer, Fritz Talbot.' Gone was the pleasant attitude and friendly smile. 'That's all I have to say.'

The door slammed.

Well hell. Jess supposed they would have to try for a handwriting analysis using the signature on his driver's license. 'Dammit.'

'I guess you can't blame her for wanting to protect her son,' Lori said as they strode toward Jess's Audi.

'But is she protecting him or helping him commit murder?' Jess settled behind the steering wheel of her faithful old car. No need for her detective's lead foot now.

Next to her, Lori snapped her seat belt into place. 'I can't get right with the idea that Todd would give up all he's attained to get even with the past. Unless he's mental.'

'I'm having trouble getting past that one myself. If the motive is revenge' – Jess started the engine – 'why wait until you've made all your dreams come true to come back here and throw it all away by committing multiple murders?'

'Maybe he thinks his success and money will protect him the way it protected the Five twelve years ago.'

'There's a difference between simply having money,' Jess reminded her, 'and having money *and* power. And why wait twelve years? Why not ten or eight or thirteen? What significance does that length of time carry? What happened to spur the killer into action? Every act of murder is driven by something.'

'We find that something,' Lori added, 'and we'll know our killer.'

The certainty they were getting close set for Jess. She checked for oncoming traffic before pulling into the street, then glanced at Lori. 'We may already know him.'

The Garage, Tenth Terrace South, 6.15 P.M.

Corlew had taken possession of his preferred stool. Lori said he could always be found here. Evidently she was correct. He'd already downed half of at least one longneck bottle of beer and appeared to be ready to knock back the rest posthaste.

'You trying to drown your conscience?' Jess asked. 'Or is this just the fastest way to kill the memories of how badly you've always managed to screw over every friend who ever dared trust you?' That was the thing about guys like Corlew. They just couldn't play nice with that massive ego hanging around their necks like a millstone.

'Jess.' He gifted her with a big old grin. 'Why don't you join me? Let your hair down. You've turned into one of those uptight cops like Burnett and his pals.'

Opting to let that comment go, Jess slid onto the stool next to him and waved off the bartender who immediately headed her way. The statuesque blonde was likely another reason Corlew liked this place. He liked his women tall, thin, and big-breasted. Jess had known when he directed that vast charm at her all those years ago that he'd only wanted to rattle Dan's cage. Blond was the only one of those three requirements she had met. And she doubted that particular one was at the top of his priority list.

But that had been a long time ago. This was different. They were all grown up and had real jobs to do. She didn't need his crap and she damned sure wasn't in the mood to play his games.

'Why didn't you tell me about Todd Penney the first time we talked?'

'I had to do a little digging of my own before I was certain that information was relevant.' He slid his empty bottle to the far side of the counter and gave the bartender a nod. 'Once I figured out Penney was in town, I suspected there might be a connection. That's why I had you meet me at the cemetery. Truth is, I wasn't sure of much until Carson got knocked outta the park.'

'But you never told me Penney was in town.' She wasn't letting that one go. This case was too big, too important to let him off the hook.

Corlew shrugged. 'Am I supposed to tell you everything? I thought you were some big hotshot agent for the FBI all those years. That should have been your first question when I told you about the case.'

If he was trying to tick her off, he had a damned good head start. 'You also failed to mention Scott Baker's ongoing affair.'

Corlew looked Jess straight in the eye then. 'I'm not a cop anymore, Jess. I'm a PI. I get paid the big bucks for two reasons.' He stuck out his thumb. 'Because I'm good at the job.' The index finger came out next. 'And I'm discreet. I don't tell people's secrets unless it's to save someone's life. The fact that Baker was keeping his pretty little high school sweetheart on the side was a threat to no one.'

'Unless his wife found out and hired someone to take care of the situation.'

Corlew laughed outright then. 'Don't waste your time on that avenue. Trisha Baker is scared of her own shadow. She wouldn't change brands of toilet paper without asking Scott first. You know the kind,' he tossed at Jess. 'The little wife who does whatever her husband tells her and is just glad he shows up every night.'

Jess couldn't deny that Baker's wife seemed to fit that stereotype. The quiet, obedient wife of the rich man. Didn't matter. Jess had an obligation to investigate that possibility, at least until now. Carson's murder pretty much changed everything.

'I'm giving you the benefit of the doubt, Corlew,' Jess said frankly. 'No one else in the department seems to harbor any warm and fuzzy feelings for you. I'd prefer not to join those ranks. Don't force my hand. I don't play games when it comes to my cases.'

He held her gaze for a long moment before he spoke. 'Fair enough. Just remember one thing about the rich and powerful in this town, Jess. They will do anything to protect that power and wealth. *Anything*. And you are still not one of them, kid.'

Chapter Sixteen

Lakefront Trail, Bessemer, 8.30 P.M.

Jess followed her sister back and forth in the kitchen as she cleaned up. Jess had offered to do it for her, especially since she'd gotten fed as soon as she arrived, but Lily insisted on doing it herself.

Lily had always been the most bullheaded, no matter what anyone thought.

'I keep forgetting to stop by Wanda's and pick up that medical history she supposedly compiled.' Jess didn't trust their so-called aunt as far as she could throw her. She hadn't cared about them when they were orphaned kids – why would she now?

Oh yeah. She'd gotten religion. Ha!

'I could have Blake go by and pick it up if you'd rather not,' Lil said, pausing with a plate in her hand. 'Or I could.'

Jess made a face. 'I will not have you or Blake going to that neighborhood. You remember where she lives.' Where they had lived for one miserable year. Putting up with their aunt's men friends and her drug habits.

Lil stuck the plate in the dishwasher and took Jess by the arms. 'The Bible teaches us to forgive, Jess. Maybe she has changed her life. We can't be judging her.'

Jess made a rude sound. 'Maybe you can't but I sure can.'

'Anyway.' Lil smiled. 'You've had a busy week. Don't beat yourself up for not getting around to that or for not calling me every day or whatever. I'm just so glad to have you back home that the idea of seeing you a couple of times a week is a dream come true.'

More guilt heaped on Jess's shoulders. She'd stayed gone over two decades. Getting home once a year had been the goal and that hadn't always happened.

'I know. I've missed so much.' She gestured toward the photos of Alice and Blake Junior adorning the fridge. 'Your kids are all grown up and they hardly know me.'

Lil scoffed. 'That's not true. I told them stories about you their whole lives. Every case you helped solve. Everything. You're a hero to those kids.' Lil pulled her into a hug. 'You're a hero to me.'

Jess didn't feel like a hero. She felt like a woman who'd run from the past and all the broken relationships – their parents, their aunt, Dan, Wesley. Maybe she was still running. She couldn't get trapped and end up heartbroken if she kept running, at least in the emotional sense.

How was that for a self-analysis? That's what happened when she allowed her thoughts to wander too far from a case.

When her sister finally stopped squeezing her, she asked, 'How're you feeling?'

Jess listened through a lengthy monologue of how her sister hated being sick. Hated even worse that everyone treated her as if she were dying. Even her minister was coming by every day or two. She'd had to force both her kids to go off to college on schedule. Alice had been waiting all year for her freedom. Now she was terrified of being away from her mother. Even Blake Junior hadn't wanted to go back to school. At twenty most guys couldn't wait to get back to school and out of their parents' home after summer vacation.

Jess laughed. 'The buzzards are circling, Lil,' she teased. 'Next thing you know, the kids'll be sneaking home and dividing up your jewelry.'

They both laughed for a minute . . . but the laughter faded and silence took its place.

'How are you, really?' Jess said softly, her throat aching with the struggle of restraining her emotions. Lil didn't need anyone else treating her like she was dying.

'It sucks to be me right now,' she admitted. 'I don't

mind all the tests and the feeling like crap. It's the not knowing if or when it'll end – whatever it is – that's driving me crazy. The test results don't come back fast enough.'

Jess understood completely. 'Dr Collins will figure this out. Give the old goat time.' He would figure it out or he'd send her to someone who could. He and Jess had already had that discussion. She doubted he wanted to hear from her again anytime in the near future.

'Hope so.' Lil reached for another plate.

'Is Blake handling everything okay?' He'd been his usual self through dinner. Laughing and talking about work. Always considerate, he'd disappeared into the den to watch TV so Jess and Lil could have sister time.

'You ask that every time we talk,' Lily complained. 'Yes, he's fine. Keeping his chin up and mine too.'

'I guess I'm getting senile,' Jess lamented.

They laughed and hugged some more and Jess headed home. She was tired and she needed to let the details of this case she'd learned today permeate.

And then she needed to sleep. She couldn't remember when she'd been so tired. Maybe last night, she mused.

9911 Conroy Road, 10.15 P.M.

Showered and with her comfiest nightclothes on, Jess curled up on her new-old sofa and cradled her glass of wine and stash of M&M's. She was so glad this day was basically over. There was a long ways to go in solving this case but the pieces were slowly but surely coming together.

If she and her team could find the right answers before anyone else died, she would be a happy camper.

Lil looked good despite the ongoing tests and frustrating symptoms. That was another mystery Jess couldn't wait to see solved.

Speaking of unsolved mysteries, her unsuspecting landlord had suffered through a search of his property today. At least it was done. Maybe things would get back to normal here at least.

She almost choked on a sip of wine. When had her life ever been normal?

Now there was a mystery she didn't even want to try and figure out.

First thing tomorrow she had a meeting with the remainder of the Five – Juliette Coleman, Aaron Taylor, and Kevin O'Reilly – at least she hoped O'Reilly would be there. They hadn't been able to locate him. But he had a voice mail waiting for him on his home, office, and cell phones. Not being able to reach the man under the circumstances had her more than a little concerned. But he had spoken to his secretary twice today – this morning and then later in the afternoon – which alleviated some of

Jess's worry and was the primary reason she didn't have an APB out on the man.

What she didn't need was another victim.

Why the hell hadn't Corlew told her about this Lenny Porter business the first time they talked? If he had, maybe, just maybe, Elliott Carson would be alive.

Between the discovery of a second victim, the ill-fated interview with Todd Penney's mother, and the come-to-Jesus session with Corlew, there hadn't been a bright spot all day. On top of all that, she'd gotten back to the office at quarter to seven to find a Post-it note from Lieutenant Prescott saying she had requested a transfer to the gang task force and Burnett had given her the go-ahead.

Apparently he hadn't considered it necessary to ask Jess. She was only the deputy chief of SPU for heaven's sake.

Jess unclenched her jaw and popped some more M&M's into her mouth. Rather than march straight to his office, assuming he'd still been there, and demanding an explanation, she'd opted to take the night to cool off. She'd needed to check on Lily and relax. Better to approach that particular confrontation in a calm, professional manner.

'Horse shit,' she muttered.

It wasn't that losing Prescott was such a hardship – far from it. It was the principle of the thing. When was he going to stop lording over her as if he had to protect her from the most mundane decisions?

Have another sip of wine, Jess. Then another wad of chocolate. Since she hadn't worked out in weeks, she might as well work out her mouth. *Dumb.* If she kept ignoring her body's needs, she'd end up going up a size or two and then Dan's mother would call her fat the way she had Lily.

How Katherine Burnett managed to invade her thoughts at a time like this was beyond explanation. She had never liked Jess. Thought a girl from the wrong side of town wasn't good enough for her one and only son.

Corlew's words echoed right alongside those frustrating thoughts. *And you are still not one of them, kid.*

She wasn't one of them. Not really. She didn't have the Mountain Brook address or the hefty bank account or the family history and prominence possessed by women like Gina Coleman and Sylvia Baron. Jess could name a dozen more of those in Dan's social circle, male or female. She wasn't one of them, and no matter what she did, she never would be, not in their eyes. That kind of status in Birmingham was bigger than what was in your wallet. It went all the way to the bone, to the very DNA. And those who had it were accepted on a level those who didn't never would be under any circumstances.

Jess had a theory when it came to social acceptance and she'd pretty much lived by that principle since she was a kid. You could spend your life wishing you were one of *them* or you could decide you wouldn't want to be one even if you could.

Worked really well unless you stupidly let yourself fall in love with one of *them*.

'That's it,' she scolded herself. 'Time to get out of here.'

A leisurely stroll around the yard would do her good. She dragged her sneakers from under the sofa and tugged them on, then marched to the fridge to stow her wine. She'd come back to that. She set the stemmed glass on the shelf and with a bump of her hip knocked the fridge door closed.

She stopped, turned slowly back to the door, and opened it again. She stared at the object on the top shelf right in front of the yogurt she probably needed to eat pretty soon. 'What in the world?'

Feeling like she'd suddenly lapsed into slow motion, she watched as her hand reached inside and picked up what looked like a Chinese takeout box. She hadn't picked up Chinese in . . . days. The box was white. No markings. Same little wire handle like the ones from her favorite takeout joint down the road.

By the time she reached the counter, a mere two steps away, her hands were shaking. A note was written on top of the box. *Are you going to fish or cut bait?*

'Shit.' Her heart battered against her sternum.

Backing up, she hit the table, almost knocked over a chair. She needed gloves. Her bag was on the floor by the sofa. She dug out a pair of gloves and her glasses. She shoved the glasses onto her face and tugged on the gloves. Ordering herself to calm down, she walked the few feet back over to the counter.

Very carefully she opened the top of the box.

'Oh . . . God.'

Jess took a breath and looked again, just to be sure.

Red wiggler fishing worms . . . *bait*.

Two quick raps at her door had her practically jumping out of her skin. She pressed a hand to her chest and blew out a breath. She stuck the box back in the fridge, ripped off the gloves, and tossed them onto the counter.

'Pull it together, Jess.'

She swiped her sweaty palms on her lounge pants and walked back to the sofa and her bag. She reached for her Glock. Her pulse seemed to slow as her fingers wrapped confidently around the weapon.

Another knock echoed in the room.

Just as she reached the door, Burnett called out, 'Jess?'

Relief weakened her knees. She tucked her gun back in her bag and drew in a deep breath. 'Coming!'

She squared her shoulders and opened the door. 'Hey.'

His gaze swept over her as if he needed to see for himself that she was okay. 'Hey.'

'What's up?' Now was *not* a good time. She needed to figure out the worms in her fridge business . . . without telling *him*. God, that sounded like a totally dumb excuse even to her. But he was already hovering. The whole department was watching. Not only was he making her look bad, but he was also making himself look bad. Somehow she had to get it through his head that she was as capable as Black or any of the others. He had to treat her the same or there would be trouble among the ranks.

The idea of those wiggly worms in her fridge had her shuddering inside instead of focusing on the man at her door.

Couldn't be Spears. But she wanted it to be . . . didn't she?

Whoever it was . . . he had been in her apartment. Touched whatever he wanted. The bottom dropped out of her stomach. Oh God.

'Jess, are you listening to me?'

She forced herself to pay attention. 'Sorry. What did you say?'

'You going to keep me standing out here all night?'

'Oh . . . come in. Sorry.'

He stepped inside and she closed the door. She tried to decide what to do with her hands. Someone had been in her apartment. *Again*. And she'd had the locks changed after the incident last week. She had to do something to protect herself and her stuff.

'I see you have your homework board already prepared.'

Jess jerked back to attention. She turned to the board she'd mounted on the only wall space in her apartment where there weren't any windows or doors. *Say something for Pete's sake!*

'Yeah.' She shrugged, gestured to the board. 'I do some of my best work in the middle of the night.'

He just sort of stood there looking at her then.

Uh-oh. Something was up. She searched his face for a clue as to what he was thinking. 'What're you doing here?'

'I need to discuss a couple of issues with you.'

If there was one thing that could get her attention in most any given situation, having him show up at her door at this hour with an ax to grind was it. 'Now that you mention it, I have an issue to discuss with you too.' She turned and walked to the sofa and sat down. 'Why don't you have a seat?' She gestured to the chair on the other side of the sofa table.

'O-kay.'

Sitting side by side was personal. Sitting across from each other was for business. This was business as well it should be. It was Wednesday after all. Hump day. The middle of the *business* week.

'Lieutenant Prescott came to my office today.'

'I heard. She left me a Post-it note.' Jess faked a smile. 'That was professional of her. It was even more professional of you to approve her transfer request without discussing it with me first.'

'I assumed you would appreciate losing the negativity in your unit.'

'You *assumed*, Burnett. That's the problem. There's a chain of command. You preach to me all the time about ignoring it. You need to practice what you preach.'

Let him argue that. He was wrong and he knew it. And she was spitting mad. She needed her glass of wine, except that wasn't possible because someone had invaded her space . . . had left her a message challenging her to do more than just cut bait. Another of those shudders quaked through her.

What the hell had she done?

'You're right.' Dan turned his hands up. 'I should have spoken to you first. I apologize for jumping the gun with Prescott. If you or a member of your team knows of a suitable replacement, consider it done.'

Keep talking until you figure this out. 'Prescott preferred GTF over me, huh?'

'She mentioned that she'd enjoyed her time there.'

'Was this move a promotion?' If he'd given Prescott a promotion, that would add insult to injury after the unprofessional way she'd behaved.

'It was not.'

Surprised, Jess said, 'But she has a good record in the department.'

'*Had* a good record,' he corrected. 'Her disloyalty to you amounted to insubordination. She needs a little more time in grade to reach her full potential, in my opinion.'

Inside, where he couldn't see, Jess went utterly still and it had nothing to do with the worms in her fridge. 'So you punished her for giving me a hard time.'

Recognition flared in his eyes. 'No. I did my job. It's my responsibility to ensure cohesiveness in the department. Proper respect for her superiors is something Prescott purposely chose to disregard.'

Jess wished she could appreciate his intent but he just didn't see what a hornet's nest he was stirring. 'Prescott and the rest of the department won't see it that way, Dan. You punished her because of me. You can't let them think you're playing favorites.'

She stood, too wired up to be still, and started to pace the room – the room some stranger had invaded. His actions were exactly the reason she kept the Spears stuff from him. The more he knew, the more he hindered her ability to do her job and the more negative attention he drew to himself. Why didn't he get that?

'What's done is done,' he said flatly. 'I admit that I should have discussed the move with you but the other was my decision to make.'

'Have it your way, then.' She hated this part. Why couldn't he see her as just another one of the guys at work?

'Maybe,' he offered, his voice suddenly tight, 'I wasn't thinking clearly since right before Prescott showed up I'd just heard from Special Agent Duvall that you've been contacted by Spears.'

Oh hell. She should have anticipated this was coming sooner rather than later. 'I haven't spoken to Wesley since the day after he left Birmingham.' She shrugged. That was the God's truth. No matter, judging by Dan's expression, he wasn't buying it. 'I don't know where he got his information.'

'I do.' Burnett flashed her one of those fake smiles. 'From Gant. You told Gant and Gant told Duvall. Problem is, no one told me.'

Oops. 'You didn't tell me about Prescott, so I guess we're even, then.' She could hope but she would never in a million years get off that easily. Regret and dread and a couple other emotions had her stomach twisting in knots.

Fury darkened his face. 'We are not even, Jess. Not by any stretch of the imagination. It's not bad enough you failed to inform me that you were contacted by the same killer who stuck a knife in my gut and who kidnapped and tortured one of my detectives, but you also showed up on the five o'clock news colluding with Buddy Corlew.'

A laugh burst out of her. 'Colluding? I wasn't colluding with anyone. He came to my crime scene with useful information about the case. What was I supposed to do? Send him packing in front of all those reporters? I assumed the best route was to stay calm and pretend all was well.' Was this Chief Burnett talking to her or Dan Burnett, the guy who still appeared to get jealous at the idea she was talking to his old high school nemesis?

'Is that what you were doing?' Dan shot to his feet, hands on hips, jaw tight with fury.

'When it comes to the case,' she snapped right back at him, 'I'm not taking chances or playing games.' That might not be entirely accurate. She occasionally did both even if she rarely admitted as much even to herself. She did what she had to do to solve the case. 'Corlew is involved. He's been involved with this case since Lenny Porter took a dive off the old *Birmingham News* building.' When Dan would have hurled an argument, she stopped him with upheld hand. 'Personal feelings aside, I need whatever he's got on this case. I wasn't here twelve years ago and he was.'

'I was here twelve years ago.' Dan pounded his chest. 'I can tell you what he's got. Nothing!'

'You were here but you weren't investigating homicides,' she argued, the fight going out of her fast at the disappointment and hurt in his eyes. 'Black and Corlew were.'

'You know he's going to slant whatever he tells you to make the department look bad.' He visibly struggled to calm down. 'That's how he operates, Jess. Harold Black did the job right. You can take my word on that.'

'I'm sure I can take your word, just as I'm sure Corlew will twist things around.' Dammit. She didn't want to hurt him and clearly she was. 'But if he's got anything at all that might help this investigation, I need to hear him out. Two people are dead. This is about finding a killer, not about egos.'

Burnett held up his hands. '*This* is getting us nowhere.'

'Amen.' She stiffened her spine against the war of emotions twisting inside her and said the rest of what she needed to say. 'You can't have it both ways, Burnett. You can't insist I follow the rules if you're not going to follow them yourself.'

'What the hell does that mean?'

'You want me to keep you fully informed, then you have to do the same. You tell me what Corlew did to turn most every cop in the department against him and I'll tell you about Spears. We have to set aside personal feelings and process what we learn. This isn't about us.' She gave her chest a thump this time. 'This is about what we *do*. The job.'

That muscle in his jaw that flexed when he was seriously angry was going at it now. 'As your chief, you have an obligation to keep me informed, Jess.'

'Oh ho,' she scoffed. 'Do as I say, not as I do – is that it? You going to teach me a lesson the way you did Prescott?'

The standoff that followed lasted long enough to make her sweat. Then he broke.

'I only want to protect you, Jess.'

There it was – the elephant in the room. She'd heard the words before but it was the fear in his eyes that forced her to see the part she'd been missing. An integral element to their relationship, personal and professional. Daniel Burnett was terrified of losing her. To danger, like the kind Spears represented, of course, but also he was afraid she would leave again. He needed to protect her from danger and those who would disrespect her like Prescott.

Her heart ached with the need to make him see that she was here to stay this time. 'I understand.' And for the first time, she did. They still had to find a happy medium, but she got it now. 'I need you to understand that I'm tougher than you think. I can and will deal with the Prescotts and the Corlews and whoever else gets in my way. I'm not going anywhere this time.'

'I plan on holding you to that.'

She laughed. 'I'd be disappointed if you didn't.'

That smile of his that made her heart go pitter-patter appeared and she wanted to hug him. This had been one hell of a day and it wasn't over yet, but they were good where it counted.

'For the first eight or ten years of his career, Corlew was a good cop.' Dan shrugged. 'He came back from the

Marines seemingly matured and with a healthy respect for the rules.'

Jess sank back down onto the sofa.

'When he was accepted into the police academy, I worked in the mayor's office.' Dan settled in the chair a few feet away again. 'Over the next few years we rarely ran into each other. He rose up the ranks and gained a decent reputation.'

'But it didn't last,' Jess suggested.

'Six years after he started in the department, I came over as the liaison. Everything changed after that. Whether it had anything to do with my presence or not, I can't say. His work got sloppier and he got cockier. There were incidents involving missing reports and misplaced evidence, including money. Mostly, I think to cover up bad police work. By the time I was named chief of police, there were rumblings of evidence tampering and he was drinking. A lot. I ended it. It was the right thing to do.'

'I had no idea it got that ugly.' Old habits were hard to break, and even when you did, sometimes the reprieve was short-lived. Sounded like Corlew had drifted back into his old habits.

Dan nodded. 'There were rumors of him sleeping with the wives of other cops. It was always something. The drinking was the straw that broke the camel's back.'

That was too bad. She'd wanted to believe Corlew had changed. No wonder he'd made so many enemies. 'Thank you for telling me. Still, he's a person of interest in this case because of his personal involvement twelve years ago. He may know details that aren't in the official case files. I'll need to work with him to some degree just to be sure I don't miss anything.'

'I can live with that.' Dan leaned forward, bracing his forearms on his knees. 'But I can't live with you leaving me out on the other. Spears is a monster. A heinous killer. You can't play this game with him alone, Jess.'

'Is that what you and Wesley decided?' Maybe she shouldn't have thrown that barb at him but she couldn't help herself. Letting go of a single millimeter of her independence was more difficult than she'd anticipated.

'What Duvall thinks is irrelevant to me. But I have to tell you that it hurt hearing it from him instead of you.'

That was one cold, hard fact she couldn't deny. She should never have told Gant without telling Dan first. Not only was the decision disrespectful on a professional level, it was hurtful on a personal one. 'I'm sorry. I didn't want to give you more reason to hover over me.'

He straightened, drawing away from her. 'Hover?'

'You know what I mean!' She wanted to scream. No matter how many times they went over this, he just wouldn't see her perspective. 'I don't want you treating me differently than you do the others. I am a deputy chief. I deserve the same respect and trust from you as Black and Hogan and all the rest.'

'You think I don't trust you?'

He wasn't listening! 'You don't trust my ability to take care of myself. Every little thing you learn like this diminishes the hope you'll ever see me as capable on all professional levels.'

He got up and came to sit down beside her. 'Jess, you are the most capable investigator I have ever known. We're all in awe of you. Some don't show it. Hell, maybe I don't. But the one thing I can guarantee you is that no one thinks you are less than capable on any level, professional or personal.'

Maybe it was the exhaustion or the realization that he meant exactly what he said, maybe a little of both, but she surrendered.

'Gant can't find any record of Spears coming back into the country. But I get a text message every now and then and he seems to know what I'm doing.' As much as she wanted to be with him this close, she resisted falling into Dan's strong arms. She had to get this said. 'Like that night at your house my first week back in Birmingham when he seemed to know I was in bed. But he could've been guessing based on the time.'

'Have the other contacts been like that?'

She shrugged. 'Pretty much. I'm leaning toward the possibility that maybe he has someone watching me. He's too smart to be here himself. He'd send someone, the way he did Matthew Reed.'

Reed had murdered an agent. He'd kidnapped Lori Wells and tortured her for days. Still, just because it likely wasn't Spears himself didn't mean there wasn't reason for concern.

'No more holding out on me,' Dan said, his tone leaving no room for debate. 'I want to know immediately when you hear from Spears or whoever the hell is acting on his behalf.'

'I will let you know. I swear.' As much as she despised admitting it, he was right. This battle might just be too big for her to wage alone.

Holy hell. Dread swelled, swallowing up the relief she felt at having reached this understanding. If she was going to keep him informed . . . he should know the rest. Just get it all on the table now.

'I should also tell you that when I hear from Spears, I respond.' There. She'd said it.

His posture stiffened. 'You respond how?'

'I try to think of something witty,' Jess admitted. She'd gone out on that ledge – no point turning back now. 'To bait him, like rubbing it in that I'm the one who got away.'

'You bait him?' Outrage or something of that order flashed in his eyes. 'Are you trying to end up a victim of this son of a bitch?'

He was going to love this. 'I figure that's the only way to lure him close enough to take him out.'

Burnett shot to his feet again, palms up in exasperation. 'You can't be serious. Spears has endless resources, Jess. He's disgustingly rich and damned brilliant. You can't possibly hope to think of all the bases he might hit. Baiting him is a bad idea. One that could get you killed just so he can prove a point.'

Okay, Jess, finish it. 'I suppose while we're on the subject, I should tell you that he may have sent me a gift. I can't be sure, of course, but—'

'What gift?' Dan glanced around the room. 'What the hell are you talking about?'

'He left me some fishing worms. You know, *bait*. With a note.' The relief at getting it all out was immeasurable. She hadn't enjoyed keeping secrets from him.

Burnett visibly struggled for patience. 'Where?'

'In the fridge.'

He looked from her to the fridge and back; then he stamped over and checked it out.

Without a word to her, he dragged out his cell and made a call. 'This is Chief Burnett. I need an evidence tech at 9911 Conroy Road ASAP.'

He turned back to her then. 'Pack a bag. You're staying at my place until we figure this out.'

It felt a little strange not calling him on his high-handedness, but he was right.

Another liberating admission. She was on a roll.

Needing a moment to herself after coming so clean,

she ducked into the bathroom and closed the door. She'd pretended for too long that she could handle this alone. She stared at her reflection in the mirror and cursed herself.

'Fool,' she muttered.

She couldn't get Spears by herself.

Her cell vibrated in her pocket. She dragged it out and glared at the screen.

I'm getting bored, Jess. I might just go fishing.

Chapter Seventeen

Parkridge Drive, 10.40 P.M.

Lori set her laptop aside and turned to Chet. 'You really believe Corlew was a dirty cop?'

Chet lowered the volume on the local news. 'He was damned good at what he did,' he allowed. 'He worked hard and seemed to be dedicated. I was a rookie. He was always nice to me. The way I heard, he just sort of started this downward spiral.'

'But you don't like him.' Lori had noticed the grimace that claimed Chet's face every time Corlew's name came up. Not to mention the cocky way he'd handled him at the Carson murder scene today.

'I don't like him.'

'Why?' Why was it a woman had to drag this kind of thing out of a guy? Women lived to talk about this stuff.

To share and commiserate. Somehow males didn't get that gene or something.

'My first partner was a veteran cop who taught me everything I know. He had twenty years in the department and he was a good guy. Good cop and a good guy.'

'Okay . . .' Lori prompted. She disliked that there was a sadness in Chet's voice as he talked about this but she really needed to know. 'This is difficult for you. I get that. I'm still spilling my guts once a week to the department shrink. But you know what?'

He turned to look at her.

'It works.' Being tortured by a serial killer for a couple days kind of fucked with one's psyche, but she was working through it. 'Talk to me, baby. I need to know.'

'My partner's first wife died before I joined the department. He'd remarried. A younger woman who made him very happy.'

Lori snuggled closer to Chet. 'Nothing wrong with that.'

'Except that Corlew set his sights on her and they ended up having an affair.'

'That sucks.' She'd gotten that vibe from Corlew. Womanizing bastard. Now she was mad and she hadn't even known Chet's first partner.

'Yeah. It sucked all right. But, in time, Corlew got his.'

She waited for him to continue, holding her breath.

'He was working a high-profile case involving a

homicide victim who turned out to be a big-time loan shark. Internal Affairs got a tip that Corlew was keeping some of the evidence – money – instead of turning it in. A search warrant found it hidden in his home. Corlew denied he'd taken it. My partner's wife left him, filed for divorce, and testified that her husband took the money to get back at her lover. The investigation got ugly and my partner ended up having a massive heart attack. He didn't even make it to the ER.'

'Damn. That's terrible. What happened to Corlew?'

'The bastard was cleared but no one looked at him the same after that. When Burnett made chief he made sure Corlew was out of there.'

'No one ever bothered to find out what really happened? What about the wife? Did she stand by her statements?'

'She did. So did Corlew. So my partner died with that mark on his record. Even if it was never official. The case was closed unsolved.'

'I'm sorry. I didn't know. I'd heard that he was a legendary investigator but that he was dirty. I never had any reason to look into it.'

'One of these days the truth will find its way to the surface.' Chet draped his arm around her shoulders and pulled her close. 'It always does.'

They watched the rest of the news. It felt good just to be, especially in Chet's arms.

And without his son around.

God, she felt guilty about that. But it was so hard.

Don't think about that, Lori. Enjoy the moment. She had to admit that things had gone better tonight. They'd taken Chester to McDonald's and spent an entire hour in the PlayPlace. The kid had actually interacted with her a little bit. The change wasn't groundbreaking but it was something. Progress. Slow, but maybe sure.

That little bit of progress made Chet happy, so it made her happy.

When the news was over, Chet clicked off the television. 'You and the chief meeting with the Five tomorrow morning?'

'What's left of them. If they're smart, they'll take her advice about lying low until we figure out what's going on in this case.'

'You ready to hit the sack?' The hopeful gleam in his eyes sent warmth rushing through her body.

'I'm ready anytime you are, Sergeant.' She kissed his jaw.

'I appreciate how patient you were with Chester tonight.' He traced a finger down her cheek. 'I know it hasn't been easy.'

'I think he's beginning to like me.'

'Come with me, Detective,' Chet teased, 'and I'll show you how much *I* like you.'

'No need to go all the way to the bed.' She pushed him

back onto the couch and straddled his lap. 'Right here works for me.'

He wrapped his arms around her and stood, holding her against him. 'We should take it to the bedroom. We don't want to get into the habit of doing it just anywhere. We might forget sometime when Chester is here.'

'Oh.' That definitely trampled her libido. 'I didn't think of that.'

He nuzzled her neck on the way to the bedroom. 'I'll teach you everything you need to know,' he murmured against her skin. 'There's all kinds of rules when it comes to kids. My ex reminded me of a few I hadn't thought of.'

When had he spoken to his ex? *She* was giving him the rules? He paused at the bedroom door, drew back to look into her eyes. Clearly he'd felt the new tension in her body.

'Did I say something wrong?'

Lori forced a smile. 'No way.' She kissed him hard. Hard enough to empty both their minds of thoughts of kids and ex-wives.

She would adapt. That was her new mantra. She could do this. She loved Chet. She could do whatever necessary. Chester would learn to like her. She'd find a way.

They tumbled onto the bed. He dragged her panties down her legs and touched the place that ached so for him. She groaned. Nothing else mattered but getting those jeans off him and *him* inside her.

Back in the living room his cell rang. He stilled.

'If it's work, they'll call your landline.' She did not want him to stop. She needed this. She needed him . . . all of him.

'It might be Sherry. Chester could be sick.' He rolled off the bed. 'That's another thing about kids,' he said as he straightened his fly and zipped it, 'if they get sick, it's usually in the middle of the night.'

Lori waited for her heart to stop pounding and her respiration to slow. She listened to the low, deep sound of Chet's voice as he spoke to the caller who was obviously his ex.

Maybe the kid wasn't going to be the real problem. Maybe it was the ex-wife.

Or maybe the problem was Lori.

Maybe she wasn't cut out for *this* yet.

Chapter Eighteen

Dunbrooke Drive,
Thursday, August 12, 7.05 A.M.

'You got everything?'

Jess saddled the strap of her bag on her shoulder. 'I do.' She tugged at her suit jacket. She really liked the rich red color but the lining was itchy. If she didn't like the skirt so much, she'd take it to that fancy thrift store Dan's friends used and donate it.

Men were the lucky ones. She admired the one fiddling with the coffeemaker. A few classic suits and shirts and the only real accessory they had to worry about were ties. Shoes were black or brown and comfortable. Lucky dogs.

'You want to take a coffee with you?'

'No thanks. I'm ready.' This was the part she hated about sleepovers. Her car was at her place. She was basically at his mercy. She liked to get up, get dressed, and get to work. She dragged her coffee with her and didn't care if she ate or not.

Dan, on the other hand, looked over the morning paper with his coffee. Nuked a prepackaged breakfast in the microwave.

She'd been counting off the minutes for half an hour.

'What time is your appointment with the security company?'

'Two.' Inside, she winced at the idea that she was going to have to turn her place into Fort Knox to satisfy Dan's demands.

'Good.' He grabbed his briefcase and nifty to-go cup and followed her to the door.

Thank God.

While he set the security system and locked up, she climbed into his fancy Mercedes SUV. It was a nice vehicle, no question. But it reminded her of that big, fat dividing line between Dan's family and hers. His family were Brookies, Mountain Brook residents, the high and the mighty. And she was from way, way across town, the low and the invisible.

He settled into the driver's seat and started the engine. 'You sure Mrs Wallace and her friends are expecting us this early?'

'They're expecting us.' Her day was already jam-packed. Meeting with the widows was a courtesy to Frances. A phone call from one of her detectives could have sufficed but she owed the lady more than that. The least she could do was follow up personally.

Frances probably had a lot more to do with Jess and Dan becoming a couple back in high school than she realized. She helped Jess see that the massive chip she carried around on her shoulder was not going to get her what she wanted out of life.

Admittedly, she was still a work in progress, but Frances had set her on the right track.

'I slept better knowing you were right down the hall.' Dan backed out of the driveway.

Jess studied his profile. He really worried about her. She'd realized that last night. He worried the way she and Lily worried about each other. In a way, Dan was closer to *real* family to her than any other man she'd had in her life – not that she'd had that many. Her one marriage to Wesley had ended almost before it started. More her doing than his. She'd pushed him away even before he'd moved across the country.

The kind of connection she and Dan shared also carried far more potential for intense pain. She knew that particular pain too well.

She made an agreeable sound in answer to his statement; then she turned her attention to the passing landscape. Everyone she'd ever had that deep bond with had left her, starting with her parents when they'd gotten themselves killed in that car accident. Then Dan after college.

Maybe she'd been pushing people away ever since. Even Lil. It was easier to be busy up in Virginia than to come home for frequent visits and get too attached. People left . . . people died.

Jess closed her eyes and wished with all her heart that Lil would be okay. Jess had wasted a lot of time . . . she didn't want to lose her sister now.

She glanced at the man next to her.

Or him.

That confession, even if only to herself, made her throat ache and her chest tighten.

Vestavia Village, 7.55 A.M.

'So we're in the clear?' Lucille, the eldest of the widows, asked.

'Yes,' Jess repeated. 'New evidence has come to light that suggests Baker's murder was not related to the Village or anyone here.'

One of the twins, Molly, harrumphed. 'He's dead and we're no better off than we were before. Clemmons isn't trying to stop the construction. He's seeing dollar signs.'

The widows all started talking at once, which was the norm for this group.

Frances held up her hands. 'We will not give up, ladies.'

Lucille argued, 'We're wasting—'

'Stow it, Lucille,' Frances warned. To Jess she said, 'Can you tell us anything about the case?'

Jess shook her head. 'Sorry. I can't talk about an ongoing investigation.'

'It's related to that ex-ball player,' Polly said knowingly. 'My son is one of his neighbors. He would know.'

'Well.' Jess stood. 'We should be going.'

Looking past ready to do just that, Dan stood as well. 'Thank you for your cooperation, ladies.'

Frances walked them to the door. 'I saw on the news that both victims once belonged to this tight little group called the Five. Has someone targeted them for what happened to that young man all those years ago?'

Jess should have realized that Frances would remember the case; she had still been teaching at the time. 'We're working every angle, including that one.'

She grabbed Jess's hand and tugged her closer. 'You two still look good together.'

Jess glanced toward the corridor outside the door to make sure Dan was out of earshot. 'Frances, he's my boss now. We're friends.'

Her too-perceptive eyes twinkled. 'Call it what you will, but I know what I see.'

Jess must have looked confused because she added, 'That young man looks at you the way my Orson always looked at me.' She smiled, her eyes watery now. 'Until the day he died.'

Jess gave her dear friend another hug and hurried to catch up with Dan.

She felt a little depressed at what Frances had said, though she was sure that wasn't her old friend's intent. Frances and Orson had lived the kind of relationship love stories were written about. Lily and Blake were like that. They were so much a part of each other it was impossible to imagine one without the other. As much as Jess loved her independence, she really didn't want to grow old alone. She and Dan had promised each other that if they were still single when they hit sixty, they would get married just to prevent being alone.

But that wasn't the same.

Could Frances be right? Jess stole a glance at Dan. Could he possibly love her that way?

Her heart pounded at the thought of relying on anyone so completely.

Give her a cold-blooded killer to face down any day over figuring out affairs of the heart.

How could she trust anyone else to make the right decisions if she couldn't even make them herself?

It was so much easier to stick with what she knew.

'We need to pick up my car,' she reminded him.

'As long as you don't go taking off on your own,' he reminded her.

'You're the boss.'

He sent her a look.

'Okay, okay. I will take every precaution.'

He reached across the console and squeezed her hand. 'I know it cramps your style, Jess, but until we know what's going on with the Allen case and have a better handle on what Spears is up to, we need to be vigilant.'

Jess smiled at him but inside she wondered if she'd ever be free of Spears again.

She didn't know why she bothered. She knew the answer.

Not until he was dead.

Birmingham Police Department, 11.02 A.M.

Jess waited until the three remaining members of the Five were seated around the conference table. 'First, I appreciate your coming.' She looked from one to the other. 'I know your schedules are busy but I believe this is a serious threat. Two of your friends have been murdered already.'

'We're very much aware of that fact, Chief Harris,' Kevin O'Reilly said pointedly. 'What we don't know is what you intend to do about keeping the rest of us alive.'

Jess just didn't see how a woman as seemingly nice as

Juliette Coleman could have ever been friends with these two overbearing, self-serving men.

Then again, in some social circles it was more about pedigrees than personalities. Both men were attractive and well dressed. Aaron Taylor was perfectly manicured from his eyebrows to his nails. Not a hair out of place. O'Reilly, on the other hand, was more what she would call money groomed. He had the bucks for the right clothes and the better hair stylist but beneath what money could buy he was rough around the edges. He'd missed a tiny spot when shaving. His striped shirt, though undeniably a designer label, didn't quite match the suit. Then there was Juliette. Like her sister, she had long dark hair and gray eyes. Either could be a supermodel or a big-screen actress. Both had that sexy, fresh-faced beauty that called out to a camera and the fashion sense and dollars to back it up.

That was something else Jess had noticed about the Five. They were all attractive and fairly fashionable while Lenny Porter and his friend Todd Penney were your typical nerds with big glasses and an unkempt appearance. Lenny and Todd had been perfect targets for the likes of these snobs. As hard as Jess tried not to hold what she'd read in those journal pages against the group, it was difficult.

And now, a dozen years later, they were looking at a double homicide. Sometimes the bullied or the downtrodden came back to get even.

'I can only help you, Mr O'Reilly, if you cooperate,' Jess explained with all the patience she intended to bother with. 'We're doing everything possible to find the person or persons responsible for Scott Baker's and Elliott Carson's murders but we need evidence and motive. These murders appear to have been well planned and equally well executed.'

'What you're saying is that you're stumped,' O'Reilly accused. 'You have no idea who killed our friends even though we've given you a suspect and his address as well as his motive.'

'You know that's not how this works,' Taylor argued. 'Just because we believe Todd Penney is picking us off one by one doesn't mean the police can just arrest him. They need proof. That attitude is not going to help us,' he warned his friend.

The two glared at each other for several seconds. Maybe not such good friends after all.

'Well said, Mr Taylor,' Jess noted when no one else seemed inclined to break the silence. 'We have no proof that Mr Penney has done anything wrong.' Other than the journal entries, which may or may not have been written by him, and the fact that his Corolla had followed Jess around that one evening, but the latter wasn't really a crime. He'd have to do it a lot more and venture considerably closer for her to accuse him of stalking.

Honestly, she had no idea why the man felt the need to follow her – if Penney had even been behind the wheel.

At this time, the one known aspect of his behavior that cast undeniable doubt on Penney was his refusal to come in to make a statement. He knew the police were looking for him. Only a man with something to hide refused to cooperate when the authorities came knocking.

'What is it you expect us to do?' O'Reilly demanded.

'The best option would be to relocate to some place safe away from your home and usual routine. If that isn't a viable possibility the department will provide a surveillance detail for each of you.' With budgets tight all over, those kinds of resources were getting tougher and tougher to come by but Jess didn't see any way around it in this instance. If the mayor complained, she would remind him that she was only taking care of his friends.

'I'm staying with my sister,' Juliette said. 'Do you think I still need a surveillance detail, Chief Harris?'

Jess opted not to say that her big sister was just a reporter, not a superhero. 'I would strongly recommend the detail.'

'I'm supposed to just uproot my family because the cops can't do their job?' O'Reilly roared. 'No way. And I won't be made to feel like a prisoner in my own home.'

The three of them started talking at once – arguing mostly.

You can lead a horse to water but you can't make it drink.

Jess stood, drawing their attention back to her, which ironically shut them up. 'I would advise you to accept my offer or to take the proper precautions as I've outlined. Avoid your routine and keep your eyes and ears open. Call nine-one-one immediately if you feel you're in danger. Do not hesitate. No one is going to complain about a false alarm under the circumstances. If you change your mind about a surveillance detail,' she said to O'Reilly and Taylor, 'don't hesitate to call.'

O'Reilly was the first out the door. No *thank you*, no nothing.

'I'm sorry for his behavior,' Juliette offered. 'He's been a wreck since Scott told us Todd was back in Birmingham.'

'Stop covering for him,' Taylor insisted. 'He's always been a jerk. If his father wasn't who he is, Kev wouldn't have a friend on this planet.' He turned to Jess. 'Thank you for the offer, Chief Harris. My wife and I will go to a friend's lake house. I'm due a vacation anyway.' He hugged Juliette. 'Stay safe, Jules.'

When Taylor was gone, Juliette lingered. 'Chief Harris, do you think you can find Todd before he tries to kill another one of us?'

'We're doing all we can,' Jess assured her. Rather than leave it at that, she pushed for more reaction from the woman. 'I'm just having some trouble reconciling the idea that a man who had achieved huge success on the West Coast would return here to have revenge for the death of his friend twelve years later.'

Todd Penney's high school records showed he'd been in counseling for depression and anxiety back then. Harper had found nothing else since. Not even a traffic violation. The night Lenny Porter died, Penney disappeared. Days later he was discovered in the psych ward after a near drug overdose. Beyond his insistence that his friend had been murdered – a statement he later recanted – there was not a speck on his record. His employer gave him a stellar recommendation when Jess called just before this meeting. But then a lack of evidence didn't mean the man wasn't guilty. It just meant they hadn't found his secrets yet.

'It has to be him,' Juliette insisted. 'There's just no other explanation.' She frowned, openly searching Jess's face. 'Are you saying he doesn't meet the criteria for cold-blooded murder?'

'All of us are capable of evil,' Jess allowed. 'It's choosing not to commit an act of evil that separates us from the bad guys. Sometimes a good person can make a mistake and cross the line. Evidence shows that once that line is crossed, it's easier the next time. Even easier the time after that. So, yes, it's possible. Whether it's probable is yet to be seen.'

Juliette looked away. She covered her mouth as if she had more to say or ask but couldn't bear to do so.

'If there's something else you need to tell me, this

would be the time. I can't help you and your friends unless I have as many of the facts as possible.'

Juliette seemed to compose herself and readied to go. 'It's nothing. Just something Scott said a long time ago.'

'A long time ago meaning shortly after Porter's death or sometime since?'

'It was a few months later. He said that sometimes the universe tests you and maybe we failed the test that night. I think maybe he was right. Maybe we failed the test and this is our fate. Maybe this has nothing to do with Todd. It could just be fate catching up with us.'

The lady had watched way too many B-rated movies. 'I don't deal in fate, Juliette. But I do deal in facts. And there are still a lot of those missing in this case. Until I know all the facts, none of you are safe. I wish you'd change your mind about staying some place the killer wouldn't know to look for you.'

Juliette thanked her and went on her way. Jess had a feeling one or all of the dwindling group knew something – possibly earth-shattering – about the night Lenny Porter died, but none wanted to share with her.

She hoped they wouldn't wait until it was too late to make a difference.

Speaking of late, it was almost noon. Jess was supposed to meet the security system technician at her place at two. If she didn't do something drastic, Dan would never allow her to go home again.

Don't kid yourself, Jess.

Spears had scared the hell out of her last night. She'd been more than ready to come clean with Dan and to get out of that apartment. She shuddered at the memory of opening that takeout box and finding a clump of worms. The evidence tech had found no prints, no nothing other than worm excrement. Not that she'd expected anything to be found. Spears was way too smart for that. Nothing would be found unless he wanted it found.

The new dead bolts she'd had installed failed to deliver the security she'd hoped for. In truth, she wasn't naïve. A top-notch thief could open most any kind of lock and then relock it when he was done.

The bottom line was she just hadn't expected Spears to make a move like that . . . this soon. She had baited him for weeks now. Hoped he would make a move. Show up back in Birmingham so she'd have a second chance to do what she'd failed to do twice already.

And yet she hadn't been prepared. Not by a long shot. She'd turned tail and run like a scared little girl. All the way to Burnett's place.

Spears was getting bored. He'd said so. Regret sank like a rock inside her. Her puny efforts to keep him entertained had been a lost cause.

When the craving started, a serial killer like Spears was hard pressed to ignore those desires. She feared it wouldn't be long now until he would start killing again.

Because she had failed to stop him when she had the chance.

Her cell rang and she jumped. 'For the love of God.' She had to get a hold of herself. It was just Harper calling. 'Harris.'

'Chief, I think you're going to want to get over to Easy Storage off Lorna Road. Looks like someone's been planning to take out the Five for a while.'

'On my way, Sergeant.'

Jess tossed her phone into her bag and dug for her keys. 'Damn.' Lori and Cook were in the field. Cook was interviewing a distant cousin of Penney's and an ex-boyfriend of his mother's. Lori was following up with Scott Baker's father about the payments to Lenny Porter's mother. Mayor Pratt had warned that Jess should steer clear of the Baker patriarch. But that didn't mean Lori couldn't attempt an interview.

Jess wasn't about to pull those two off task. Waiting for an escort would be a waste of time and resources. It was no big deal. She was driving straight to the location where Harper waited. She was certainly capable of driving herself across town in broad daylight. Dan needed to be reasonable.

Just in case, she took the stairs. The chances of running into him were far less likely along that route. She smiled for the security guards in the lobby and hurried out of the building. Careful to remain aware of her surroundings, she reached her reserved spot in the parking garage in record time. Minutes later she was in her Audi and on the street. She breathed a huge sigh of relief.

It felt good to have her car back. And her freedom, even if only for a few hours. The need for precautions was important but she liked being in charge of her own movements. She hated having a babysitter. Except for last night. She'd been really glad to have Dan with her after finding the gift Spears had sent her. Not only had he called for an evidence tech, but he'd also called Gant. Saved her the grief Gant would have given her.

Looking at the situation in the light of day, she realized that certainly Spears had hired someone to do the job. As Dan said, the man had endless resources. Well, his resources wouldn't do him any good when she got her security system installed.

'Dammit!'

She felt around for her phone and put through a call to the tech who was scheduled to show up at her apartment. There was no way to know how long it would take to go through this storage unit but she needed to reschedule to the latest appointment the man had available today. It wouldn't wait until tomorrow.

She needed her own place back.

Was that idea of staying with Dan really so unappealing? She felt a little hitch in her chest.

Wait. What was she thinking? Of course it was. Their positions allowed no room for flaunting a personal relationship.

That remark Corlew made haunted her again.

Jess had known Dan and his family for better than two decades. Could she be that kind of wife? The one who attended all the right functions on his arm? The one who stood in the background . . . and applauded his self-lessness and success?

Maybe she'd just wait until they were sixty and see what happened.

The twenty minutes she'd needed to reach Harper's location went more smoothly than she'd expected. No pileups or traffic jams. She eased ahead of a poky minivan. As she passed the vehicle, the carload of children, most young enough that they were strapped into safety seats, tossed toys at each other. No wonder the woman was poking along. Her sanity had likely gone out the window several miles back.

Jess made up her mind then and there. If she ever had children, she would not allow them to behave like untamed little beasts. Her children would show respect and have manners.

Not that she'd given it that much thought. Images like the one she'd just passed stuck in her brain and reminded her whenever she had a brief lapse in reason.

Sixty was looking better and better.

As she slowed for her exit, a dark sedan roared up close behind her.

'Almost missed your turn, did you?' She harrumphed. 'Probably texting.' She hated texting. She hated even worse that people did it while driving. 'Idiots.'

Jess slowed as she cruised to the bottom of the ramp and made the posted stop before crossing Highway 31 onto Lorna Road. She checked for oncoming traffic, left then right and—

Her Audi bumped forward.

'What the hell?' The car behind her had nudged her bumper. She checked the rearview mirror. 'What do you th—'

The driver's face was obscured by the gun he aimed right at her head.

Jess rammed the accelerator.

Traffic on her left registered.

She cut the wheel. Bounced off the shoulder of the road.

Horns blared as angry drivers who had just missed plowing into her whipped and whizzed by.

Heart thundering, she twisted around. The car was gone. She surveyed the intersection of streets around her . . . tried to recall the color and model. Dark but definitely not the Corolla. Black or navy? No larger than her own vehicle. What was that emblem on the front . . . ?

Think! An upside-down V? That was it.

Hands shaking, she reached for her cell as she carefully navigated across Highway 31 and onto Lorna Road.

She hit the necessary numbers and waited for dispatch. 'This is Deputy Chief Jess Harris.' She recited her badge number. 'The male driver of a black or dark blue sedan, possibly an Infiniti, was waving a handgun around at the intersection of Highway 31 and Lorna Road. I didn't see which way he went. Patrols in the area should be aware.'

Dispatch thanked her and Jess sat for a minute to gather her wits.

Could have been just a crazy waving a gun. It happened. Random shootings were becoming an everyday affair in larger cities across the nation.

Didn't mean it was Spears.

Or someone Captain Allen had sent to finish the job – if he was even still alive. A shudder quaked through her at the idea that he could be dead because of her.

Her cell vibrated with an incoming text.

She pressed a hand to her throat as she lifted the phone to view the screen.

Bang! Do you like this game so far?

Rather than get angry or more terrified, Jess grew oddly quiet inside. Well, now she knew. Spears wanted to play for real now. No more tap dancing around the concept. He'd sent a friend to start the games.

This was what she'd wanted, wasn't it?

Forcing her respiration to slow, she carefully chose her words, tapping the letters into the text box, then, holding her breath, she hit send.

Afraid to make your own moves, Spears?

Dan wouldn't be happy about this.

She blinked back the emotions that threatened. 'Just do what you came here to do, Jess.' Hands still shaking, she maneuvered back onto the street.

Harper was waiting for her.

Easy Storage, 2134 Lorna Road, 12.45 P.M.

The storage locker was a ten-by-ten. Not that large but covered from floor to ceiling with photos and newspaper clippings. And more importantly, page after page of the journal. Jess skimmed entry after entry that cited more cruel acts committed by the Five against the writer and his friend. The final entry appeared to be from the night before Lenny Porter died. Todd Penney, assuming he was the author, and his friend were excited about graduating and getting out of Birmingham.

'The locker's rented to a T. Penn,' Harper explained. 'He rented it one week ago according to the paperwork.'

'Was there a copy of his photo ID?' These places were supposed to have a photo ID on record.

'Negative. The owner says there was a lot of that going on. That's why he fired the guy he had running this place. When he got here this morning, he found this unit open. Says he knew trouble when he saw it so he called it in.'

'There's no security video?' She'd seen the cameras posted around the property.

'He claims the system's been broken for years.'

Jess didn't doubt it.

She surveyed the photos and newspapers clippings. Penney or whoever had done this had been keeping up with the Five all these years. In every photo, an X had been swiped over their faces.

'Evidence techs on the way?'

'Yes, ma'am.'

Jess studied the collage created apparently in the last week. If Todd Penney had been in California all this time . . . had his mother collected the newspaper clippings for him?

'Sergeant, let's see if we can determine how often Mr Penney has come home for a visit. Did he fly or did he drive as he did this time? How long did he stay? If he hasn't been back, then who collected these?' Maybe the mother had kept a shrine of sorts. Or maybe . . . 'Also, let's find out what Lenny Porter's mother has been up to. Maybe all these clippings and the journal are from a shrine to her son.'

Jess wasn't sure how far they would get with the last since Mrs Porter was out of the country.

'I'm on it,' Harper assured her. Even though the evidence techs hadn't arrived yet, he glanced around as if to ensure they were alone. 'May I ask you a question, Chief?'

She reminded herself not to frown. Bad for her complexion. 'Absolutely. Ask me anything you'd like.'

'Is it true that Lieutenant Prescott transferred to GTF?'

'That's right.' Jess shrugged. 'I guess she couldn't get past her feelings that I got the job she felt she deserved.'

'Will we be bringing anyone new onboard soon?'

'I sure hope so, Sergeant. We're a skeleton crew as it is.'

'Corlew called me this morning.'

Jess was surprised he hadn't called her. 'Did he have something new to share?' She wanted to believe he meant well getting involved with this investigation, but she had far too many reasons to doubt the idea.

'He says Mrs Porter's ship is coming back into port on Sunday. He suggested we have someone waiting for her.'

'I have a better idea.' Jess had been thinking she needed to get a firmer grasp on what Corlew was up to. After talking to Dan last night, she'd made up her mind. 'When you're caught up here, track down Corlew. Tell him you need to have a look around his home and office.

If he doesn't want to cooperate, let's get a search warrant. If he wants to get more involved in this investigation, let's give him a written invitation.'

Harper grinned. 'My pleasure, ma'am.'

Jess's cell clanged.

Harper's must have vibrated because he reached for his.

Burnett. He'd already heard.

Harper stepped out of the locker to take his call. Jess bit the bullet and hit accept.

'Harris.'

'Where the hell are you?'

'I'm on Lorna Road at an Easy Storage with Harper.' She didn't mention that they were in separate vehicles.

'What happened with the Infiniti and the driver with a weapon?'

'He nudged my car and when I looked in the rearview mirror, there was a gun pointed at me. I didn't see his face.' And unless Todd Penney had traded way up, it wasn't him. Not that she thought for a second the incident had anything to do with her ongoing case.

'Do not leave your location until I get there. That's an order.'

Jess hit END CALL. 'Great.'

'That was Officer Cook,' Harper announced as he stepped back into the unit. 'He just got back to the office. The hospital called.'

Fear closed Jess's throat. She prayed Lily was okay.

'Your friend Frances Wallace is in the ER with chest pains.'

Jess had to get to her. 'You know what to do here, Sergeant.'

'I've got it under control, Chief.'

Jess hesitated at the door. 'When Burnett gets here, tell him I'll call him as soon as I know anything on Frances.'

Dan shouldn't be surprised when he arrived to find her gone. If he didn't know by now she wasn't very good with orders, then he hadn't been paying attention.

She never had been good with authority. Otherwise she wouldn't have been voted most likely to rebel her senior year.

Come to think of it, Corlew had gotten that same vote.

Apparently neither one of them had changed much.

Chapter Nineteen

University of Alabama Hospital, 2.00 P.M.

Jess paced the waiting room. Frances had seemed fine this morning. Obviously Scott Baker's murder had taken a heavy toll on her. Finding the body of a murder victim haunted a person.

At some point she'd stopped counting how many victims and their killers she had viewed and analyzed.

No matter that she was surrounded by others, also waiting to hear news on their loved ones, Jess realized that until coming back home a month ago that was pretty much all she did – analyze evil and murder.

Maybe that was still her top priority. Her sister would certainly say that Jess was all work and no play unless the players were a part of her work. Like Spears.

He appeared to know that about her and intended to utilize those vast resources of his to taunt her. She had a bad feeling he also understood that she would do just about anything to prevent him from going *fishing*, as he called it in his text message. If he started another murder spree, there was no telling how many people would die before he was stopped.

'Chief Harris?'

Jess reeled her thoughts back to the present. She hurried to the AUTHORIZED PERSONNEL ONLY doors. 'I'm Chief Harris,' she said to the nurse who had called her name.

'Mrs Wallace would like you to join her.'

'Thank you.' Relief rushed through Jess. 'Is she all right?' She followed the nurse along the wide corridor. The sterile hospital scents invaded her nostrils. She hated the way hospitals smelled.

'She's doing fine. She'll explain everything to you.' The nurse stopped at a closed door. 'The doctor has released her, so she's free to leave. I think your aunt just needs a little extra patience.'

Her aunt? Jess thanked the nurse again and entered the room where Frances Wallace sat atop the exam table wearing a generic print gown. 'That color is you,' Jess said, her chest tightening at the weary mask of fatigue her old friend wore.

'It's a classic,' Frances complained. 'Unfortunately one that never goes out of style in these joints. Otherwise they'd have something new by now. These are the same old rags they had when my daughter was born.'

Jess laughed. 'You know, I think you're right. I've never been in a hospital that didn't have those same damned gowns.'

'Exactly my point.'

'So.' Jess walked over to stand beside her. 'What's the prognosis? Will you live?' She bit her tongue when the other question on her mind bounced to the tip of her tongue. Where was her daughter?

'I'll live,' she said with a shrug. 'It was only a panic attack. Or maybe gas. The child they called a doctor couldn't say for sure. But I'm fine now and' – she gave Jess a look – 'more relaxed than I've ever been in my life.'

'Drugs will do that,' Jess teased. 'I guess you didn't realize how Baker's death affected you?'

She patted her meticulous bun. 'Possibly. Mostly I think I shouldn't have eaten Thai for lunch.'

'Maybe not,' Jess agreed, hoping it was that simple. 'You do understand that Baker's death had nothing to do with you or the widows, don't you? I explained that already.'

'I'm not dense, Jess. Certainly I understood. I didn't kill the little shit and neither did any of my friends.'

That was plain as day. 'I'm going to have an attorney Dan knows look into this business at the Village,' Jess promised. 'Maybe he can find a way around the clause in your contract that gives the board the right to screw you over.'

She reached for Jess's hand and hopped off the exam table. 'That would be very nice of you, dear.'

'Why did you tell the nurse I was your niece?' Not that Jess minded but she suspected there was a motive behind the move.

'The only way they'd let you take me home is if you're family. You have a problem with that?'

Jess gave her the universal gesture of surrender. 'Absolutely not, Aunt Frances.' She grinned. 'Just remember your favorite niece in your will.'

'I've already taken care of that,' she assured Jess as she reached for her clothes. 'I'm leaving you my tell-all biography. You're to see that it's published so all the old geezers I used to know can roll over in their graves and their highfalutin offspring can be properly mortified.'

'It would be my pleasure.' Jess turned her back when the cotton gown hit the floor. 'I'm not in this book, am I?'

'Of course you are.' The rustle of clothes underscored her words. 'I spent several chapters analyzing your life and raved on and on about how I helped shape your future.'

'That's sweet.' That was one biography she couldn't wait to read.

'That's me,' Frances announced as she gathered her purse. 'Sweet as honey and a whole lot less sticky.'

Jess offered her arm and Frances took it. As they approached her car in the ER parking garage, Frances brought them to a halt. 'I didn't call my daughter.'

'Is there a reason you didn't?' Jess located the fob and unlocked her Audi.

'She's not strong like you, Jess.' At the passenger side door, Frances turned to her. 'God love her, she's like her father. She needs everything to be normal and calm. This would have gotten her all worked up for nothing.' She smiled sadly. 'Besides, like her father, she thinks I'm immortal. I can't have her believing otherwise.'

Jess patted Frances's arm. 'Your secret is safe with me.'

'That means a great deal to me, Jess.' Frances smiled but Jess saw the glitter of emotion in her eyes.

She moved around to the driver's side. When they settled into the front seat, Frances turned to Jess. 'After you and your handsome boss left this morning, I made a few calls. I had a long chat with a former colleague of mine who taught at Carver High School.'

Jess had read the records on both Porter and Penney. But firsthand accounts generally provided better insights. 'Do tell.'

'The young man who died, Porter, was quite besotted with a lovely young lady from Brighton Academy.'

Juliette Coleman. 'Were there any particular incidents your colleague recalled?'

Frances shook her head. 'Just that she thought it was very sad for Porter. She said he and his friend Todd Penney were very nice young men.'

'I appreciate the information but you really don't need to bother yourself with this investigation, Frances. You have enough to worry about with that construction.'

'Too late.' She smiled crookedly, probably the drugs. 'I also spoke with an old friend who taught at Brighton. Scott Baker and his friends were smart, polite, and hardworking in school.'

Jess felt a twinge of disappointment. 'The perfect students.'

'Hardly,' Frances mused. 'They all had a wicked streak a mile wide. When they thought no one who mattered was looking, they could be quite nasty.'

'I may need to speak with this old friend of yours.' This case was not nearly as cut and dried as it appeared on the outside.

'You let me know. I'll be happy to arrange it.'

As Jess drove across the parking lot, Frances touched her arm. 'You're a lot like me, Jess.'

She flashed a grin. 'I'll take that as a compliment.'

'Maybe you shouldn't. I know how fiercely independent you are. That can be a good thing. But it can also leave you lonely and needy when there's no one around to lean on because they've all been trained to stay out of your way.'

Jess couldn't decide how to respond to that.

'We all need a strong shoulder once in a while, Jess. Take my advice and let someone else be the strongest from time to time. You'll regret it if you don't.'

9911 Conroy Road, 5.40 P.M.

Jess had gotten to her apartment just in time to cover her murder board with a sheet before the technician from Atlas Home Security, Harry Watson, arrived. Dan had been too furious that she had left the storage facility alone to show up here, so he'd sent Lori instead. Jess knew he would reserve his explosion for when they were alone.

She couldn't wait. For now she and Lori followed Watson around the room as he explained what he had done.

'That' – he pointed to a small object in the corner near the ceiling above her bed – 'is a motion detector. If anyone comes through that door' – he indicated the only entrance to her place – 'this sensor will set off the alarm. If there is any movement at all in the room, the same will happen.'

She'd had a system in Virginia. She understood that the motion sensor was for when she was away from home. Otherwise she might wake up in the middle of the night and set it off when she got up to pee.

'Each window' – he indicated the windows around the room – 'has a sensor. If the window is opened, the connection is broken and the alarm goes off.' He then pointed to another little beige box he had installed on her wall, this one above her murder board. 'That's a glass break sensor. It's triggered by the sound of breaking glass and will set off the alarm as well. Your entry door has a sensor the same as the windows. If the door opens, off the alarm goes.'

'What's to prevent a professional from shutting down the system somehow?' Jess wanted to know. The old-fashioned systems like she had in Virginia worked through a landline. Cut the phone service outside the house and the system was useless. She'd never upgraded since she was rarely home anyway.

'This system is totally cellular.' He directed their attention to the modem-like box he'd placed atop Jess's chest of drawers. 'Complete with battery backup that continually recharges in case the power goes out.'

That was a huge relief. 'You did something outside?' Lori asked. 'You were working on the stairs.'

'Since that door and the staircase is the only way in or out of your place,' Watson explained, 'I felt you needed to know if someone was approaching. So I placed motion sensors at the bottom of the staircase and then another set about midway. They're attached on the underside of the railing so you won't see them and they won't pick up a cat or dog the way they would if they were at the tread level.'

'Sounds like I'm covered.' Jess was impressed. According to Burnett, this was the top security company in the city.

'All I need now is your security code, four digits, and a code word or phrase.'

Jess went with the day and month she returned to Birmingham and for the code word she decided on *Glock*. Who would ever guess that?

With the work done, all she had to do was write the massive check. God, her checking account balance was dwindling and her puny savings wasn't much better. The locksmith had come while the security guy was doing his thing. Now she had new locks *again*.

Once the technician was out the door, all she needed to do was fumigate her place. The idea that some stranger had been in here made her shudder. Lori had helped her check the place for bugging devices, audio or video. They'd also checked every cupboard and drawer and they'd taken apart her bed all the way down to the box springs to make sure nothing else had been hidden there.

'Man, you are state-of-the-art,' Lori praised. 'I wonder if you can count this as a tax deduction since it's work related?'

Jess snorted. 'I won't hold my breath. Since the technician was here already when I finally made it, how about an overview of what you and Cook learned today.' She curled up on the sofa and motioned for Lori to join her.

She settled at the other end and opened to the notes in her phone. 'The cousin and mom's ex both claim Todd hardly ever comes home. His job takes up most of his time and he swore when he left Birmingham he was never coming back.'

Jess knew that story line. 'Did Cook get anywhere on relatives of Mrs Porter?'

'No luck. Her house is locked up tight. Cook had hoped to at least get inside if there was a house sitter. No relatives we can find. She doesn't work, so no coworkers to question. If she goes to church, none of her neighbors know where.'

'Try getting through to her ship. Maybe she'd be willing to answer at least a few questions.'

Lori entered the notes into her phone's notepad. 'I'll get on it. Depending on the time zone, I may be able to get through tonight.'

'Anything from Harper on Corlew's reaction to our request?'

Lori smirked. 'Oh yeah. Corlew is mad as hell. He said his lawyer would contact you.'

'We'll give him until noon tomorrow.' Jess shouldn't

be getting any glee out of this but she was. If Corlew thought he was dragging her into his grudge with the department, he had another thought coming. Nor would she tolerate him muddying this case.

There was no point putting it off. Dan was waiting for her at his place. Talk and dinner. The dinner she looked forward to. She was starving. The other, not so much. She'd promised to do better just last night and already she'd gone back on her word.

'Thanks for hanging out with me while this was done,' she said to Lori. At this hour Jess was cutting into the detective's personal time.

'Not a problem. We all want you to be safe.'

'I appreciate that.' She gathered her keys and her bag. 'I guess I'm headed to Burnett's house for dinner and a scolding.'

Lori waved her phone. 'Yeah. I'm supposed to take you there.'

Jess started to argue but decided that she'd give Dan that, considering how badly she'd broken her promise today. She locked up and set the alarm. That way he'd have to bring her home and then he could see that with the new locks and the security system there was no reason she wouldn't be safe right here.

'We took Chester to McDonald's last night,' Lori said as they descended the stairs.

'How'd it go?'

Lori nodded. 'Better.'

'All it takes is time.'

A crash inside the garage had both Jess and Lori going for their weapons. Neither said a word as they flattened against the stone walls and eased toward the side door.

The door was ajar.

Jess's gaze collided with Lori's.

Lori nodded and Jess reached for the door.

She swung it open and Lori went in, weapon leveled and ready. Jess was right behind her.

Mr Louis staggered a step or two, then reached up and righted his eyeglasses.

'Mr Louis, are you all right?' Jess skirted the old Caddy and hurried to the elderly man's side.

He gestured to the overturned ladder and a box lying on the floor, its contents scattered. 'I lifted the box to put it on the shelf and lost my balance. The next thing I knew I was going down, ladder and all.'

'Are you hurt?' She looked him over. 'You really shouldn't be up on ladders like that.'

Lori started gathering the scattered items. Old sewing patterns and dozens of spools of thread. Squares of fabric.

'I'm fine. Really.' He dusted himself off. 'I feel a little foolish, that's all.'

Good Lord. The man was as bad as Frances overdoing it like this. Jess crouched down to help Lori. Then again, she suspected she would be doing the same thing at their age.

'You're not hurt. That's all that matters,' Jess assured him.

'My sister's things.' He shrugged. 'I should have cleaned out her room years ago.'

'Next time let me know and I'll help.' He'd been so kind to her that was the least she could do.

Lori righted the ladder and climbed up to reach the shelf Louis had been aiming for. Jess lifted the box to her. It really wasn't that heavy. Louis, being on the short side, must have overreached. A hazard of working on a ladder.

'Thank you, ladies. I feel quite foolish.'

'Happy to help, Mr Louis.' Lori smiled at him and Jess could swear he blushed.

Jess waved a goodbye. As she and Lori made their way to the door, the empty space under the breaker box caught her eye.

The old wooden box she'd stubbed her toe on was gone. Maybe he'd just moved it. She figured that George Louis was a doer. Always piddling at something.

As they drove away, Jess decided she should get an alarm system for her old Audi as well. If she'd had one last week, she would have known if it was Ted Allen who'd tried tampering with her car.

Or if it was Spears.

Spears had caught her off guard last night. She

wouldn't kid herself. He'd scared the hell out of her. But she was okay now.

Let him come.

Dunbrooke Drive, 6.30 P.M.

The smells coming from that commercial-grade stovetop were making her mouth water. Maybe she'd been wrong when on her first visit to his home she'd taken one look at this fancy kitchen and laughed. What did a man who ate out all the time need with all this? Maybe the guy did cook occasionally.

Jess leaned against the island counter, her arms crossed over her chest and prepared for whatever Dan opted to throw her way after he heard what she had to say to his suggestion she would be safer here.

'I'm not staying here again tonight.' He froze mid-stir. 'The security system is installed and online. There's no way anyone's coming in without me knowing it. I sleep with the Glock under my pillow. I'm good to go.'

As unsettling as all these events were – the break-ins, the vehicle tampering, someone aiming a weapon at her – she had to do this the right way. She didn't have to remind him that he wouldn't be inviting Black or Hogan to spend the night with him. Protecting the integrity of their positions in the department was critical.

He continued stirring the array of fresh vegetables he had dumped into the wok along with the chicken. The rice had already boiled and the tempting smell of whatever sauce he'd prepared was driving her wild and she hadn't even tasted it yet.

'Apparently you've made up your mind. I guess there's nothing left for me to say on the subject.'

That sounded good but she knew the man better than that. He would not let the subject go without a fight. Though they had spent the past twenty years about a thousand miles apart, it had only taken her just over a month to see that he was even more hardheaded than before. He was ridiculously overprotective of her, and nothing she said or did appeared to sway him one iota.

He cared about her. He wanted her to be safe.

'If we're done discussing my living arrangements, I'll get the plates and open the wine.'

Since he opted not to answer, she took her time arranging place settings before opening the bottle of pinot grigio he had taken out of the fridge twenty or so minutes ago.

Silence still choking the air out of the room, she gathered two stemmed glasses and poured a generous serving for them both. She had a feeling they were going to need it to get through this meal.

As if he'd taken lessons from Guy Fieri himself,

Burnett placed a bed of rice on each plate, then spread the chicken and veggies like juicy, colorful icing.

Mercy, it looked as good as it smelled.

He grabbed his glass of wine, gestured for her to take her seat at the island, and then chugged the pinot.

Oh yeah. His feathers were ruffled.

Whatever. She intended to eat.

The first bite had her moaning in spite of her best efforts to eat quietly. Until she'd started taking on so, you could've heard a pin drop in the room.

'Good?' he asked.

'Amazing,' she confessed.

'Gina taught me this recipe. She takes cooking classes over at the Cook and Bake Company as a way to relax. She says it helps her achieve her Zen goals.'

The deliciousness exploding in her mouth fizzled like a flat soda. 'That's interesting.' At least Gina taught him something useful. It took every ounce of restraint Jess possessed not to say exactly that. She had no right to be jealous of the woman. No right at all. But it was hard not to be. Gina Coleman was gorgeous and smart and a good cook who took lessons for her Zen whatever. La-tee-da.

Jess would bet a hundred dollars that the woman couldn't change a tire if her life depended on it. She probably couldn't qualify with a weapon either. Or take down a bad guy with a few precisely placed moves.

'Do you remember my cousin Ronald?'

Jess about suffered whiplash from the abrupt subject change. 'Vaguely.'

'He graduated high school two years after us,' Dan went on. 'Anyway, he and his wife had their first child. A baby girl named Serena. They've asked me to be her godfather. The christening is at two on Sunday. If you don't have plans, would you like to come?'

'I'd love to.' Who wouldn't want to sit on a hard church pew and listen to a baby scream while everyone in the room oohed and aahed about how beautiful it was?

Stop being mean, Jess. For those who didn't have children, a christening wasn't exactly a fun time. It was hard to relate to people who had decided their entire lives should now be focused on this tiny human who had only higher taxes and fewer job opportunities to look forward to.

'I'll pick you up about one-thirty, then.'

'Sure.' If she had said no, would he have invited gorgeous Gina?

Then it hit her. The whole reason he had told her about Gina teaching him to make this lovely meal was so she would jump at his invitation. The sneaky—

'I don't want you to go back to your place tonight, Jess.'

In spite of her very best efforts to stay strong, the worry in his voice tugged at her heart. She laid her fork down and turned to him. 'We can't keep skating into dangerous territory, Dan. We already have enough trouble keeping our professional relationship professional. Black and the others aren't blind.'

She needed more wine. She reached for the bottle but he beat her to it. He refilled her glass.

'I know we're supposed to be taking this slowly but I'm almost forty-three. I don't want to take it slowly anymore.' He poured himself some more wine before putting the bottle down. 'I want to spend the rest of my life with you, Jess. I want to love and protect you for as long as I live. If something happened to you...' He shook his head. 'I couldn't bear it.'

The whirlwind of emotions his words launched had her head spinning. 'What're you saying?' Had he just proposed? And told her straight up that he loved her too. *Oh my God!*

'I'm saying that I love you. I want us to take it to the next level. I want a commitment.'

'Boy, that was a mouthful.' Reeling, she didn't know what else to say to his revelation.

'If you don't want the same thing, for God's sake say so and put me out of my misery.'

Take it slow and careful, Jess. 'I can't say that I don't want the same thing.' Okay, that wasn't so hard.

'Then why the hesitation? Is it about having children?'

That she wasn't sure about. 'There was a time when I was certain I'd be spending the rest of my life with you.'

She smiled but her lips wouldn't quite hold the gesture. 'Being back here. Being with you feels right. It feels like it was meant to be but . . .'

As if Frances had abruptly walked into the room, her voice rang in Jess's ears. *It can also leave you lonely and needy when there's no one around to lean on because they've all been trained to stay out of your way.*

'But . . .' he prompted, hurt in his voice and on his face.

'I'm terrified, Dan.' Just tell him the truth. 'It feels like we have this incredible and unexpected second chance. A *gift*. A do-over opportunity that most people don't have the privilege of stumbling upon. And I don't want to screw it up. We have to be careful. Take it slow and be patient. We have to, Dan. We just have to. This is too important to rush or jump the gun.' She drew in a big breath. 'I have to learn to lean on someone besides myself sometimes. You have to learn not to smother me.'

'I just want you safe.'

'I know you do but we have a job to do and at work you can't treat me different. We have to learn to separate those aspects of our lives. We talked about this last night. Otherwise your position as chief of police could be damaged. We have to be smart about how we do this. We have to do it right.'

He took her hand in his. 'You make a number of valid points. I shouldn't be rushing things but when I think of

Spears getting close to you, I'm the one who's terrified.'

Jess kissed him on the lips. 'I love you, Dan.' The happiness that lit in those blue eyes of his tightened her chest. If he could say it, she damn sure could too. 'Thank you for admitting you're afraid too. I don't like being terrified alone.'

He kissed her firmly, then drew back. 'Eat.' He winked at her. 'Then you can tell Gina how much you appreciate all she taught me.'

Jess narrowed her gaze. 'That will cost you, mister.'

He leaned down and kissed her again. His lips lingered until she melted against him and kissed him the way he wanted to be kissed. The way they both wanted to be kissed.

When they were gasping for breath, he whispered against her cheek, 'I want to make love to you.'

She looked up at him and smiled. 'I hope this shirt didn't cost too much.' Before he could say a word, she ripped it open. Buttons flew over the granite counter and the wood floor. Her hands were on his skin and she didn't care about anything else.

They made it as far as the sofa. She wasn't sure whose fingers fumbled the most; she only knew that it took them working as a team to get his trousers open. She wrapped her legs around his and somehow he got her panties aside and pushed into her.

He did exactly what he'd said he wanted to do . . . he

made love to her. Fast and hard the first time and then slow and softly the second.

Jess didn't know why she had bothered to fight it . . . this was where she wanted to be.

At least until daylight . . . when duty called.

But she would always come back . . . because this was where she belonged.

Chapter Twenty

Cahava Valley Road, 11.01 P.M.

Aaron sat by the pool. The lights deep beneath the water were the only ones illuminating this sultry summer night. Even the stars were hiding from the devil that had been let loose. He almost laughed. Oh yes, he had always possessed a flair for drama. An uncanny ability to size up the situation and tell it like it was.

Like the fact that he and the survivors of their tight little group were royally fucked. 'Is that descriptive enough, old chap?' He raised his tumbler of bourbon and toasted the air. Who knew if Lenny Porter was in heaven? But one thing was abundantly clear. He wasn't in hell because that was right here. On earth. In this city.

Aaron had lost count of the number of times he'd filled his glass. Didn't matter. He was royally fucked, right? Who cared? Not his pretty wife, that was for sure.

She was out getting fucked by someone else because he couldn't bear to do the job himself.

There had been a time when he could rise to the occasion and make that woman scream with pleasure. But he just didn't have it in him to pretend any longer. The love of his life – the man he would give anything and everything he owned to be with tonight – had finally had his own fill. He could not live in secrecy any longer. He wanted a real life with a real partner.

Aaron could not give him that. Not if he hoped to achieve Alabama Supreme Court justice one day as his grandfather had. As his father now served. The Taylor men were bred for greatness. He certainly could not fail his heritage even if that duty meant failing his own heart.

So he waited out here, alone and in the open, to face what Fate would bring him. Scott and Elliott were dead. They had paid for their sins.

'Hallelujah, brother!' he shouted. Everyone knew the wages of sin was death.

They had sinned.

They had all sinned.

Now they would pay.

He really had intended to go to the lake with or without his wife, but as he'd sat here alone contemplating the best course of action, he'd decided it would be best to face this head-on. To negotiate a mutually beneficial resolution. That's what he had been born to do. Why fall down on the job at this important juncture? Of course, he had consumed a healthy portion of bourbon by then.

To hell with it. If O'Reilly was man enough to stand his ground without the cops backing him up, Aaron sure as hell was too.

Then he'd found the envelope someone had shoved under his front door. His eyes had trouble focusing on the words at this point but he already knew them by heart. He'd read them over and over.

May 15

I want to kill Aaron Taylor.

Why stop with him? They had all tortured us. Why not kill them all? School pretty much sucked but they had made senior year the worst of them all.

Just because they could.

Selfish bastards.

They'd taken him to the rock quarry with them and gotten him drunk. He didn't even like beer. But he'd done it to please her. Then he'd gotten sick and he called me to come get him. By the time I got there he was passed out. He'd puked all over himself. That wasn't the worst of it. When I drove up that faggot Aaron was pissing on him.

They just laughed as I picked him up and walked away.

I hate them. I hope before they die they know how it feels to be in the kind of pain my friend has suffered.

Only a few more days until graduation and then we can get out of this shit hole.

Aaron dropped the page as he stood on shaky legs and walked toward the lighted pool. 'Come out of the shadows, sir,' Aaron demanded. He had sensed someone was watching him a while ago. At first he'd thought it was only the bourbon but then he'd felt the subtle shift in the air around him.

Penney was here . . . to have his revenge. And Aaron had no one to blame for his ill preparedness but himself.

'You've made your point.' He turned slowly around, swaying a bit. 'Rather than take another life, why not enjoy the fruits of your labor. I have one million dollars with your name on it. Money offers a great deal of healing power.' Aaron sighed. 'I know this well. I have healed myself over and over.'

He shook his head. Tossed back the last of the bourbon. He grimaced at the burn. 'What we did was wrong. So fucking wrong.' He shook his head again, the movement stilted. 'We allowed a young man to be buried with the world believing he had killed himself. We tarnished both your reputations and never looked back.'

Aaron staggered over to the table next to his favorite

chaise lounge and filled his tumbler yet again. 'There's no need to hurt anyone else,' he promised. 'I'll call the police right now and tell them the truth.' He probed his trouser pocket for his cell phone. He stumbled back a few steps but recaptured his balance. He waved his phone. 'See, I have my phone. I'm going to make the call just as I said. We'll pay for what we did. Isn't that what you want? Our public humiliation and downfall?'

He promptly dropped the phone. 'Shit,' he muttered as he reached down for the blasted thing.

When he rose, something slammed into the back of his head. Aaron plunged forward into the pool. Something splashed into the water with him. He watched the small cast statue of a child – the symbol of what his wife would never have as long as she was married to him – sink to the bottom of the pool.

His vision was blurred and he felt oddly heavy.

For a moment he just sort of lingered beneath the surface but then adrenaline must have kicked in because he started to kick and flail his arms in an effort to reach the surface.

Don't breathe . . . don't breathe.

He had to get out of the water!

Why wasn't he going up? As drunk as he was, he knew that with the air still in his lungs he should float to the surface. All he had to do was hold his breath and stroke upward until he reached the surface.

Above him was a blurry image. A man standing at poolside . . . with the skimmer pole.

A sharp jab at his shoulder and Aaron understood. He was being held beneath the water with that damned skimmer.

Fear roared through his veins.

He had to get away . . . had to get to the air . . .

He didn't want to die like this. He tried to keep fighting but his arms and legs just wouldn't work anymore.

Aaron watched the bubbles going up around him and he knew the air had just seeped from his lungs. Water rushed in to take its place . . .

Chapter Twenty-One

Friday, August 13, midnight

Kevin was struggling for breath by the time he reached his car. His hands were shaking and he dropped his keys twice before he could hit the damned unlock button.

He reached for the door, relief starting to seep into his veins. He'd made it. Thank God.

It was damned dark out here but he kept looking over his shoulder just in case. The feeling that someone was watching him just wouldn't go away. But he'd been extremely careful to ensure he hadn't been followed.

The bastard couldn't be that stealthy.

He glanced back once more just to be certain. He didn't see a damned thing.

'Idiot.' He laughed at himself. No one was there.

All he had to do was get the hell out of here. He would

get some sleep in the recliner with his gun right where it was now – in his waistband.

He didn't give a shit if Todd Penney was watching him or not. He wasn't taking Kevin down. He was smarter than the others. He'd figured out exactly how to protect himself from that bastard. 'Fuck you, Todd.'

Kevin opened the driver's side door and—

A strong arm closed around his neck. The gun was plucked from his waistband before he could react. The cold, hard muzzle rammed into his temple.

'No. Fuck *you*, Kevin O'Reilly.'

Chapter Twenty-Two

Dunbrooke Drive, 4.59 A.M.

Jess locked the bathroom door and sat down on the edge of the whirlpool tub. Dan was still asleep. The shirt she wore smelled like him. If she never smelled anything else the rest of her life, his scent would be enough.

God, this was hopeless.

She rested her head in her hands. 'What in the world?' She bit her lip and fought the wave of tears. He wanted to move to the next level – a committed relationship. It wasn't that she didn't. She loved him. Yes. She'd told him. Out loud. But she needed time – time to get used to the idea. To wrap her head around not being totally independent of those kinds of commitments. He didn't want to wait and God almighty she was weak. So weak.

'Suck it up,' she muttered as she straightened her back and squared her shoulders. She was a grown woman.

Locking herself in the bathroom and whining was no way to find an answer or a comfortable place for her emotions to land.

She needed a shower. The red skirt and matching scratchy jacket would just have to do until they dropped by her place for a change of clothes on the way to work. Which meant they would have to leave early. She needed to get a move on.

With renewed determination, she dragged her bag onto her lap and prowled for the little compact that held her birth control pills. That was something else she had to do. This was her last refill. She needed to get a doctor here.

'Definitely not Collins,' she muttered. Though he really was a good doctor, he was one of the many who at times pooh-poohed the unique health issues that women faced. Her sister's case was a perfect example of that mentality. She'd squared that away with a face-to-face with the good doctor.

How come she could clear up everyone else's problems but never her own?

And why was it this damned frustrating packaging required her to pry it open every single time? They really should design these things better.

She stared at the number of pills left. Wait. That wasn't right. Today was the thirteenth. She should be having her period by the fifteenth, which meant she should be into the blue-green pills now, not still in the white ones.

Searching her bag again, she unearthed her phone and checked her period calculator. Wasn't that a handy app?

There it was. She was right. There should only be one of the white pills left, at most. But there were four. Not a good thing.

A trickle of terror kicked her heart into higher gear.

Surely she hadn't forgotten as many as that? Yeah, she'd forgotten one here or there in the past but never more than one in a month.

Jess shoved her hair back from her face. Had she gotten behind after her room at the Howard Johnson Inn was vandalized? Things had been a little crazy for a few days and she'd gotten abducted by that crazy little gangbanger. Lil had gotten sick in the midst of all that.

And she wasn't even going to throw Eric Spears into the mix. He had turned her life completely upside down. She shuddered when the image of that gun pointed at her flashed in her head. What if that guy had pulled the trigger? What if…

He hadn't. She couldn't think about the what ifs; she had a bigger problem at the moment. There were lots of excuses for why she might have forgotten this many pills but none were good enough. This was serious business.

No . . . this was *life-altering* business.

'Okay. Deep breath.' The chances that she had missed

two or more days in a row were slim. So, this might not be as bad as it looked.

And maybe her calculations were off. She could be right on schedule. Maybe she'd entered the dates wrong in the app in the first place.

'That has to be it.'

Jess popped a pill into her mouth and ducked her head under the faucet. She swallowed and felt better already.

She swiped her mouth with the back of her hand and stared at her flushed skin and tousled hair.

The fear attempted to swell again. Shaking her head, she turned her back to her reflection. She peeled off Dan's ruined shirt and climbed into the shower.

She was worrying for nothing. The Pill was 99.99 percent accurate, wasn't it? Something like that.

There were better odds of winning the lottery than of her getting pregnant. Hadn't she read that somewhere?

7.30 A.M.

Since Jess had showered first, she'd scrambled eggs and made toast while Dan showered and shaved. They sat together at the kitchen island and asked the usual questions.

'You sleep well last night?'

'I did.' She sipped her juice. 'You?'

'Like a rock.'

They sounded like an old married couple. Very few things had ever scared her more.

Afterward, Dan loaded the dishwasher while Jess grabbed her stuff and readied to go. The meal wasn't as elegant and delicious as one Gina Coleman would have whipped up but it served the purpose.

'Cooking classes, my ass,' she muttered as she headed back into the kitchen. She could take a cooking class if she wanted to, but she didn't have time. She was too busy stopping killers and keeping Birmingham safe.

Maybe that was a little over the top.

Loading up in his SUV and heading to the office together was another of those couple things. She'd stayed overnight with him a few times during the last Spears ordeal when she first got back to Birmingham, but things had been so frantic then that she hadn't really thought about how it felt to take each of these steps. Only how it looked to everyone watching them.

This morning felt . . . comfortable yet awkward somehow.

Didn't make any sense but there it was.

'I'll just pick up my car when we stop at my place. I hate being stranded.' It made her feel completely powerless.

'I know how you feel about that,' he ventured, 'but I

just don't think it's a good idea for you to be alone out in the open in a vehicle he can tie you to. Not after what happened yesterday.'

As much as it annoyed her that whenever he learned about an incident that involved her safety, he wanted to take control and protect her, he had a point she couldn't ignore.

'I won't go anywhere without Wells or Harper. And I'll ride in their vehicles. You have my word.' She wasn't a fool. The guy had scared the bejesus out of her. 'The Audi will stay in the city parking garage.'

Her cell clanged. She checked the screen. *Lori.*

'Harris.'

Jess heard Burnett answer his phone as well. Simultaneous calls were never a good sign.

'Chief, there's been another murder. It's Aaron Taylor. The maid found him a few minutes ago.' Lori gave Jess the address.

Why the hell hadn't the guy gotten out of town like he said? Or at least accepted a surveillance detail? What was wrong with these people? 'I'm on my way.'

And then there were two.

Cahaba Valley Road, 9.00 A.M.

Like his friends, Aaron Taylor lived in a mansion. A

modern beauty with an infinity pool that flowed practically right up to the French doors at the rear of the house.

Paramedics had pulled Taylor out of the pool but he'd been long dead. Overnight at least. The skin around his hands and feet was wrinkled and loosening from the body. His eyes glistened, which indicated he had been underwater since his death.

Jess leaned down to peer into his open mouth. She couldn't see any vomit or pink froth from the battle to draw in oxygen but it might have washed away. Lividity along the face, chest, and abdomen told her that he had been facedown on the bottom of the pool since his heart stopped beating. A nasty lump on the back of his head suggested someone had either rendered him unconscious or attempted to. Either way, he had died just the same.

'One of the techs is going into the pool for the small statue near where the victim was recovered. That may be the weapon used to give him that massive lump.'

'What about the skimmer?' She looked from the pool to Harper. 'That's too light to have been used for cracking his head. Maybe it fell in accidentally or was already there?'

'They'll retrieve that as well.'

Jess had unbuttoned the victim's shirt to check the lividity along his chest. She pushed the material away from his shoulders and found a mark on his left shoulder.

She pointed to it. 'Maybe the blow to the head didn't put him down the way the killer hoped. He had to use the skimmer pole to hold him under the water until he stopped struggling.'

'There's a nearly empty fifth of bourbon over there,' Harper mentioned. 'He may not have done a lot of struggling.'

'True. As fit as this guy was, that pole wouldn't have held him under if he hadn't been incapacitated to some degree.'

Just another reason to stay sober when your friends were dropping like flies. Dammit. Why the hell hadn't he listened to her and gone to that lake house? Or at least accepted the surveillance detail she had offered?

Lori joined them on the patio. 'The house is untouched as far as we can tell. No ransacking. The maid says everything appears to be right where it's supposed to be.'

Jess stood. 'Does she know where Mrs Taylor might be?' Jess hoped they didn't have another victim around here somewhere. Taylor had mentioned taking his wife out of town; maybe he'd sent her on ahead and had intended to join her but waited too late.

His checkbook and a pen waited on the table next to the dwindling fifth of bourbon. Maybe he'd thought he could negotiate his way out of this. Evidently he'd thought wrong.

'She said Mrs Taylor's makeup bag isn't here, which means she didn't stay here last night.' Lori glanced around and added, 'Apparently the lady of the house often spends nights away from home.'

Do tell. 'We need to track down the lady.'

Reporters were already gathered in front of the house. No matter that the mayor wanted this investigation kept low-key, Taylor's murder was going to turn the tide. Carson's death hadn't been connected to Baker's in the media. Most of the coverage had been about his former celebrity status as a pro ball player. With this third murder, the connection would click. Three murdered friends in the space of four days. The blitz would hit by the evening news whether the mayor liked it or not.

'Man, I hope the rest of this day goes better than the beginning,' Lori grumbled, dragging Jess's attention back to her. 'I had a flat on the way over here.' She frowned at Jess. 'And you're wearing the same clothes you wore yesterday.'

'Does the maid know how to find Mrs Taylor?' Jess asked, ignoring her comment.

'She gave me her cell number.'

That reminded her. Jess glanced around the patio. 'Did you find Taylor's cell phone?'

'It's in the water,' Harper answered. 'Right next to the statue. And for the record,' he added with a pointed look at Lori, 'I mentioned yesterday that tire looked a little low.' He turned to Jess and gave his head a shake. 'Don't worry, Chief. I didn't notice the outfit was the same.'

Before Jess could summon a witty comeback, her detectives had gotten back to the business at hand. Damn but they needed to find this Todd Penney. If he was the killer in this case, he had just reached a status that wouldn't make his mama so proud.

Serial killer.

'Found this in the shrubbery.'

Jess turned to Officer Cook, who held a familiar wrinkled page.

Another journal entry. 'Bag it and let's have a closer look.'

An evidence tech placed the page into a protective bag and passed it to Jess.

Lori and Harper gathered around to read another glimpse of Todd Penney's and Lenny Porter's encounters with the Five.

As much as she needed to stay objective, Jess couldn't help feeling bad for Todd and Lenny. Aaron Taylor had been a total asshole in high school but that didn't mean he deserved to die like this.

'I guess he got his wish,' Lori noted, referring to the author's frustration.

'Cook.' Jess passed the journal entry back to him. 'Nudge that handwriting expert. We need to know if he can confirm from Todd Penney's DMV signature if this is his handwriting. He's taking far too long to give us an answer.'

'Yes, ma'am.'

'Sergeant, where are we on locating Penney? He has to be close.'

'His face was in all the newspapers again this morning,' Harper said. 'He's lying low somewhere because everyone in the city knows we're looking for him as a person of interest in this case and no one has laid eyes on him.'

'He hasn't reported back to work,' Lori added. 'As soon as I was notified of Taylor's murder, I called Penney's boss at home. Then I called his mother. She isn't answering her phone,' she added before Jess could ask.

Damn. Damn. Damn.

'Lori, find Taylor's wife before she hears about this.' Jess scowled. Hells bells. She needed her car. 'You'll have to drop me at the office first. I'm going to round up the final two of the Five. One or both knows more than they're telling. I'm betting if they want to stay alive, they'll start talking.'

Birmingham Police Department, 10.52 A.M.

'Do you have any idea where your friend Kevin is this morning?'

316

Eyes red from crying, Juliette Coleman shook her head. 'I tried to call him three times on the way over here. He's not at home and he's not answering his cell.'

Gina hugged her sister close but kept her comments to herself.

'His wife has no idea where he is?'

Juliette shook her head. 'She said he worked late at the paper last night and she went to bed. She had no idea he hadn't come home until she got up this morning. But no one at the paper has seen him this morning.'

Looked as if they were going to need to issue another APB in this case. Unless they already had another victim whose body just hadn't been found yet. Her frustration cranked up another couple of notches.

'Juliette, I'm going to be totally honest with you.' Jess readied to finish ruining the woman's day. It was Friday the thirteenth after all. And another man was dead. Not to mention yet another was unaccounted for. 'We've had no luck finding Todd Penney. He's here in Birmingham. We've confirmed that much with his mother. But we can't find him. He's lying low and he appears very good at it. But that alone doesn't make him a murderer.'

'It's him,' Juliette insisted. 'It has to be him.'

'How do you *know* it's him?' Jess gave her a second to absorb the impact of that question. 'His friend died twelve years ago. Penney has a very successful life out in California. Why would he come back out of the blue and start killing people? It's not the anniversary of Porter's death. No special date has passed at all as best I can tell.'

Still Juliette said nothing.

'That leads me to believe there's a reason we haven't uncovered yet,' Jess reasoned.

'What are you implying?' Gina Coleman asked.

'For a man to start a killing spree, there has to be a motive. Considering the one event all three victims have in common, we have to assume the motive is related to Lenny Porter's death and that it's been festering all that time. And now, after twelve years, he's decided to do something about it. The problem is, we haven't found a trigger.'

'A trigger?' Juliette asked, looking confused or guilty, maybe both.

Jess pushed a copy of the latest journal entry across her desk. 'Yesterday we discovered a storage unit,' she explained to the two women. 'That storage unit was covered with pages like this.' Anger and disgust started to build inside Jess. 'Long narratives detailing how five smart, attractive, rich kids tortured two young men whose only shortcoming was that they didn't have it all.'

Plain old pissed off now, Jess spread crime scene photos of Scott's, Elliott's, and Aaron's bodies in front of the women. Juliette gasped. Gina glared at Jess.

'Your three friends are dead not just because they were selfish assholes when they were teenagers.' Jess struggled to contain her outrage. 'They're dead because something occurred recently. A conversation, a meeting, something. And that something triggered their murders. There's only you and Kevin left. Are we going to let whoever is responsible for these murders just keep following this obvious pattern or are you going to start telling me the whole truth?'

'Are you accusing my sister of something?' Gina demanded.

Jess looked her square in the eye. 'Absolutely. I'm accusing her of not telling me the whole story.' She turned to Juliette then. 'Three of your friends are dead,' she repeated. 'Another is unaccounted for. Are you going to keep pretending that you don't know anything until you're all dead?'

'We need a lawyer,' Gina announced. 'Let's go, Jules.'

'Just one more little detail.' Jess opened a folder and withdrew Scott Baker's phone records. She'd gotten to the office this morning to find them waiting for her. Why the hell it sometimes took as much as three days she would never understand. They were still waiting for Todd Penney's, Elliott Carson's, and now Aaron Taylor's. Evidently she needed to add Kevin O'Reilly to that growing list. 'Scott called Todd Penney just over one week before he died. They spoke again the day before he was murdered. You and Scott were lovers. Did he mention to you that he'd spoken to Todd?'

Gina stood. 'Don't say anything else.' She kept that glower tuned at full power on Jess.

Juliette held up her hands. 'Okay.'

Mouth gaping, Gina stared at her sister.

'We were doing drugs that night.'

'Oh my God!' Gina cried.

'If you'd like your sister to leave the room,' Jess said to Juliette, 'we can go on without her.' Jess ignored the mega evil eye that earned her. Gina would need a few more cooking classes to get her Zen after this.

'No.' Juliette shook her head. 'I want her to stay.' She fell silent for a long moment; then she began, her voice taking on a distant quality. 'None of us did drugs. We didn't even smoke pot.' She glanced at her sister. 'But that night was the last night of our youth, you know? Starting on graduation day, we would be adults. College, jobs, marriage, and children lay ahead of us.'

Jess didn't prompt her with more questions. Just let her talk.

'We decided that one night would be ours. Completely. We could do anything we wanted and it didn't count. We swore never to talk about it. Like it never happened.'

'How did Lenny Porter become involved?' Jess had a feeling he didn't just show up.

'The guys wanted guinea pigs. We'd spent the whole year screwing around with them – why not include them in the big bash? So Scott and the others invited Lenny and Todd.' She stared at her hands. 'Lenny did everything they told him. Whatever stupid thing it was, he did it. He took the drugs but not just the pot and coke we did – the hard stuff, like acid. He was their puppet. They were getting off on watching his reactions to the drugs.'

'What about Todd?'

'He played along at first but then he tried to get Lenny to leave. Finally he left without him. But he was tripping too. The acid really screwed with their heads.'

As much as Jess wanted to explain to this woman that four people were dead and she was partly responsible, she waited for the rest.

'The guys started goofing around close to the edge of the building. Scott, Aaron, and Elliott were acting totally insane. I sobered up pretty quickly. I begged them to stop but it didn't do any good. They just kept getting closer and egging each other on. I was done. I told them I was leaving. I turned my back for a second. A *second*! And Lenny jumped.'

'So the three who have died, your friends, were at the edge with him but he was the only one who jumped.'

She nodded. 'We went home and pretended it never happened. But Todd knew. No one believed him but he knew. And now he's having his revenge.'

'What about Kevin?' Had she forgotten about him? He was there that night as well. What was he doing during that pivotal time?

321

She laughed, then pressed her hand to her mouth as if she hadn't meant to do that. 'Are you kidding? He's terrified of heights. There was no way he was getting near the edge.'

'Juliette,' Gina said, breaking her silence, 'has always been the good girl in the family.' She smiled at her sister. 'She wasn't a rebel like me. She didn't give anybody any grief.'

'Except Lenny Porter,' Jess reminded her. 'And his friend Todd Penney. You read the journal entries.'

Both women stared at her in something like disbelief. Juliette was the first one to speak. 'I was always nice to Lenny.' She shrugged. 'Why wouldn't I be? It was the guys who were mean to him. I didn't like being a part of that. I tried to smooth things over. I felt sorry for Lenny. The poor guy loved me.'

'But you couldn't love him back enough to make your friends stop,' Jess suggested. Before she could respond, Jess moved on. 'Thank you, Juliette.' She passed a notepad and a pen across the table to her. 'I want you to write down everything you've told me.' She turned to Gina then. 'When she's done, take her home and keep her there. Do not go anywhere or do anything that might cause the two of you to become separated from your surveillance detail.'

'Of course.' Gina wore the shocked look of someone who had just learned that people, even little sisters, sometimes kept deep dark secrets.

The door to Jess's office opened just a crack and a head poked in. 'Oh, excuse me.'

The door closed as fast as it opened.

What was Corlew doing here?

'I'll be right back, ladies.'

Jess got up and walked out of the room. Corlew was already halfway to the elevator. 'Hold up, Corlew,' she called after him.

He waited for her to catch up to him.

'You wanted to see me?' she asked.

'There was another murder last night? Aaron Taylor?'

'That's right. Do you know something about it?'

'I'm not sure. Is there some place we can talk?'

'There's a conference room.' Since they had to walk right past the lounge, she had to have more coffee. Corlew declined.

Once the conference room door was closed, she started things off with a simple question. 'What's on your mind?'

'Twelve years ago, after Lenny Porter died, Todd Penney insisted that the Five had something to do with his death. But the cops who worked the case cleared those kids.' He shrugged. 'Who was going to drag the offspring of Birmingham's biggest big shots through the mud? So Penney ends up looking like a total fool and a bad friend because he wasn't there to save his friend, whose death was ultimately ruled a suicide.'

Jess sipped her coffee and sent him a disinterested look. 'I got all that, Corlew. Where's the new stuff?' The better question was, what information was compelling enough to bring him *here*? Or was he angling for her to change her mind about the search warrant?

'All these years later, Penney finally returns home for a visit and people start dying,' Corlew went on. 'But I don't think Penney is killing anyone.'

She had her doubts about Penney's involvement as well. 'I'm in the middle of taking a statement. If you have something relevant to say, forget about setting the stage and just say it. And don't forget you have until noon to comply with my request.'

If he was here to offer a bone that might put her off his scent, he could forget about it.

His cheeks puffed with frustration. 'All right.' He looked around the room as if he didn't know where to begin. 'I haven't been totally up front with you, Jess.'

If she hadn't already suspected that was the case, she would be mad as hell. As it was, what she wanted was for him to spill his guts. 'I warned you not to yank me around, Corlew. I will get that search warrant and I will make your life miserable from this day forward if you don't tell me the truth right this minute.'

He held up his hands in surrender. 'I got it. That's why I'm here.'

'That better be why you're here,' she warned. If

playing his games had cost her team precious time, he would regret it. 'Let's hear it.'

'Keep in mind,' he said sheepishly, 'that sometimes the end justifies the means.'

She glared at him so he would get on with it.

'Monday night I was at Vestavia Village.'

Outrage rushed through her. 'The night Scott Baker was murdered you were there?'

'He was still alive when I left, but yeah.' Corlew tucked his hands into the back pockets of his jeans. 'It's like you said before, I discovered his ongoing affair with Juliette Coleman during the investigation for Frances Wallace. I decided maybe there was something there, so I went back to compile the necessary evidence.'

'You went back for pictures.' She shook her head in disgust. 'You intended to blackmail Scott.' It wasn't a question. She understood exactly what he was up to. How the hell could he still be that guy? The one who cared about no one but himself?

Worse, he had the unmitigated gall to look disappointed at her for calling him on it.

'I wasn't going to blackmail anyone. You know how things work, Jess. I figured the photos would be good bargaining power in the future if I found myself in a tight negotiation. In my line of work, collecting insurance dividends is a necessary evil.'

'Start from the beginning,' Jess ordered. 'Don't leave

anything out. And when we're done here, you're going to write an official statement.'

He heaved a long-suffering sigh. 'I arrived at Vestavia Village just after six Monday evening. Juliette typically arrives around seven, so I wanted to be in position. I parked on the street that runs parallel with the front of the property and cut through the trees on foot. I settled in between the hydrangeas.' He looked straight at Jess and said the rest. 'Five, ten minutes before seven, two men exited the lobby and stood outside the main entrance for another couple of minutes. I could tell by their body language that the discussion was not exactly a friendly one, so I zoomed in with my camera.'

Jess reminded herself to breathe.

'One of the guys was Scott. He had something in his hand. A notebook or something. The other man I didn't recognize at first, so I zeroed in closer on his face.' He made a long, low whistle. 'I knew that face but I couldn't believe what I was seeing.'

'It was Todd,' Jess surmised.

He nodded. 'They talked or argued a minute more and then Penney got into his Corolla and drove away. Scott went back inside. Juliette drove up about that time.'

'And you got your photos, is that right?' Jess was kick-the-crap-out-of-him furious. Not only could he confirm Penney had met with Scott that night, but also he could likely confirm what time Juliette left. All of which was immensely relevant to her investigation.

'Nope.'

Unable to hide her surprise, she echoed his answer. 'Nope?'

'I decided I was more interested in what was up with Penney's return. I rushed back to my Charger and followed him. He drove to one of those geeky places he used to frequent back in the day and that's where he stayed until around midnight when he went to his mother's house.' Corlew scrubbed a hand over his face. 'After that I drove back by the Village and saw all the official vehicles and I knew I'd picked the wrong guy to watch.'

Jess wanted to shake him. 'I could've used this information days ago.'

'All it proves is that Penney didn't kill Baker,' Corlew argued. 'And that maybe you need to look more closely at Juliette's alibi. Where the hell were the rest of her buddies that night? Have you looked into that? I'm telling you, the Five were responsible for Lenny Porter's death and at least one of them is responsible for what's happening now.'

'You're determined to prove it's one of them, aren't you?' Jess had her suspicions along those lines as well, but there was no concrete evidence yet and she damned sure couldn't nail down a motive unless Penney was blackmailing one of the Five. If that was the case, no one was telling. And the suspect pool was getting mighty slim.

'What I'm determined to do,' Corlew said, 'is right the wrong that was done the first go-round.'

'What wrong? Stop beating around the bush and get to the point.' She needed specifics not innuendos.

'When Porter took that fatal plunge, Daniel Burnett was the liaison between the mayor's and the chief of police's offices. He made sure Deputy Chief Black closed that case the way the rich daddies of the Five wanted it closed. Call me an asshole but this is my opportunity to take Danny boy down a notch or two with the truth. That's why I didn't tell you. You weren't going to listen to me over Dan. I decided to do it myself. I thought I could nail the killer, close this case, and prove the department screwed up last time, but I was wrong. I kept an eye on O'Reilly's house all night last night. Once again I picked the wrong guy to watch.'

'O'Reilly never made it home last night,' Jess said, the scenarios whirling in her head. 'He worked late.'

Corlew shook his head. 'He didn't work late. I called his office and asked for him at six. His secretary said he'd already gone for the day.'

'His wife hasn't seen him since he left for work yesterday.'

'Taylor's dead,' Corlew offered. 'That just leaves the

princess. She was banging the first victim and all four of those guys always rallied around her like she was the last female on a dying planet.'

'There was a cop sitting in front of her house all night last night.'

'That doesn't mean she didn't go out the back,' he countered.

That was true. A surveillance detail was to help keep trouble away from Juliette, not prevent her from sneaking off to find it. That was her sister's job.

'What about Penney? Where has he been all week?'

'That's the thing.' Corlew shrugged. 'I haven't been able to locate him again since that first night. The guy is too sharp even for me.'

She opted not to comment on that last part. 'Anything else?'

'Ask yourself, Jess, why Penney would kill Carson and Taylor and not Baker? Doesn't add up.'

That was indeed the question of the day. 'I need your statement in writing and I need any photos you took of Baker and Penney Monday night.' If that notebook Baker had been holding was the journal, she wanted to know it.

That might very well be how the killer got his hands on it.

As she headed back to her office, Corlew in tow, she put in a call to Harper. She needed him to ramp up the efforts to find the former manager of that storage facility.

So far they hadn't been able to catch the guy. His cell phone had been turned off and he'd gotten evicted from his apartment. If he could be located, maybe he could identify the person who rented that storage unit.

Jess was pretty sure the person who'd decorated that storage unit and the killer were one and the same.

Kevin O'Reilly or Juliette Coleman? Either one could have easily accessed the material that covered the walls of that unit. But only one had admitted to being with Scott Baker the night he was murdered. Corlew saw Juliette arrive. Baker possibly had the journal in his hand. And they'd had wine and sex.

Jess's cell startled her. 'Harris.'

'Jess, it's Blake.'

Her sister's husband. Jess's heart did a dizzying flip-flop. 'Is Lily all right?'

'I . . . don't know. She collapsed again and we're at the hospital. They don't like what they see in some of her blood work, so they're admitting her. She wants you here.'

'I'll be right there.'

Chapter Twenty-Three

University of Alabama Hospital, Noon

Jess sat on the side of her sister's bed, worry eating away at her. 'Has the doctor told you anything?'

Lil shook her head, her own worry palpable. 'They're doing more tests. They've alerted Dr Collins. My liver numbers are wrong. This doctor said something about hepatitis and cirrhosis. How is that possible?'

'Cirrhosis?' Her sister scarcely even indulged in a glass of wine. But then, there were other causes besides alcohol consumption. 'This is ridiculous,' Jess said. Why the hell couldn't they figure this out?

'Blake is about to have a nervous breakdown. Alice and Blake Junior don't know the half of what's going on.' Lil dropped her head back onto the anorexic pillow. 'We're afraid to tell them too much and have them running back here. They need to be focused.'

Blake had gone for coffee and to give them a few minutes.

'We'll get to the bottom of this,' Jess promised.

She couldn't help feeling guilty for being so busy this week. She'd scarcely managed one brief visit with Lil. She'd always let the job take over everything else. The whole time she'd lived away, she had been too caught up in the job to be here for much of anything. She should be ashamed of herself for letting it happen this time. Things were going to be different from now on. Lil needed her.

And that damned medical history.

'Dammit,' Jess muttered.

'What?' Lil looked at her expectantly. She looked so tired. So afraid. So vulnerable.

'I've had three murders in as many days and I keep forgetting to pick up that medical history from Wanda. Dammit!' Jess stood and started to pace. How could she be so negligent? She had one thing to do for Lil and she'd fallen down on the job. What kind of sister was she? Never mind, she didn't want to know the answer to that question.

'I doubt anything she can tell us will help,' Lil offered. 'Her brain's probably fried from all the alcohol and drugs.'

Jess made a face. 'I don't doubt it.' Still, she'd made a promise. 'I'll do it as soon as I get a break from this case.' She made the mistake of checking the clock on the wall and suppressed a groan. This day was half over and she had a new victim, leaving her with three unsolved murders and a killer out there somewhere trying to have his revenge.

Corlew's latest revelation had her leaning away from the possibility that Todd Penney was the killer. Yet, he had the most glaring motive.

Bullying was a serious matter. If one or all of the Five had taunted Lenny Porter or encouraged him to take his life, they were guilty of intimidation, a hate crime, and possibly other charges. These were smart kids with everything going for them. She hated the idea of what that meant about society.

Some called bullying nothing more than the innate human survival-of-the-fittest instinct. Jess called it evil.

One never knew what the face of evil would look like. She thought of Juliette Coleman and her tight little group. All smart, wealthy, and attractive. Yet, something evil happened that night and all these years the ugly secret had been kept hidden beneath the money and the power. Why had Scott Baker called Todd Penney now? Had something she hadn't discovered yet triggered Penney's need for revenge after all these years?

Or had Scott Baker's own son's trials at school reminded him of what he'd done to Lenny Porter? His wife was convinced that Baker considered his son's troubles a penance for some past wrong. Maybe he'd set out to make things right . . . only something had gone very wrong.

A knock on the door had Jess putting aside those worries for another. Was Blake or the doctor back with news?

A large peace lily sitting atop a cart was the first thing she saw. Her heart skipped a beat at the memory of the same plant being delivered to Burnett's hospital room after Spears stabbed him. Then the young woman who was pushing the cart came into view, snapping Jess back to the here and now.

The volunteer in the pink uniform smiled. 'Good afternoon, ladies.'

'Oh my goodness,' Lily said. 'Blake must have ordered this.'

Jess hated peace lilies. Reminded her of death and she got enough of that at work. She sure didn't want to think of it when she was in a place like this with her sister as a patient with some unidentified ailment.

'There's a card.' The girl in pink, whose nametag read BARBIE, plucked it from the ridiculously large plant.

Jess took it from her before she could pass it to Lily. 'Thank you, Barbie.' She gestured to the plant. 'Just put it wherever it'll fit.'

'Yes, ma'am.'

'Who sent it?' Lil demanded. 'Blake or Dan?'

Jess hadn't even called Dan. She really had to get better organized this afternoon.

'Y'all have a great day!' Barbie called as she pushed her cart out of the room.

Don't let this be from him. Jess noted the name of the local florist on the front of the small envelope, then held her breath as she opened it.

It was a simple card. *Get well soon.*

Beneath those generic words was a single letter.

E

Of course Eric Spears hadn't signed that initial . . . the local florist had.

But he knew her sister was in the hospital almost as quickly as Jess had known.

The memory of staring at the business end of a weapon in the hand of a man whose face she couldn't see erupted in her brain.

Someone was watching her . . . *and the people she cared about.*

3.00 P.M.

After listening calmly to her update on her sister and getting a heads-up about the plant from Spears, Dan sent Sergeant Harper to the hospital to pick Jess up. Corlew had given her a ride over here. She wasn't sure who was the biggest speed demon, him or Lori. Corlew had promised to write up his statement and get it back to her ASAP. She wasn't holding her breath. But she had what she needed from him for now.

Since every minute counted, Jess used the driving time to make sure she was up to speed. 'No one has seen or heard from Kevin O'Reilly?' She just didn't get this. If the killer had gotten to O'Reilly, why hadn't his body turned up? And if he hadn't, where the hell was the guy?

'His wife has no idea where he is,' Harper added. 'O'Reilly's father and the mayor are keeping Burnett busy putting out public relations fires.'

Jess would never understand how Dan tolerated his job. Corlew's accusation nudged at her. She refused to entertain his conspiracy theories when she had far more pressing issues. 'What happened to the department's PR liaison? I thought he was supposed to be back from baby leave this week?' Oh, God, having kids meant taking time off work. She could not have a child. She couldn't. She just couldn't.

'Trent Ward.' Harper glanced at her. 'He's back but the chief feels he should handle this situation himself.'

Corlew's accusation echoed in her ears again. *Fine, just get it over with, Jess.* 'You were in the department back when Corlew was on the force, weren't you, Harper?'

'I never worked directly with him but I knew him, yes, ma'am.'

'He said something to me today that just won't stop nagging at me.'

'What's that, ma'am?'

'He said Burnett was a part of the Lenny Porter case getting shut down without a proper investigation. Do you remember hearing any such thing?' She felt like a dog even asking that question.

'May I be candid, ma'am?'

'Please.'

Harper stared at the road ahead for a moment before speaking. 'Corlew is a piece of shit alcoholic. I wouldn't trust a word he says.' He sent another look her way. 'Whatever he's up to, he has an agenda you won't like and it will benefit no one but himself.'

Jess chewed on that for a minute. 'Thank you, Sergeant. I appreciate your candor.'

This was a subject she would take up with Dan as well. He had a right to know what Corlew was saying about him.

'Here we go.' Harper made the turn onto Pansy Street.

Still no Corolla at the Penney residence. Where was this guy? The APB for him and his car had gotten negligible results. The guy apparently knew how to hide.

Ramona Penney sat in the swing on her front porch. She watched as Jess and Harper got out of the SUV and walked her way. She made no move to stand or to welcome them to her home.

'Mrs Penney, I'm sorry to bother you again,' Jess said as she stepped up onto the porch. 'You may or may not know we've had another murder and I'm very concerned about your son.'

'No need, my boy's just fine. He called me a few minutes ago and told me he had nothing to do with these murders.'

Jess gestured to the vacant chairs on the porch. 'Do you mind if we visit for a bit?'

'Suit yourself.' She lifted her glass of tea. 'I'd offer you refreshments but this was the last glass.'

'That's all right. We can't stay long.' Jess settled into one of the chairs. Harper opted to remain standing near the steps.

There was very little likelihood that she was going to get any cooperation from this lady but there was one tactic that just might work. 'Mrs Penney, there's a chance your son is in danger. I mentioned the last time we spoke that I was worried about Todd. We now have reason to believe that someone is attempting to make him look guilty.' If Todd hadn't posted those journal pages all over that storage unit, someone had. 'Whoever that someone is, Todd's life may be in danger.'

The dismissive expression on her face instantly shifted to one of suspicion laced with a hint of fear. 'I don't know what you mean. My son has done nothing wrong. He just wants to be left alone. The world will know the truth soon enough. He told me so.'

Since Penney was no prophet, that sounded like a threat to Jess. 'Three people have been murdered since your son returned to Birmingham. The one thing they all had in common was Lenny Porter's death. A journal we've confirmed was handwritten by Todd named every one of those victims. The last entry we discovered included threats related to those same victims.'

'That journal was written when he was in high school. Teenagers are emotional,' she argued. 'They say stuff they don't mean.'

So she did know about the journal. 'Do you know what happened to his journal?'

'He kept it all this time but then he decided it was time to let the past go.' She dabbed at her eyes. 'He was finally ready. So he got rid of it.'

'Did he throw it away?'

'He gave it to Scott Baker.' She shook her head. 'I told him it would only stir up trouble but he did it anyway.'

Jess's instincts moved to the next level. 'You're certain he gave it to Baker?'

'That's what he said.'

Scott had the journal when Corlew saw him talking to Penney. Juliette had arrived right after that. Their killer was looking less and less like a he and more and more like a she.

Jess put that revelation aside for the moment. 'Here's the problem we have,' she explained to Todd's mother. 'If your son is not the person who committed these heinous crimes, then he is most assuredly on the killer's list. We need to find him for his own safety.'

That got her full attention. 'Has this killer left some clue about my son or said something about him?'

'He leaves a page from the journal at each scene. He's killing the folks, one by one, who were with Lenny Porter the night he died. Your son was with Lenny that night. He left him on that rooftop. Maybe this killer sees him as guilty too. Would a real friend leave like that?'

Her shoulders stiffened. 'Todd was the only friend Lenny had. They were like brothers. Todd left him on the roof that night, yes. He hoped Lenny would follow him. After he stormed out of the building, he couldn't get back in. He called up to Lenny and the others, over and over and no one would listen. The drug he took had him freaked out. My boy didn't do drugs. He couldn't handle it.'

She fell silent, tears brimming in her eyes. Her chest shook with a shuddering breath. 'He had to find someone who would let him use their cell phone to call the police after Lenny fell. We didn't have the money for one and most businesses in that part of town were closed at that hour. It was awful for him. Just awful.' She looked straight at Jess. 'I can't tell you where my son is because I don't know, but I can tell you one thing for sure. He hasn't killed anyone.'

'I appreciate your honesty, ma'am. Just one more question. Did Todd see Lenny fall?' Jess steered clear of saying Lenny jumped; she needed Ramona cooperative not defensive.

'He was standing in the parking lot,' Ramona confirmed. 'He watched those other kids playing around the edge like fools. Then Lenny fell. But just before he fell, that girl, the selfish little bitch, whispered something in his ear.'

'What girl do you mean?'

'Juliette Coleman, who else? Lenny was in love with her. He would have done anything she asked. Even walk off that building, especially since he was all drugged up.'

He loved me.

Had he loved Juliette Coleman enough to jump?

Jess had suspected Juliette wasn't being totally open with her but if she really was the reason he jumped, then why wasn't she the first victim?

Maybe because she was the killer.

Chapter Twenty-Four

Kevin froze.

He was coming back.

Oh sweet Jesus! He was coming back.

He tried not to breathe so hard but he couldn't help himself. His wrists and ankles were raw from trying to work free from his bindings. He'd shit himself because the bastard had left him here for fucking hours. Tied in this damned chair.

'What do you want from me?' Kevin shouted. 'I didn't hurt you or your friend! It was the others, not me!'

The son of a bitch didn't say a word, just walked into the room and turned on the light. Kevin didn't know where the hell he was. Some cheap motel or something. Maybe an abandoned house. He couldn't tell.

'You may think you'll get away with this but you won't,' he warned the fool. 'The police will figure you out. They've got your face all over the news. They're all looking for you.' Dumb bastard. Did this lowlife really think he could get away with this eleventh-hour bullshit?

Todd Penney leaned down, his dark hair as unkempt as it had been back in high school. His eyeglasses looking like a midcentury castoff. Kevin instinctively drew away from him.

'You'd better hope they don't find me,' he warned.

Kevin refused to show him any fear. 'I'm not afraid of you, you stupid shit!' Kevin had Penney's number and it was zero. Z-E-R-O. 'I hope they find you and put you away for the rest of your worthless life.'

'You,' Penney advised, 'should be dead by now.'

Kevin stiffened. What the hell did that mean? Okay. Okay. Okay. Maybe he didn't want to know. 'If you let me go now, I won't tell anyone about this. You can disappear and we can forget this ever happened.'

Penney laughed. He put his face right in Kevin's. 'If I let you go, you're as good as dead. Now who's the stupid shit?'

'You're wrong,' Kevin urged. 'Really, you have to listen to me.'

Penney started walking away. 'Don't worry, O'Reilly. You're not going to miss the showdown. You'll be center stage.'

Chapter Twenty-Five

Birmingham Police Department, 6.48 P.M.

'Still nothing on Penney or O'Reilly,' Lori reported.

Jess paced back and forth before the case board. She'd added the photos Corlew had e-mailed her and updated the timeline with Penney's visit to Baker's office. It had been a hell of a long day and it was only going to get longer.

There had to be something here they were missing.

'We have three choices.' Jess turned to the photos on the board. 'If it's not Penney out for revenge, then it's Juliette or O'Reilly. What are we looking at in terms of motive?'

Harper approached the board and grabbed a marker. 'Fear.' He wrote the word under both Juliette's and O'Reilly's photos. 'Depending on exactly what one or both did, they're looking at prison if found guilty.'

'Humiliation, financial ruin,' Lori added. 'Either one would have a lot to lose, besides their freedom.'

'We could say the same about Penney,' Jess noted. 'He has a lot to lose as well. But it doesn't add up that he would kill the others and not kill Baker.'

'We only have Corlew's word on that,' Harper argued.

Jess put up her hands, relinquishing the point. 'True.' God knew she shouldn't trust anything he told her. Somehow, this part she did.

Moving on. She surveyed the board. 'Let's look at the reactions of these two over the past few days.'

'Juliette came forward with information first,' Lori reminded her.

'She was more than ready to accept a surveillance detail when O'Reilly refused,' Jess recalled.

Harper pointed to Baker's photo. 'At the first indication of trouble, Scott Baker sent his wife and son away. Elliott Carson sent his family to his mother-in-law's. Neither man wanted to risk his family's safety.'

'Even though Aaron Taylor and his wife didn't go away as he'd planned,' Lori picked up where Harper left off, 'the wife stated that he had suggested they go but she had other plans. She left and he stayed home.'

'Yet' – Jess turned to O'Reilly's photo – 'Kevin O'Reilly never sent his family anywhere.' Adrenaline fired through Jess. 'His wife didn't even seem to be aware there was a reason to be afraid.'

'O'Reilly could have easily gotten all those newspaper clippings to use in the storage unit,' Harper pointed out.

'His family owns and operates *Birmingham News*. He absolutely could,' Jess agreed. There was another loose end they hadn't been able to tie up since the former manager remained MIA.

Chad Cook stood, sending his chair banking off the wall behind his desk. 'Holy crap!'

Everyone in the room turned to the youngest member of their team. His job was to carefully go through the DMV records, fingerprint databases, whatever electronic files were at their disposal, of all persons of interest in this case. Those still breathing had priority.

'I've got Channel Six on my iPad.' He hunkered his shoulders. 'I hope that's okay.'

Jess motioned for him to get to the point.

'That ex-cop, Buddy Corlew, just called Chief Burnett out in a one-on-one interview with Gerard Stevens.'

Stevens was the male counterpart of Gina Coleman at Channel Six. Both were attractive, beloved, top investigative reporters. The only difference was that Stevens had his own half-hour show that aired every afternoon.

Harper grabbed the remote for the big flat panel on the wall. He selected Channel Six. Sure enough there was Corlew running off at the mouth about the Porter case.

'That son of a...' Jess should have known he would get back at her for forcing his hand.

She grabbed her cell and called Dan. 'Are you watching this?'

'I am.'

She sighed. Dammit. 'He's doing this because I pushed him into a corner.'

'Don't sweat it.'

He was sure taking it a lot better than her.

'I was just about to head your way,' he said.

'What's up?' She chewed her lip, giving herself a sec to brace for trouble. Like she didn't have enough already. 'We're working on the case.'

'I just got off the phone with Gant.'

The rhythm of Jess's heart shifted and the noise in the room faded. 'You told him about the plant?'

'And the driver with the gun. He's not happy.'

Like she was. 'He's never happy.'

'There's a new development, Jess.'

She steeled herself. What now?

'They've found a discrepancy in the passport verification log for Chicago. He can't say for sure, but he believes Spears reentered the country last Saturday.'

That reality hit her in the face like a bucket of ice water. Why the hell was she surprised? She had known it would happen eventually. She'd done everything she could to hasten it along with all those antagonizing responses she'd sent him. But somehow she wasn't prepared.

He could be anywhere . . . he could be *here*.

She needed to warn Lori and Harper. Dear God. She hadn't considered the full impact of her decision to taunt Spears. And Lily and her family. Fear pumped hard through her veins.

'We need to talk about what this means.'

Not right now. She couldn't go there yet. 'I should get back to work.' She glanced around at her team, who were still mesmerized by the attention-drawing antics of a grudge-carrying ex-cop. 'Thanks for the update.'

Since his secretary passed him a note that he was wanted in the mayor's office, Dan let her off the hook with the promise they would talk more about this later. All Jess could think about was how to keep Spears focused on her and away from the people she cared about.

Her cell clanged. She jumped like she'd been shot. *Damn. Damn. Damn.* She scrubbed at her forehead; damned creases were turning into more wrinkles every day. Most of them had Spears's name written on them. Bastard. 'Harris.'

'My sister is missing,' Gina Coleman said, her voice hollow.

Oh shit. 'Are you at home?'

'Yes.' A shaky breath rasped across the connection. 'She said she wanted a nap before dinner. I went to check on her just now and she's gone. The patio door is standing wide open . . .'

Jess grabbed her bag. 'Was there any other indication someone may have taken her?'

'There's no sign of a struggle.' Gina made a frantic sound. 'My car is still in the garage. Unless she left on foot, someone had to have taken her.'

Or she left on her own . . . to finish what she'd started.

'We're on our way,' Jess promised. She ended the call. The members of her team waited expectantly for whatever bad news she had to deliver. 'Juliette Coleman is missing. Sergeant, get whoever is on surveillance detail at the Coleman house inside now. I don't want Gina talking to anyone else or going anywhere until we get there.' She turned to Cook. 'Get a couple of evidence techs over there.'

'Yes, ma'am.'

Then she turned to Lori. 'Make sure the unit watching Ramona Penney's home is on full alert.'

Everyone went into scramble mode. Jess was out the door and in the corridor when Harper stopped her.

'Hold on, ma'am,' he said to his caller. He turned the cell away from his face. 'Chief, this is dispatch. A janitor from the *Birmingham News* has called in trouble on the roof of the building. He says there's at least three people up there and one of them has a gun.'

Jess went cold. Maybe Scott Baker was right . . . maybe Fate was about to catch up with the last of the Five.

4th Avenue, the Birmingham News, 8.25 P.M.

'You know this one's a new building. The one Lenny Porter fell off or jumped from was torn down a few years ago,' Lori mentioned as they moved into position.

Jess had heard about that. The new *Birmingham News* was right across the street from where the old one had been. 'I remember Lil mentioning something about it.'

'We definitely have warm bodies on the roof,' Harper confirmed. He passed the binoculars to Jess. 'We have one on the ground but moving. I think that's Juliette. O'Reilly and Penney are huddled together a few feet away. I believe Penney's the one with the gun.'

Jess was immensely grateful for the sergeant's state of preparedness. The man carried most everything necessary to collect evidence, fight a small war, or to break out of prison in the back of his SUV.

She was also very thankful for the big-ass lights on top of the building. Otherwise they wouldn't be able to see a damned thing.

'Yep, that's Penney with the weapon all right.' Dammit. She had hoped he wasn't the one. 'What's the status on SWAT?'

'Still ten minutes out.'

That was way too long. Even when they got here, time would be needed for getting into position. 'Be sure the commander knows we need a hostage negotiator.'

'On it.'

En route Jess had spoken to the janitor. He had assured her there was no one else in the building. He and his coworker had exited, leaving a side door open for the police to enter.

Jess turned to Harper and wished she had backup here now. 'I don't want to keep waiting. This could be over before we even get up there.'

Maybe no one would die. Maybe Penney just wanted Juliette and O'Reilly to understand what he and Lenny had felt that night. Or maybe he just wanted the truth. Whatever he wanted, three people were dead. She didn't need him or anyone else adding to that body count.

One of the three on that rooftop was a killer.

'Let's do it,' Harper suggested.

'I can go,' Lori offered. 'SWAT will need you, Chief.'

'Hold your position, Detective.' Jess used her firmest voice. 'We'll need you to keep us informed of the movements on the roof until we're in position up there.'

Lori didn't argue, though she clearly wanted to. She took the binoculars from Harper. 'Be careful.'

'That's the plan,' Jess promised.

She followed Harper, staying close to the other buildings, hugging the brick walls and wishing she had worn jeans and sneakers today. If she was going to be a hands-on deputy chief, she needed to consider dressing the part. She thought of Gina Coleman and Sylvia Baron and decided maybe that wasn't such a great idea. Neither one would be caught dead in sneakers and jeans on the job.

The side door the janitor had told her about was open.

Inside, they hurried to the elevator. Jess wasn't a fan of elevators under the circumstances but they didn't have a lot of options right now. At least they didn't have to take it all the way to the roof.

Once they were in the car headed up, Harper gave her an update. 'SWAT is getting into position. Wells still has a visual on Penney.'

'At least that's some good news.' So far no one had flown off the roof and backup was here. If only their luck held . . .

'Chief Burnett has arrived as well. And so's a whole posse of reporters.'

'An audience,' she mused. 'Fabulous.'

The elevator bumped to a stop on the uppermost floor. Jess and Harper moved to the side of the doors and assumed defensive positions.

Jess's heart rate climbed higher and higher.

The doors glided open. The corridor was empty.

Jess felt the fresh burn of adrenaline rushing through her veins as they moved toward the final blockade between them and the roof. The stairs were narrower than the typical public stairwell but that didn't slow them down. At the top, they exited into the small corridor the janitor had told them about.

Beyond the six- or seven-foot corridor was the door that led onto the roof. It was a solid door so there was no way to see outside and determine where Penney was relative to their current position. Jess couldn't recall seeing the door . . . she'd been too busy looking at the man on the roof.

She sent Lori a text to see if she had a better visual.

Directly behind Penney's position.

'Good answer,' Jess murmured. She showed the screen to Harper.

As good as that news was, there was always the chance Penney could turn around just as they opened the door. Or that there could be two doors.

Jess's cell vibrated.

Penney and O'Reilly moving away from your position toward the edge.

Shit! Jess relayed the new message to Harper. 'Let's go.'

Harper slipped into a crouch at the door while Jess moved to the side. He reached up, eased the door open, and checked out the situation.

And then he was up and moving.

'Freeze!' he shouted.

Jess was out the door right behind him.

Juliette Coleman, hands secured with duct tape behind her back, was seated midway across the roof while Penney and O'Reilly were maybe two feet from the roof's edge. O'Reilly's hands appeared to be secured behind his back as well. Penney had the business end of a handgun rammed into the back of his hostage's skull.

Juliette started to wail as soon as she saw them. 'Please,' she pleaded. 'He's going to kill us!'

Penney yanked O'Reilly in front of him as he wheeled around. 'Tell the truth, Juliette! Who wants to kill whom?'

'I can take him,' Harper murmured. He had a bead on Penney, who was a head taller than O'Reilly.

'Wait,' Jess ordered. This was wrong. Statements and scenarios and those photos of him with Baker were swirling in her head. If Penney had wanted either of these two dead, they would be dead already. But they were alive, the same as Scott Baker had been when he'd left him. Penney wanted them to talk.

'Who does want to kill whom?' Jess shouted to Penney. 'I'm a little confused here.'

No matter that it was Dog Days in Alabama; it was cooler up here, the breeze stronger.

'Why don't you ask the princess?' Penney suggested. 'She knows everything. Gets everything. Except the one thing she wanted most.' Penney laughed as if he weren't in the bead of both Jess's and Harper's weapons. 'You could never have him, could you, Juliette.'

'Shut up!' Juliette screamed between sobs.

'Chief,' Harper murmured while Penney and Juliette ranted at each other, 'SWAT is in position awaiting your signal to take him out. The hostage negotiator wants you to wait for him to catch up.'

Jess didn't want this to end the way she feared it would. And waiting for the hostage negotiator to get up here was out of the question.

She wanted the truth and she didn't want anyone else to die.

Was she going to *fish or cut bait*?

A cold shiver danced along her spine but she was going for it. 'Tell the commander to hold his position,' she whispered to Harper; then she took a breath and dove in.

'They killed your friend,' she said to Penney. 'I get it. The problem is, right this very minute, SWAT is standing by waiting for me to give the signal so a sharpshooter can take you out, Todd. Do you want to die that way? Just another screwed-up head case who couldn't deal with life? Or do you want the world to know the truth?'

Jess lowered her weapon just enough to buy a little

trust – she hoped – and stepped forward. 'Tell me the truth and I'll make sure the right person pays.'

'What the hell are you doing?' O'Reilly screamed. 'He's going to kill me!'

Next to her and one step behind, she could hear Harper arguing in a fierce whisper with someone on his cell, most likely the SWAT commander. There had been no time to set up proper communication links.

'Bring him away from the edge,' Jess said to Penney. 'We'll get the answers you want. You have my word.' She dared to take another step toward the two men. 'But you have to come away from the edge.'

'You want to know what happened?' O'Reilly attempted to pull away from his captor. 'I'll tell you what happened,' he said, his tone frantic, his face flushed with fear. 'Scott suddenly grew a conscience and decided he couldn't live with the way we treated poor, poor Lenny. He didn't care if his decision ruined our lives too. He always was a selfish bastard. He called Todd up and then announced to Juliette he was done with her. You can figure out the rest, Chief.'

'You bastard,' Juliette screamed; then she burst into sobs. 'He's the selfish coward who doesn't care about anyone but himself!'

'Tell her,' O'Reilly demanded, 'or I will! Tell her what you did!'

'Ma'am,' Harper said, barely loud enough for Jess to hear.

She leaned toward him, not daring to take her attention off the two men.

'The negotiator is coming up the elevator now. He won't wait unless we can get those two away from the edge.'

Dammit. 'Todd, if you don't bring Kevin away from the edge,' Jess urged, 'SWAT is going to move in. I can't stop them.'

Penney whirled around, dragging O'Reilly with him, both men teetering dangerously close to the edge as he surveyed the buildings and streets around them in search of the sharpshooter. Jess's heart swelled in her throat.

'You have to listen to me, Todd,' she pressed. 'Move toward me and everything will be fine. Just a couple of steps. Please.' That was all she needed. The opportunity to keep everyone alive while they got to the truth.

'She killed Scott,' O'Reilly announced. 'She called me bawling.' He glared at Juliette as if she were worse than pathetic. 'She said if she couldn't have him, then no one was going to have him. She lost it for a minute and killed him.'

'I didn't mean to kill him,' Juliette wailed. 'I was angry. I hit him. I couldn't believe I did it . . . It happened so fast.'

'See!' O'Reilly ranted. 'I told you! Then she called me to help clean up her mess!'

Jess considered Juliette's words. 'If you didn't mean to

do it, Juliette, why did you hit him again?'

Juliette stared up at Jess, the expression on her face one of true shock. 'What? I didn't hit him twice. I threw down the statue as soon as I hit . . . him . . . I ran outside and called Kevin.'

Jess turned her attention back to O'Reilly. 'And you came to her rescue. Only your friend wasn't dead and you had to hit him again. After all, he'd called Todd and opened this can of worms.'

'She just told you she killed him!' O'Reilly shook his head. 'I'm not taking the fall for what she did. No way.'

The pieces fell fully into place for Jess. 'Where's your journal, Todd?'

Todd blinked as if her question had dragged him from some faraway place. 'I gave it to Baker.'

'Why did you do that?'

'Because he called me. Wanted to make amends for his part in what happened.' Penney made a weary sound that might have been an attempt at a laugh. 'I figured he was just trying to buy absolution from me. But it wasn't for sale.' Fury tightened his face. 'I wanted him to remember just what they had done, so I gave him the journal.'

'Yes, you did,' Jess agreed. 'And Scott Baker was so devastated by the anguished words he read there that he ripped out the pages that referred to how badly he had treated Lenny. He hid those damning pages before Juliette arrived. That's why they weren't found at the scene. But Elliott Carson and Aaron Taylor didn't get a chance to hide anything. The person who killed them made sure the pages from your journal were in plain sight so we would find them.'

As if hearing that revelation startled him, Penney's hold on O'Reilly loosened, and O'Reilly jerked away. He backed up the meager two steps that separated him from the very edge of the roof.

Jess stopped breathing. 'Don't move, Kevin. Just stay right there.' She lowered her weapon to the ground and held her hands out to her sides in a gesture of good faith. 'All we want to do is clear up this mystery. There's no need for anyone to do anything he might regret.'

Thankfully Juliette had dissolved into sobs and was no longer arguing with O'Reilly. Harper had a bead on Penney even though the weapon in his hand wasn't aimed at anyone just now.

'Todd, why don't you put your weapon down and kick it away? If you do, Sergeant Harper will lower his weapon as well. Then we can all talk about this calmly.'

'You killed Scott,' Juliette cried. 'You let me believe I did it and it was you.'

'What difference does it make?' O'Reilly snarled. 'You had murder in your heart when you hit him. Poor Juliette, her perfect image is shattered. Tsk tsk.'

Mesmerized by the exchange taking place between O'Reilly and Juliette, Penney slowly responded to Jess's request. He placed the handgun on the ground and toed it away.

Jess looked to Harper and he lowered his weapon. Since the door from the stairwell didn't open, she assumed the negotiator had backed off.

Air expanded in her lungs once more. 'We'll get this sorted out, Kevin,' Jess promised. 'Just come away from the edge and tell me what really happened. You have my word that I'll protect you.'

He laughed so hard he lost his breath, had to double over in a coughing fit.

Goose bumps zipped over her skin as Jess prayed he realized just how close to the edge he was.

'I don't believe you,' O'Reilly argued. 'You think I killed them.' He shrugged. 'You believe I killed Scott and took the diary.' He nodded adamantly. 'I know what you're thinking.'

'I don't know that, Kevin. Juliette had access to Scott and the diary the same as you did. She may be the one.'

Juliette started wailing again.

'You killed Lenny!' Penney accused, snapping back to the conversation. 'You and the others. You just kept badgering him. You *made* him jump.'

Kevin just shook his head and laughed some more, somehow finding humor in this precarious situation. 'I didn't kill him, you idiot.' He pointed at Juliette. 'She did!'

'He's insane,' Juliette screamed. 'Can't you see that? Why don't you do something?'

Kevin howled as if every word she said was ridiculously funny. 'You're right. I'm definitely insane.' He shrugged. 'I did it,' he confessed. 'I killed Scott and Elliott and Aaron. They were all assholes anyway. They always thought they were better than me. But I showed them. The journal was a stroke of genius.' He sighed dramatically. 'I left the journal pages to make it look as if Penney were the guilty one. I decorated that damned storage unit to look as if he'd been plotting his revenge since he came back.' He shook his head. 'What can I say? I didn't want to go to prison. And Scott had fucked us all by making that goddamned phone call.' He looked at Jess then. 'That's the truth. But I didn't kill Lenny Porter. She did,' he snarled.

'No!' Juliette wailed. 'I didn't! I swear I didn't.'

'Then what did you do?' Jess demanded. Her patience with the woman had expired. 'Tell me right now before I have to arrest you for murder.'

'We were high.' She turned her red, tear-stained face toward Jess. 'We were all out of our minds on drugs. They'd been playing games with Lenny all night and he said something like "None of you would give a shit if I just jumped." And they all started chanting at him to do it. It was a joke.'

'Who chanted?' Jess demanded. She had zero sympathy for the woman.

'Scott, Elliott.' She glared at her friend. 'Kevin and Aaron. They all did it. "Jump, Lenny!"' she mimicked. '"Jump! Jump!"'

'But he didn't,' Kevin roared. 'Not until you went over and whispered in his ear. "Do it for me, Lenny. Jump, Lenny!"' he mocked Juliette's whiny voice. 'You were so stoned you bragged about it. "Look! He really did it. Oh my God!"'

'I only did what the rest of you were doing. I'm no guiltier than you!'

'But he loved you,' Jess reminded her of her own words. 'He did it for *you*.'

'There you go, Chief,' O'Reilly called out. 'Mystery solved.'

Jess stiffened. The hair on the back of her neck stood on end at the sound of resignation in his voice. 'You need to ensure she doesn't get away with it,' Jess urged. 'I'll need you to help me with this, Kevin. Your testimony will seal her fate.'

The laughter was gone. O'Reilly just shook his head. 'It's over.'

Jess didn't dare move toward him. 'You did the right thing, Kevin. You told the truth.'

'I know.' For a split second he stared at Jess; then he jumped.

For one startling moment, Jess felt frozen . . . then she swiped at her eyes and struggled to gather her composure.

Behind her, Juliette Coleman wailed hysterically.

And then there was one.

Chapter Twenty-Six

9911 Conroy Road,
Saturday, August 14, 2.20 A.M.

Lori parked in Jess's drive.

They both just sat there for a bit.

Four people had died this week. All because no one had been paying attention when they were hurting others. The Five had taken bullying to the ultimate level. The true victims in this tragedy that sprawled across more than a decade were Lenny Porter and his friend Todd Penney.

Twelve years ago, Juliette Coleman and Scott Baker had been madly in love. Yet everything changed the night Lenny Porter died. Scott turned to another woman and rushed into a marriage with her in an attempt to forget. But he'd still been in love with Juliette and they began a torrid affair. For years he promised Juliette that he was leaving his wife and they would finally have the life they deserved. Then children came along and Scott never came through with his promises.

The story was as old as time.

It took more than a decade, but Scott Baker finally grew that conscience Kevin O'Reilly mentioned. He watched his own son suffer and he realized he could no longer carry the burden of guilt, so he called Todd Penney and asked for forgiveness.

Five teens who'd had the world at their feet and the stars in their eyes had effectively killed another. And this week fate had caught up with them.

Usually Jess didn't rely on fate, but this was one of those rare instances when it worked out. Sort of.

'You think the DA will levy charges against Penney?'

'I don't think so. They'll want to keep this as quiet as possible. Juliette is another story.'

'It's difficult to feel sorry for her,' Lori admitted.

'I do feel sorry for her family.' Jess would never forget the devastation on Gina Coleman's face when she learned the whole truth.

'It's not a pretty story,' Lori said. 'I can't believe Coleman is doing an exclusive on it tomorrow afternoon.'

Jess laughed. 'I get where she's coming from. Juliette is her sister. Gina feels it's her responsibility to set the record straight. Besides, you don't get to the top and stay there by letting someone else scoop the story. She has to do something to steal back some of the spotlight Stevens stole with that Corlew interview.'

'I guess I'll never be at the top, then. And Corlew's an ass.'

'He is.' He was now officially on Jess's bad side. 'Don't worry about the top. They don't call it a lonely place for nothing.' Jess had been there and she had nothing to show for it. Well, except for an obsessed serial killer.

'Dr Baron was not a happy camper when she arrived on the scene.'

'I was too busy to notice,' Jess fibbed.

Sylvia was not pleased at all about the call. Jess had evaded her at all costs. Hadn't been difficult since the SWAT commander and the negotiator were standing in line to chew her out.

Sitting here wasn't going to get her up those stairs. 'Thanks for the ride.' Jess reached for the door handle.

'See you on Monday.'

'Lord willing and the creek don't rise.' Jess laughed as she climbed out of the car. What she should have said was *if Spears doesn't show up to play*.

He was close. Gant's call about the security breach in Chicago was all the confirmation she'd needed.

As if the same thought had occurred to Lori, she parked the Mustang and climbed out. 'I should walk you to your door. Make sure everything's as it should be.'

Burnett had trained her detectives well.

Jess dragged herself up the stairs, Lori on her heels, and unlocked her door. She disarmed the security system and waited while Lori had a look around.

'All right. I'm out of here.' She grimaced. 'Wish me luck. We're taking Chester to the zoo this afternoon.'

'Remember,' Jess said as she walked her to the door, 'patience and persistence.'

'I'll try.'

Jess waved her off and locked up. When the alarm was reset, she went in search of a glass of wine.

Half an hour later she was perched on her glider, her Glock tucked next to her and a bottle of wine right next to that. Who wanted to move for refills? Maybe she'd just sit here and watch the sun rise.

She had every right to celebrate. The case was closed.

She smiled when Dan pulled into the driveway. She'd known he would come as soon as the PR stuff was done. This had been a high-profile case and people wanted answers. She'd stayed out of the limelight on this one.

He ascended the top step and smiled at her.

He was so damned handsome. And charming. And kind.

Yes, his friends were still the rich and powerful. His family still lived in the mansion on the hill. He was an organizer, a mover and a shaker of whole communities … a man who could change the course of a city's history with one decision. Jess was a worker bee. She recognized her place and was perfectly content finding the bad guys and ensuring they couldn't harm anyone else.

Corlew was right; she didn't really fit in Dan's world. She probably never would.

But somehow she fit with *him*.

'What're you smiling about?' Jess inquired. Inside she was doing the same.

'Is that other glass for me?'

She'd brought out a second glass just in case she didn't finish off the bottle before he got here. 'It is. Join me.'

He sat down next to her and held his glass as she filled it. He noticed the Glock. 'Good girl.'

'I told you I wasn't taking any more unnecessary chances.'

'You mean like you did on that roof?'

She should have known he'd nail her on that one. 'That one was necessary.'

'You almost gave the SWAT commander a heart attack. Rob Barlow is pissed.'

Barlow was the hostage negotiator. He'd given Jess hell at the scene.

'They should get used to it.' She had her own way of doing things.

'I warned them about that already.'

'Did you talk to Corlew?' He'd proven just how underhanded he could be with that interview . . . even if he had been right about the Five.

'No need. If I give him enough rope, he'll hang himself. He's done it before.'

That was Dan. Always taking the high road.

'Whatever racket Corlew makes,' he assured her, 'the facts speak for themselves. Black did everything he could twelve years ago. He had his suspicions about the Five back then but with no evidence and all the political pressure on the DA, there was no way to convince him to prosecute.' Dan shook his head. 'You can't win a case without evidence. No DA is going to trial without it. Black's hands were tied and the case was closed.'

'I know you, Daniel Burnett, and no matter how much pressure the mayor or anyone else exerted, you would never cave unless you believed it was the right thing to do.'

He reached up, traced her cheek with his finger. 'Thank you. That means a great deal to me.'

They drank their wine and rocked back and forth on the glider for a while. Then he reached into his jacket pocket and removed an envelope. He passed it to her.

'What's this?'

'The medical history from your aunt.'

Her jaw fell slack. 'You went by her house?'

'You've been pressed for time all week. This morning I had a meeting at the mayor's office. Afterward I swung by before going back to the office. It took twenty minutes. Now it's done.'

Jess smiled. 'Thank you.' The truth was, her aunt was a part of the past she didn't want to revisit, and she'd used work to avoid doing so. Just another aspect of her problem with uber-independence. It was far easier to be strong and independent if you never looked back. Easier to pretend you didn't have a problem if you didn't recognize past mistakes.

The man sitting next to her was a very good reason to try harder to work through those issues.

'You're welcome. Now drink your wine. I'm planning on seducing you.'

'You're behind the curve, Burnett. I already started seducing you.' She lifted her glass. 'Cheers.'

She kicked aside the worry about Spears that tried to invade.

It was Saturday. The case was solved and she and Dan were off duty.

No more thoughts about bad guys and cases.

Dan carried her inside and left her on the bed just long enough to lock out the world.

They made love until the sun came up.

Chapter Twenty-Seven

Parkridge Drive, 6.00 P.M.

Lori picked at her French fries. Chet wished she would stop worrying so much about how Chester acted around her. He was a child, still a baby for the most part. He would learn to love her. Maybe not as much as Chet did, but enough.

'I'm beginning to think you're not a big fan of Mickey D's,' he teased.

She set her plate aside on the end table and curled her legs under her. If their relationship ever ended, God forbid, he would never be able to keep that sofa. She looked so beautiful, so perfect on it. This whole place would never be the same without her.

'Chester loves McDonald's.' She glanced longingly at Chet's son, who was eating his French fries right off the coffee table, his attention on *Toy Story 3*. 'I want him to be happy.'

Lori didn't know it but she was thinking like a mother already. 'Well, I have something that might make you happy.'

She perked up, the corners of her lips lifting into a smile. 'A surprise?'

Chet nodded. Seeing her smile made his heart beat a little faster. 'Chester, go get Lori's present.'

Chester looked at his daddy and grinned. ''kay.'

The boy galloped off to his room.

Lori laughed. 'What're you boys up to?'

Chester ran back into the room squealing at the top of his lungs. He climbed onto the sofa next to Lori and stuck the white box with the pink ribbon in her face.

'Sorry about the ketchup.' Chet grimaced. His son had gotten ketchup all over the white wrapping paper.

'It would probably taste about as good as those fries.' She giggled. 'Thank you, Chester.'

'Open!' he ordered, pointing a ketchup-stained finger at the present.

Pride swelled his chest so tight, Chet could hardly breathe. Picking out the secret gift for Lori and letting Chester be a part of surprising her was working. The boy was leaning against Lori, his eyes big with excitement as she opened the gift.

Chet prayed this would help break the ice between them.

'Wow!' Lori lifted the pearls from the case. 'They're beautiful.'

Chester reached up and touched the necklace. 'Loowi's su'pwise.'

'Thank you, Chester. I love it.'

He smiled at her and Chet saw the tears glittering in her green eyes.

He couldn't help himself. Chet got down on his knees in front of her and gave her a kiss on the cheek. 'I love you, baby.'

She hugged him and he felt the dampness of her cheek against his face. Tears welled in his own eyes.

'Me too! Me too!' Chester squealed. He dove into the hug.

They laughed and hugged like one big family.

For the first time, Chester let Lori get him ready for bed. Chet watched from the door as she tucked him in.

She kissed his forehead. 'Night, Chester.'

He yawned. 'Night, Lo'wee.'

She joined Chet at the door, her face beaming. 'Your turn, Dad.' She tiptoed and leaned close enough to whisper in his ear, 'Then I'm tucking you in.' She left a kiss on his jaw and disappeared toward their room.

Chet ensured his boy said his prayers, gave him a goodnight kiss, turned out his light – leaving the room aglow with the Spider-Man night-light – and softly closed the door. Anticipation making him hurry, he headed down the hall.

In their room, candles flickered from every flat surface.

The covers were turned back but there was no Lori on the bed.

He closed the door as quietly as possible and locked it. 'Hey!' he called out in a loud whisper. 'Where are you?'

'In here,' she whispered back.

He started toward the bathroom door, felt something under his bare feet. She'd left a trail of rose petals on the floor. He followed the path and stalled at the door to take in the view.

More candles and a bottle of wine waited on the counter. Two stemmed glasses. And there was Lori, neck-deep in bubbles, in the garden tub. He'd figured that thing would come in handy when he'd added the shower to this bathroom and opted to leave the big-ass tub.

'Climb in here while the water's still warm.'

When he'd stripped off his clothes and slid into the water, he wasn't surprised that she was naked but he was surprised that she was wearing her pearls.

'You like?' She pressed her hand to her throat, showing off the necklace.

He pulled her against him, aligning her body atop his. 'I love it all.'

She kissed him until he gasped for breath. 'Thank you,' she murmured.

Then they stopped talking . . . stopped thinking . . . and focused on *feeling*.

Chapter Twenty-Eight

The Falcon Center,
Sunday, August 15, 10.00 A.M.

Sylvia met him in the solarium-style lobby.

Dan took a long look around. Marble floors and soaring ceiling, and beyond the glass walls the lush gardens stretched for acres around the private clinic located just outside Birmingham. 'Impressive.'

'If you saw the check they get every month, then you'd really be impressed.' She looked around the elegant lobby. 'Too bad they couldn't help her.'

This was a part of his past he'd tucked neatly away. He didn't want to remember. But today, he needed to do this for the family. And maybe for himself. Mostly, though, he was here for Nina. 'She'll do better in New York.'

'Maybe. I appreciate very much that you came, Dan.' Sylvia shrugged. 'It will mean a lot to Father as well.'

'I don't know that seeing me will help.' The screaming and the cold, hard muzzle of the nine-millimeter flashed in broken pieces through his brain. The tie he wore suddenly felt too tight. 'But I'm happy to do what I can.'

It was the least he could do.

'She loved you, Dan. As much as she was capable of loving anyone.' Sylvia wrapped her arm around his. 'You made her happy. I think those months with you was the only time in her adult life that she was really happy on a personal level.'

As she led the way, to her sister's room he assumed, he couldn't help asking the question that had burned in the back of his brain all these years. 'You all knew she was . . . ill. Yet you never said a word. You let the whole thing play out. Why didn't anyone warn me?'

Nina's illness was the family's deep dark secret. At the time she and Dan were married, Nina would go months without any symptoms of the schizophrenia. Then she'd go over the edge. The last time she'd almost taken Dan with her. The entire Baron family insisted there had never been an episode like that before. Somehow, Nina hadn't been able to find her way back from that one. It was as if she'd locked herself away deep inside her head and refused to come out.

If he'd known, maybe he could have done things differently. Made sure he was home on time. Focused a little more on her needs.

But he hadn't gotten a clue from anyone, including Nina.

That crushing sensation settled on his chest. He'd failed her. There was no one else to blame.

'We thought somehow her love for you would be enough. That you were her savior.'

But he hadn't saved her. He had come home that evening and climbed into the shower. When he'd come back into the bedroom, Nina had the weapon they kept in the closet for protection in her hand. She had screamed and ranted at him while he tried everything he knew to coax her into putting down the weapon. Finally, she turned it on herself but she hadn't released the safety, buying him just enough time to take the weapon from her.

Sylvia paused outside an unmarked room. No numbers or names. This was an exclusive facility. Each patient was given as close to total anonymity as possible. She searched his eyes for a long moment. 'Dan, whether you realize it or not, this is more for you than for Nina.'

He wanted to argue with her reasoning but he couldn't find the words.

'One day you'll look back on this moment and be grateful for the closure. She loved you. She never meant to hurt you. None of us did. But more importantly, you didn't do anything wrong. You need to forgive yourself and move on with your life.'

How could he forgive himself?

Sylvia rapped softly on the door, then opened it. Nina sat in a chair near the windows on the far side of the room. Her brown hair was shorter now. She was thinner, paler. But she was as beautiful as ever. His chest tightened with emotion. No matter that he had thought he was prepared for this; he wasn't. Seeing her this way just reminded him of how badly he had failed her.

'I brought someone to see you, Nina.'

Nina didn't acknowledge her sister or Dan. No indication that she even realized they had entered the room showed on her face or in her posture.

He moved around in front of her and crouched down to her eye level. 'How are you, Nina?'

As if she'd abruptly realized someone said her name, she looked at him without the slightest recognition. 'It's not time for my medication.'

Sylvia pulled up another chair and sat facing her. 'You remember Dan. You've told me stories about when he would take you to dinner and a movie. You love movies, Nina.'

She turned to Sylvia. 'Is it time for lunch yet? I don't want the peas.'

Dan followed Sylvia's lead and tried making conversation. If Nina understood anything they said or even who they were, she showed no indication.

She was gone. Just like that evening when she'd held

his gun in both hands and tried to shoot, the woman he had fallen for and married was gone.

When the attendant came to take Nina for her walk, Dan said goodbye. Profound sadness shrouded him for all that she had lost. He hoped the miracle she needed would be found at the next clinic.

He turned to Sylvia and she seemed to visibly gather her uncharacteristically scattered composure. 'Well, thank you again.' She cleared her throat. 'I'm glad you and Jess are coming to the barbecue. I didn't want to leave her out. She's actually growing on me.'

Dan managed a strained laugh. 'Jess will do that.'

Sylvia squared her shoulders. 'Be sure to mention to her that next time she has a jumper to call someone else. I don't do jumpers.'

Dan walked Sylvia to her car, then climbed into his own. As he drove away, he realized Sylvia had been right. He had needed to see Nina again.

He might never be able to forgive himself for not being what she needed but he could acknowledge the fact that he had tried.

That was enough for now.

That and the knowledge that Jess was waiting for him.

Chapter Twenty-Nine

St Francis Church, 3.00 P.M.

Jess had watched in morbid fascination as Dan's cousin's firstborn was christened. The child hadn't screamed as much as she'd expected and she was really a beautiful baby. The christening gown was Irish and handmade. According to one of the ladies she'd overheard, it had been in the mother's family for several generations.

Afternoon refreshments were being served in the gardens, and thankfully it wasn't hot enough to melt what little makeup she was wearing off her face. Jess munched a cookie, homemade no doubt, and wandered through the gardens. The service had been lovely. Dan had looked so handsome and so excited to be named the baby's godfather.

Mostly Jess was in shock over how she hadn't been able to take her eyes off the baby. It was like she needed to see every wiggle and stretch.

She was just freaking out. That was all it could be. By her calendar she should be on her period by now. Could she be pregnant? Not likely. She was probably worrying for nothing. Worst-case scenario, if there was no period by Tuesday she would take one of those high-tech tests that were supposed to give immediate results. She'd figure the rest out from there.

Her heart bumped into a funny rhythm at the thought. *Just stop, Jess.*

She scanned the garden for the beverage table. Where was that lemonade she'd heard everyone making a fuss over?

'Well, don't you look lovely today?'

Dread settled like a big rock in her belly. Jess turned to face Dan's mother. The queen. The woman who was sure Jess would never in a million years be good enough for her one and only boy. The thought of having this woman as grandmother to her future children was all the reason Jess would ever need to remain childless.

'Katherine.' Jess drummed up a smile.

'They were talking about you on the news yesterday.' Katherine nodded, her expression somber. 'You solved a triple homicide and exposed the truth about a murder more than a decade old. Gracious.' She set her silk fan to fluttering. 'Too bad you couldn't prevent that young man from jumping. His family is devastated. Just devastated.'

That was Katherine's specialty. Always find the negative in everything except her own actions.

'Oh.' Jess waved her off. 'But think how much money I saved the taxpayers. No trial, no having to house and feed the poor guy. Why, I just feel he did us all a huge favor.'

'Well.' Katherine cleared her throat. 'Better luck next time.'

She strolled away before Jess could dredge up a fitting response. Just as well. She was Dan's mother. She couldn't exactly box her up and ship her to Siberia.

Jess found the lemonade and had herself a nice tall glass. Whoever had organized this little party had fabulous taste. No plastic or paper cups for this crowd. No sirree. The real thing. Crystal stemware and delicate little bone china plates.

Dan came up behind her and whispered in her ear. 'We can escape now, if you'd like.'

'I would like that very much.'

Jess left her glass on the nearest table and hurried with Dan to his SUV. As soon as they were out of the church parking lot, she relaxed.

'My little goddaughter is the most beautiful baby I have ever seen,' he bragged.

'She really is.' Cute and cuddly and smelling all like baby powders and lotion. Normally Jess was allergic to those smells but not today.

'How do you feel about that?' He glanced at her. 'Kids, I mean.'

They'd had this discussion about twenty years ago and agreed that careers and financial stability should come first. At this point both those arguments were out the window to some degree.

'I think there has to be a committed couple first. Babies need two parents.'

'I get that.' He maneuvered the needed turn. 'But do you want children someday?'

Generally she would argue that the window was closing on that opportunity but she opted to keep her mouth shut on that topic. Mainly because she got the feeling he wanted kids. She'd seen the look on his face in that church when he held that tiny little human.

'I'm not opposed to having children. Obviously you want to. I saw the twinkle in your eyes back there.'

'I do. Absolutely.'

Her throat got a little tight. Was he saying that there was no hope for them unless she wanted to have children?

Wow. She hadn't considered there was a shelf life on where they were just now. If she dallied too long, she would be out of the baby-making business and it sounded like that would present an issue.

Unless the baby-making had already begun. *Don't be ridiculous, Jess. You're not even late yet.* At least not according to her pill pack.

'I went to see Nina this morning.'

Nina? He couldn't be talking about the crazy Lopez woman who had kidnapped her. She was on house arrest out in LA. Wait, wait. He was talking about *Nina*. His second wife. Sylvia Baron's sister. The senator's daughter.

Like she didn't know that and wasn't dying to hear more.

'You never told me anything about her, remember?'

'It's a long and sad story.'

She shifted in the seat and faced him. 'We have all evening.'

He nodded. 'Okay. I'll tell you everything and then you'll tell me everything about Wesley.'

'You know everything about Wesley,' she argued.

Dan cut her a glance that challenged her statement.

'All right,' she agreed. 'We'll get that out of the way too.'

At least they weren't talking about babies anymore.

As he drove along the quiet Sunday afternoon streets, he told her about how he'd met Nina at a fund-raiser for her father's bid for reelection to the senate. Nina had been an up-and-coming attorney and they'd hit it off. He'd bypassed thirty and decided it was time to try the marriage thing again.

Jess knew that feeling, only hers had come at forty. Wesley had just been in the right place at the right time. Or maybe not since they'd divorced barely two years later.

By the time Dan parked in her driveway, Jess understood why he'd been reluctant to talk about that particular marriage. She was glad he finally had. She also understood Sylvia a lot better. No wonder she made it so difficult to get to know her – or to want to, for that matter. The kind of dark and painful secret her family had been keeping made opening up difficult.

'You had no idea about her mental illness?'

'None.'

Just went to show that even growing up in a community and thinking you knew someone didn't mean you really did. Geez Louise.

'I'm sorry. That was really awful for you.' The idea that he had come so close to being killed by someone he trusted so completely was terrifying.

He parked next to her Audi. 'Maybe she'll get the help she needs in New York.'

'Maybe so.'

He sounded so sad when he talked about her. Ten years was a long time to grieve. When they'd gotten out and headed for her stairs, she ventured into that sensitive territory. 'You do understand that what happened wasn't your fault?'

'I have my moments,' he admitted, 'when I can see how it wasn't.'

'We'll have to work on that.'

As they climbed the stairs to her door, her cell started

that annoying clang. She dragged it from the clutch purse she'd carried to the christening and was surprised to see a Virginia number. 'Harris.'

'Jess, this is Patricia Lanier.'

The real estate agent who had the contract on her house. Hope dared to rear its head. 'Patricia, great to hear from you. Do you have news for me?' Besides the possibility that her house had burned to the ground or been blown up?

'I do. We have an offer for full asking price.'

That was way better news than she'd dared to hope. 'That's great.' On the landing, Jess turned to Dan and gave him a thumbs-up. 'What do we need to do next?' Getting that mortgage payment off her back would be a tremendous relief.

'I'll fax you the necessary papers and we'll set up a closing date.'

'Thank you so much!'

'Congratulations! You'll be hearing from me again soon.'

Jess ended the call and let out a whoop. 'We have a full asking price offer on my house!'

'Sounds like a celebration is in order.' He leaned down and picked up a package that waited at her door. 'You expecting something?'

'No.' She hadn't ordered anything. But she just might start when that mountain of debt was lifted from her shoulders.

The package was a priority box from the post office. Medium size.

Their movements seemingly perfectly choreographed, they stared first at the package, then at each other.

'We should check this out before we open it.'

She wasn't going to argue.

Dan set the package back down and they returned to his SUV. He called a bomb tech and an evidence tech. And for the next forty-five minutes they waited.

If Mr Louis was home, he never came outside. Even so, she kept getting that creepy-crawly feeling she experienced when someone was watching her. Each time she looked around, there was nothing. No one.

Finally their backup rolled in.

Bomb tech found nothing. The evidence tech lifted a number of fingerprints but those could be a postal worker's. No suspicious residue on the outside and nothing inside that posed a hazard.

The bomb tech opened the package and shook his head. 'Looks like a scarf.'

A scarf? Who would send her a scarf?

The answer to that question slammed into her brain. *No.* She shook her head as if that would make it so. *No. No. No.*

With a gloved hand, Dan lifted the silk scarf from the box. Beneath it were three wallet-size photos. All three were female. All three were brunettes. All were gorgeous.

No names or markings on the front or back of the photos.

The air seemed to avoid filling Jess's lungs even with her heart pounding a hundred miles an hour. This was wrong. He never sent photos. This couldn't be . . .

She felt the cell phone in her purse vibrate. As she was digging for it, Dan was already getting Gant on the line.

Jess stared at the screen and the bottom dropped out of her stomach.

Eeny, meeny, miny, moe . . . let's play, Jess.

'Spears?' Dan demanded.

The floor seemed to shift under her feet. She closed her eyes and tried to steady herself. Gant had warned that he suspected Eric Spears was back in the country. She had sensed he was watching her . . . had known this moment was coming . . . but none of that knowledge made this any easier.

She nodded in answer to Dan's question. 'He's back. And one of these three women is about to become his next victim.'